12/12

L...
when s...
fear that s...
left with nothing m...
teaching, business management and mo...
dream of writing back a few years, but she ...
her first novel in 1993. Since then her books ha...
the contemporary, historical and paranormal genre...
recipient of many industry awards, including the PRISM for
Dark Paranormal Romance. Lori lives in Wisconsin with
her husband, two sons and a yellow labrador named Elwood.
She can be reached through her website:
www.lorihandeland.com

PRAISE FOR LORI HANDELAND'S
NIGHTCREATURE NOVELS

'Handeland has the potential to become as big as, if not
bigger than, Christine Feehan and Maggie Shayne'
Publishers Weekly

'Hold on to your seats! Handeland delivers a kick-butt
heroine ready to take on the world of the paranormal.
Blue Moon is an awesome launch to what promises to
be a funny, sexy, and scary series'
Romantic Times

'Handeland has more than proved herself a worthy author
in the increasingly popular world of paranormal romance
with these slick and highly engrossing tales'
Road to Romance

Also by Lori Handeland

MIDNIGHT MOON

LORI HANDELAND

PAN BOOKS

First published 2006 by St Martin's Press, New York

First published in Great Britain in paperback 2008 by Pan Books
an imprint of Pan Macmillan Ltd
Pan Macmillan, 20 New Wharf Road, London N1 9RR
Basingstoke and Oxford
Associated companies throughout the world
www.panmacmillan.com

ISBN 978-0-330-45134-5

1 3 5 7 9 8 6 4 2

A CIP catalogue record for this book is available from
the British Library.

Printed and bound in Great Britain by
Mackays of Chatham plc, Chatham, Kent

For Miriam Kriss:
Who knows so much and is always willing to share.
Your joyous passion for books is infectious.

MIDNIGHT MOON

Prologue

Last night I dreamed of the beach in Haiti. The rolling waves, the smooth, warm sand, turned white beneath the light of a glistening silver moon.

The dream continues to haunt me because on that beach I said good-bye to everything I'd been and welcomed the woman I would become.

Once I was a stay-at-home mom with a big house in the Southern California suburbs. I drove an SUV that was far too large for carting a five-year-old girl to ballet lessons; I was married to a man I thought was my soul mate.

Then, in the way of a picture-perfect life, everything went to hell and I became a voodoo priestess. When I change lives, I do it right.

I did have a little help from the witness protection program. Although they weren't the ones who suggested I spend years studying an ancient African religion, travel to Haiti and be initiated, then style myself

Priestess Cassandra, owner and operator of a voodoo shop in the French Quarter. No, that was all me.

I chose the name Cassandra because it means "prophet." Voodoo priestesses are often called on to see the future, but I'd never been the least bit psychic. Despite the name, I still wasn't.

Voodoo is a fluid religion, adaptive and inclusive. Practitioners believe in magic, zombies, and love charms. I like pretty much everything about it, except one thing.

Their stubborn insistence that there are no accidents.

Me, I have a hard time believing it, because if there are no accidents that means my daughter died for a reason, and I just can't find one. Believe me, I've looked.

I'm not the first person to have trouble with certain tenets of their religion. That doesn't mean I don't believe.

In Haiti, on that beach, I committed myself to voodoo wholeheartedly. I had a very good reason.

I planned to raise my daughter from the dead.

1

I got off the plane in Port-au-Prince for the second time in my life about midafternoon on a sunny Thursday in October. Not much had changed. Heat wavered above the asphalt, shimmering, dancing, making me dizzy.

Inside the airport, a man whose starched white short-sleeved shirt and khaki trousers emphasized the ebony shade of his skin hurried over. "Priestess Cassandra?"

I winced. What had been good business in New Orleans sounded pretentious in the shadow of the mountains where voodoo had first come into its own.

"Just Cassandra, please," I murmured.

I wondered momentarily how he'd known me. Perhaps my being the only white woman who'd gotten off the plane was a pretty good clue. I'm sure my blue eyes and short dark hair weren't all that common around here, either. But what usually made me stand out in a crowd was the slash of pure white at my temple.

The oddity, which had appeared in my hair shortly after my daughter died, had gradually lost pigment from its original gray. I probably should have covered it with dye—I was, after all, in witness protection—but the white strip served to remind me of my daughter and my mission. As if I needed reminding.

The streak also served as my penance. I hadn't done the one thing a mother was supposed to do—protect her child against everyone. Even her father.

The man in front of me dipped his head. "I am Marcel, Miss Cassandra."

His accent hinted at France. A lovely lilt in English; in Creole, the language of the island, he'd sound fabulous.

I opened my mouth to tell him my last name, then realized I no longer had one. Once I'd testified against my scum-sucking, drug-dealing pig of a husband I'd become Priestess Cassandra, one name only—à la Cher, the Rock, Madonna.

WITSEC, short for witness protection folks, had been unamused when I'd refused to acknowledge the need for a last name. Of course very little amused them. They'd slapped Smith on my records, but the name wasn't any more mine than Cassandra.

"Monsieur Mandenauer has arranged for a room at the Hotel Oloffson," Marcel said, taking possession of the single bag I'd carried onto the plane.

I'd recently joined a group of government operatives known as the *Jäger-Suchers*. That's Hunter-Searchers if your German is as nonexistent as mine.

The *Jäger-Suchers* hunt monsters, and I'm not using

the euphemism applied to so many human beings who belong in a cage. I mean *monsters*—the type whose skin sprouts fur, whose teeth become fangs—beasts that drink the blood of humans and only want more.

Edward Mandenauer was my new boss. He'd sent me to Haiti to discover the secret of raising a zombie. I loved it when my personal and work interests collided. Almost made me give credence to that "there are no accidents" theory.

"This way, please." Marcel awaited me at the door of the airport.

I hurried after him, leaving behind the shady, cool interior of the building and stepping into the bright, sunny bustle of Port-au-Prince.

Though Haiti is horrendously overpopulated—the newest estimates say 8.5 million souls—there is also a vast amount of uncharted, unexplored, and nearly unexplorable land in the mountains. I was certain any secrets worth uncovering lay in that direction.

I glanced at the teeming crowd of humanity that made up the capital city. Secrets certainly couldn't be kept here.

Marcel had parked at the curb in direct defiance of the signs ordering him not to do so. He held the passenger door, and I climbed inside, nearly choking on the scalding air within. After tossing my bag into the back, Marcel jumped behind the wheel, cranking the air conditioner to high, before setting off at a speed meant to crush any slow-moving bystanders.

In a very short time, we squealed to a stop in front

of a large Victorian mansion. The Hotel Oloffson was originally built as a presidential summer palace. Used by the marines as a hospital during the initial U.S. occupation of 1915, it became the first hotel in Haiti.

Marcel led me up the steps and into the foyer. The hotel was expecting me, and in short order I followed Marcel into one of the veranda rooms with a view of the city.

He dropped my bag to the floor with a thud. "Monsieur Mandenauer has arranged for you to meet a friend."

"Edward has friends here?"

Marcel slid me a glance. "He has friends everywhere."

Of course he did.

"This friend will help you find what you seek."

I frowned. "You know what I seek?"

"There was a little trouble with a curse, *oui*?"

I wouldn't have referred to the beast ravaging New Orleans as a "little" trouble, but it sounded as if Marcel knew the basics.

In the Crescent City I'd seen amazing things, but none as fantastic as a man changing into a wolf and back again.

Werewolves are real. You might think this would be an upsetting bit of knowledge for a former PTA member, but it wasn't. Because if the werewolves of legend exist, doesn't it follow that zombies do, too?

"Edward told you why he sent me?"

"To remove a curse, you need the voodoo queen who performed it, and she is dead."

"For about a hundred and fifty years."

Marcel lowered his voice to just above a whisper. "You must raise her from the grave. Zombie."

Not exactly. To raise a shuffling, decaying, frightening nightmare was not what I aspired to do. Though a George Romero *Night of the Living Dead* type zombie might be enough to satisfy Edward, it was not enough to satisfy me. I couldn't sentence my child to become such a creature.

I'd been searching for a way to bring life from death since I'd left here the last time. All I'd found was more death. Then I began to hear whispers of incredible power in these mountains, an ability beyond the mere reanimation of a corpse. However, I hadn't had the means to return to Haiti, neither the funds to search the island the way it needed to be searched nor the cash to pay for what a secret like that must cost.

Until now.

I strolled onto the veranda and stared at the distant hills. Somewhere out there was a voodoo priest who, according to the latest rumors, could raise the dead to live again.

As if they'd never been dead at all.

2

Can you imagine? No more death.

I had a hard time believing it myself. But I wanted to.

In New Orleans I'd often spouted platitudes about death being the beginning, not the end, a new plane, a different world, an adventure. Maybe it was.

I still wanted my daughter back.

I turned away from the city, moving into the room where Marcel waited. "When will I meet Mandenauer's friend?"

"The friend will come to you, Priestess." At my scowl Marcel corrected himself. "*Miss* Cassandra."

"When?" I repeated.

"When it is time." On that helpful note, Marcel opened the door and disappeared.

I didn't bother to unpack. As soon as I had a direction, I was out of here.

Exhausted, I fell asleep across my bed still wearing

my travel outfit of loose jeans, a black tank top, and black tennis shoes. When I awoke, night had fallen.

The noises of Port-au-Prince seemed louder in the still, navy blue darkness. Under a new moon, the sky was as devoid of shining silver as my jewelry box had been before I discovered werewolves.

My beringed fingers sought out the shiny crucifix around my neck, worn not for religious purposes but for protection. These days I overflowed with the stuff. I'd once thought it best to keep protective amulets hidden, but I'd learned it didn't hurt to have them displayed, either.

I turned on my side and froze. The door to my room was open, and someone stood on the veranda.

"Hello?" Slowly I sat up. "I'm Cassandra."

"Priestess."

The word was a hiss, reminding me of Lazarus, the python I'd left in New Orleans. He'd been my only friend until the crescent moon curse had brought Diana Malone into my life.

A cryptozoologist sent to New Orleans to investigate tales of a wolf where one didn't belong, she'd gotten the surprise of her life when she'd found a whole lot more than a wolf. She'd wound up in my shop investigating the voodoo curse, and we'd bonded, as women sometimes do.

The hovering shadow continued to hover, so I murmured, "Come in, please."

As soon as the words left my mouth, the figure glided

over the threshold. I flicked on the light, my eyes widening at the sight of the woman in front of me.

Tall and voluptuous, she was also gorgeous and ancient. Her skin café au lait, her eyes were as blue as mine. She was clothed in a long, flowing purple robe, and a matching turban covered her head. This was what a voodoo priestess should look like. Too bad I'd never be able to carry it off.

"I am Renee," the woman murmured. "You wish to learn about the curse of the crescent moon?"

Her accent was French, her diction upper-class. She might be from here, but she'd learned English somewhere else.

That, combined with the shade of her skin and eyes, marked Renee as mulatto—a nonoffensive term in Haiti, referring to the descendants of the free people of color from the Colonial era. Their mixed race had afforded them great wealth, as well as the rights of French citizens.

Why I'd expected Mandenauer's friend to be a man I wasn't quite sure. Maybe because he was so old the idea of a lady friend kind of creeped me out. Like catching your grandparents in flagrante delicto on the kitchen floor. I wanted to stick a needle in my eye to make *that* image go away.

"Uh, yes. The crescent moon," I managed. "Is it true a voodoo curse can only be removed by the one who did the cursing?"

"Yes."

"And if that person is dead?"

"Ah, I see." Her head tilted; the turban didn't move one iota. Impressive. "You have come to learn of the zombie."

I couldn't think of any reason to be secretive about it. "I have."

A crease appeared in Renee's nearly perfect brow. She didn't have many wrinkles, so why did I think she was ancient? Must be something in the eyes.

"Raising the dead is a serious and dangerous proposition," she murmured.

"But it can be done?"

"Of course."

I caught my breath. "Have you done it?"

"Such a thing is against the laws of both man and God."

I didn't worry about either one anymore. There was nothing the law could do to me that was worse than what God had already done.

You'd think that after what happened to my child I wouldn't believe in God. And for a while I hadn't. I'd begun to study voodoo for one reason—Sarah—but I'd been seduced by what I'd found there.

Voodoo is a complex religion—adaptable, tolerant, monotheistic. A lot of what I'd learned made sense. For instance, there can't be evil unless there's good.

And I believed in evil. Much more than I'd ever believed in anything else.

Renee frowned, as if she'd heard my thoughts. She'd probably just read my expression. I cared about nothing but raising life from death. That kind of obsession could be hazardous to everyone's health. I knew it, but I couldn't change what I felt, what I needed, who I was.

"Have you ever raised the dead?" I repeated.

"No."

I released my breath in a hiss of disappointment.

"But I know someone who has."

Anticipation made me dizzy. "Where can I find this person?"

"Raising the dead is an act performed only by a *bokor*. You know what that is?"

"A *houngan* who serves the spirits with both hands— an evil priest."

"There are no absolutes," Renee murmured. "Any *houngan* must know evil to fight it, just as a *bokor* must at one time have embraced good to hold any hope of subverting it."

Sometimes I longed for the days of black-and-white, or at least their illusion.

"What if you're raising the dead for good?" I asked.

"Nothing good can come of such a thing. In death there is peace everlasting. Though the living fear it, the dead embrace it. They do not wish to come back here."

"And you've talked to many dead people?" I snapped. "They've told you this?"

"Death comes to all of us when it is our time. There are no accidents."

"I don't believe that!"

My voice was a little too loud, a little too strident. Renee's eyebrows lifted.

I needed to be careful. The woman wasn't stupid.

She'd figure out I was in Haiti for a reason other than *Jäger-Sucher* business, and I'd discover nothing.

"What I believe doesn't matter," I said more calmly. "Edward wants me to find a way to end the curse of the crescent moon. From what I've been able to discover, that means bringing back from the dead the voodoo queen who did the cursing so she can remove said curse. Can you help me learn how to do this?"

Renee studied me for several ticks of the clock, then lifted her long, slim hands—which didn't appear very old, either—and lowered them. "There is a man in Port-au-Prince—"

"I heard there was one in the mountains," I interrupted.

Renee's eyes flashed. "He is not someone you wish to learn from."

"He who?"

"Names have power," Renee whispered. "I will not give voice to his."

I agreed with the names-have-power sentiment. In legend and myth, many curses could be broken by the use of someone's name, although in practice, I've never found this to be true.

You could call a werewolf's human name until you were three inches from dead and the beast would not change form. I'd heard it said that a key part of the ceremony for raising a zombie involved calling the departed's name three times. Since I didn't know the rest of the ceremony, I'd never been able to discover if that particular name game was true.

"I need to meet this man," I said.

"No, you do not. To raise the voodoo queen you must only learn the ceremony. Bring her out of the grave for an instant; she will do as you ask; then you will put her back where she belongs."

"And the man in the mountains?" I tried to keep the eagerness from my voice, but I doubted I was successful. "He does something different?"

Renee turned toward the veranda. For an instant I thought she might glide right out the door, and I took a single step forward. Foolish, really. I doubted I'd be able to stop her from doing anything she wanted to do. I sensed great power in Renee. Though it wasn't voodoo, it was something.

However, she didn't move, merely stared at the distant rolling hills, turned the shade of evergreen beneath the ebony skies.

"Have you ever heard of the Egbo?" she asked.

"No."

"In the bad times, when the people of Africa were stolen away and sold into bondage, there was a tribe known as the Efik of Old Calabar. They came to control all the slave trade on the coast."

"A tribe that sold its own people?" This I hadn't heard.

"Not its own. In Africa, then and now, there are divisions, wars, hatreds. One group would fight another; then the victor would sell his prisoners to the Efik, who in turn sold them to the white traders."

I shook my head. People, regardless of color, just weren't very nice to one another.

"The Efik had a secret society known as the Egbo. They began as a group of judges, but eventually the Efik had so many slaves in their possession, they had to find a way to keep them under control. The Egbo became a feared clan who imparted vicious punishment for the slightest wrong. The very whisper of their name was enough to cow captives into submission."

I could see where that would be helpful. Slave revolts were a reasonable fear when the population of the oppressed was often double that of the oppressor. In fact, Haiti had been the location of the only successful slave revolt in history.

"This is all very interesting, Renee, but what does it have to do with me?"

"The man in the mountains is said to be of the Egbo."

3

"Why would there still be an Egbo? There aren't any more slaves."

"Are you certain of that, Priestess?"

"Slavery's illegal. Isn't it?"

"Things are only illegal if you are caught doing them."

"No. They're always illegal."

She smiled. "So young and innocent despite the pain in your eyes."

I didn't want to discuss the pain in my eyes with her or anyone else.

"Are you trying to tell me the *bokor* is a slave trader?"

"Of course not. That is definitely illegal."

I rubbed my forehead. "What *are* you saying?"

"I will not tell you of the *bokor*. I will not take you to him. You are to stay away from the man. He is wicked and, I have heard, not quite sane."

Too bad he sounded like just the guy I needed to see.

"Fine." I lowered my hand. "When can I learn how to raise the voodoo queen?"

"I will send a *houngan* to meet with you."

"I thought only a *bokor* could raise the dead."

"Only a *bokor would*. Any priest or priestess may know how."

Too bad I'd never met one.

"Is raising the dead worth losing yourself?" she asked quietly.

I lifted my chin, met her eyes squarely. "Yes."

Renee held my gaze for a moment, then gave a sharp nod and stepped onto the veranda. By the time I followed, she was gone.

I returned to my empty room. I had to find the *bokor,* and I needed to get out of Port-au-Prince before Renee figured out what I was up to, if she hadn't already.

She'd tattle to Edward. He'd come down here, or send someone else. Then we'd have the shouting and the arguing and the dragging me home.

I didn't know Edward well, but I knew that much. He didn't like his orders disobeyed. I had not been sent to confront a possibly insane, violent man. I wasn't trained for it.

I'd be yanked out; one of Edward's minions would be sent in, and the only hope I had of getting my daughter back would explode in a burning ball of fire—the common *Jäger-Sucher* method of dealing with problems. Although, come to think of it, werewolves exploded when shot with silver, I wasn't sure what happened to evil voodoo priests.

I could not allow that to occur before I found out what I needed to know, so I locked my door and snuck out of the hotel.

Money talked, everywhere, and thanks to Edward I now had quite a bit of it. Less than two hours and several hundred dollars later, I entered a bar in a seedy section of Port-au-Prince—though, really, most of the city was iffy at best.

Blocked roads, huge potholes, open drains, and burning piles of garbage—I'd have been scared if I cared all that much about living. However, since I did care about my daughter, I carried the knife Edward's influence had allowed me to bring into Haiti in a sheath at my waist. I wasn't much good with guns, but the knife was a different story.

After my whole world fell apart I'd been understandably twitchy. I'd learned a little karate and how to handle a knife. I could even throw the thing, end over end, and hit a target on a tree eight times out of ten. So if a tree ever attacked me, I was in excellent shape.

Over the last few hours, I'd discovered there wasn't a Haitian alive who'd go near the *bokor*. But Devon Murphy would. For the right amount of cash, he'd sell his soul.

While the description made my lip curl—my husband had been obsessed enough with money to throw everything worthwhile away—nevertheless, I needed just such a man to lead me into the mountains.

Inside the Chwal Lanme—Creole for Seahorse if the icon on the sign was any indication—the scent of beer was overwhelming, and the crowd was thick. The tavern resembled an old-time sailors' haunt, with a teakwood bar and a ship's wheel as a chandelier. A lone white man slumped at an empty table, eyes half-closed, beer mug half-full.

"Murphy?" I asked.

His black gaze was beady in the bloated confines of his face. His beard gray and scraggly, he had to be fifty, maybe sixty. If he knew where the *bokor* lived, I didn't care if he was a hundred.

"May I?" I pulled out the empty chair.

He drained the last of his beer, then, setting the glass down with a click, motioned to it.

Lifting my hand for a refill, I sat. After the bartender brought the drink, waiting at my elbow until I paid—I guess running a tab wasn't an option in a place like this—I got right to business. "I hear you're the man to see if I need to go into the mountains."

Murphy grunted.

"How much will it cost to take me to the *bokor*?"

White, bushy brows slammed together as he drained the beer in one long sip. His mouth opened; no sound came out. His eyes rolled back, and he passed out, slumping forward until his forehead kissed the tabletop.

"Son of a bitch," I muttered.

"Is that any way for a lady to be talkin'?"

I spun around, and then I gaped. The man in the doorway was—

My mind groped for a word; all I could think of was *exotic*. His hair hung to his shoulders. Once light brown, it had been streaked nearly blond by the sun. Tangled in the strands were beads and feathers of unknown origin.

His skin had darkened to just short of bronze. Burnished gold bracelets were clasped around the honed biceps revealed by the torn-out sleeves of his once white shirt. Khaki trousers had been similarly attacked below the knees, leaving his sinewy calves as bare as his feet.

But what really drew my attention was his face. With sharp cheekbones, a square chin, and eyes that hovered between blue and gray, he was stunning.

When he tilted his head, a hoop flashed in his left ear. Before I could stop myself my hand lifted to my own pierced but no longer adorned lobe.

He smiled and instead of softening his face, the expression, combined with the hoop, made me think of marauding pirates and Errol Flynn.

"Were you looking for me, mademoiselle?"

His first words had sounded Irish; now his accent had traveled to France. I glanced at the sloppy drunk spread out on the table in front of me. "God, I hope so."

"Which makes two of us. Step into my office."

He disappeared through the door. I hesitated only long enough to stroke my fingertips over the hilt of my knife before following.

As I entered a narrow alleyway, the heat of a tropical night caressed my face. The man leaned against a chain-link fence that separated the Chwal Lanme from another business of unknown origin. He lifted a bottle of beer to his mouth and drank.

Fascinated, I watched his throat work, captivated by a single drop of liquid that raced down his neck before disappearing into the collar of his shirt. I swallowed, the sound an audible click in the silence that stretched between us.

He wiped his mouth with the back of his hand and offered the bottle to me. The idea of putting my lips where his had been unnerved me so much I stuttered. "Wh-who are y-you?"

"Who do you want me to be?"

"What?"

"For the right amount, I'll be whatever or whoever you want."

His accent was American now. He made me dizzy.

"I don't understand."

He lifted the beer, drank, then lowered the bottle. "Who are you looking for?"

"Devon Murphy."

"Then you've come to the right place."

"You're Murphy?"

"I am."

I was no longer sure if I was happy about that or not.

He took a step closer. I took a step back. My shoulders skimmed the wall of the tavern. He towered over me, which wasn't hard since I wasn't tall, but I figured he was well over six feet of wiry muscle.

My fingers crept toward my knife. His closed over them before they got there, and my gaze locked with his.

"No," he said softly, squeezing to a point just short of pain before releasing my hand.

He didn't move, continuing to crowd me, his body so close I swore it brushed against mine. All I had to do was bring up my knee, fast, and he'd go away—or perhaps go down—but I didn't do it. I didn't want to.

What was it about Devon Murphy that fascinated me? His beauty? His mystery? His strength?

Perhaps it was just my deprivation. I hadn't been with a man since I'd learned the truth about my husband. Before that, there'd only been Karl. I'd thought I was dead inside, but I guess I'd been wrong.

"Back off," I ordered.

His eyes widened; his lips twitched, but he moved. Suddenly I could breathe again. Unfortunately, all I could smell was him.

Why didn't he stink like a half-naked tavern-dwelling beer drinker should? Why did he smell like soap, rainwater, and sunshine? I had a thing for sunshine.

I shook my head hard enough to make it ache. When my vision cleared, he was still gorgeous and right in front of me. I thought of my daughter and why I had come.

"I heard you know the mountains."

He shrugged. "As well as any man can know them."

"Will you take me somewhere?"

"That depends upon where that somewhere is."

"I don't know where it is. I only know what I need to find." My lips tightened. "Make that who."

"You're searching for someone in the mountains? I haven't heard of any tourists being lost."

"Do I look like a tourist?"

"Except for the knife, I'd say yes."

"I'm not."

He lifted his hands in surrender. "My mistake. There aren't a lot of tiny white women running around Haiti. What are you?"

"None of your business. All you need to know is that I can pay, if you deliver."

"Deliver what?"

"Me. To the *bokor*."

His mouth flattened as the light in his eyes brightened. "Mezareau?"

I experienced a sudden chill despite the heat of the night, as if someone were staring intently at the center of my back. I glanced around, even though no one was here but us.

I shook off my unease, excited to hear the man's name at last. "You know him?" I asked.

"Not personally. No."

"You know where he is?"

His face became guarded. "Perhaps."

I tried to refrain from sneering. "How much?"

"A hundred thousand."

I laughed. "Dollars? Try again."

He shrugged. "No skin off my nose."

"I heard you'd do anything for money."

While that should have been insulting, Murphy merely smiled.

"What's so bad about the mountains?" I asked. "Why won't anyone go there?"

"It's not the mountains that keep people away, but Mezareau. He's . . . not right."

"Who is?"

Murphy tilted his head again, and I was distracted by the glint of his earring. Was the thing hypnotizing me? "What happened to make your eyes so sad and your voice so sharp, Miss . . . ?"

"Cassandra," I supplied.

He continued to wait for my last name, but he'd be waiting a long time.

"Hmm," he said when I didn't answer. "Secrets, *mon cher*?"

This time he spoke French with the accent of the Irish.

"How do you do that?" I demanded.

He spread his hands, trying to appear innocent but failing. "I didn't do anything."

"You change accents every other minute. Where are you from?"

"Everywhere. Nowhere. Here."

"Secrets?" I mocked.

"You tell me yours," he winked, "and I'll tell you mine."

"When hell freezes over."

"You don't want to share?"

"Sharing always gets me into trouble."

He smirked and my cheeks heated.

"I doubt you'll tell me anything anyway," I continued, "or at least not the truth."

He put his hand against his chest in a dramatic gesture. A silver ring encircled one thumb. "You don't trust me?"

"No."

"Yet you want me to lead you into the darkest jungle," he said.

"There isn't a jungle anymore."

The majority of Haiti was marked by a complete lack of tree cover. Deforestation caused by a total reliance on wood as energy and charcoal for cooking had decimated the country before the twentieth century. There were only a few forests left, and they were national parks.

"Figure of speech." Murphy's mouth curved. "How do you know I won't take the money and run?"

"Because I won't be giving it to you until we get back."

"How do I know you have it?"

"I do."

He shook his head. "I have a better idea."

His gaze wandered over me and I rolled my eyes. "Get another idea."

He laughed. "Sadly, that one seems to be stuck in my mind."

"You and most men."

"Yes. We are a disgusting lot."

Now he sounded English. I resisted the childish urge to kick him in the shin. "Is there anyone else I can hire?"

He leaned against the fence, crossed his arms. His muscles bulged against the golden bracelets. The jewelry, the beads, the feathers, should have made him effeminate, but they strangely had the opposite effect.

"What do you think?" he murmured.

I didn't bother to answer. I'd already been from one end of town to the other. Everyone was terrified of the *bokor,* if they would even admit to knowing what one was or that one existed. The single person who didn't seem afraid, merely wary, was Murphy. He was also the only man who'd known the *bokor*'s name or seemed to have any idea where to find him.

What was a hundred thousand dollars compared to both the life of my child and the death of the crescent moon curse? I was certain Edward would agree. I'd just opened my mouth to accept Murphy's terms when he spoke first. "You tell me why you want to meet Mezareau, and I'll take you to him for a reasonable fee."

My teeth snapped together, narrowly missing my tongue. "Why?"

He shrugged and glanced away. "You seem desperate."

And he didn't seem the type to care.

"What's reasonable?"

"Ten thousand plus expenses."

That *was* reasonable. If you didn't count baring your soul to a stranger in the mix.

"All right," I said, offering my hand.

His fingers enveloped mine, so long, so supple and clever, I was reminded of a pianist, until heavy calluses rubbed against my skin. My gaze flickered over the numerous cuts, scrapes, and scars on his.

Murphy held on too long, and when I realized I was letting him, I yanked my hand away, making no effort to hide my unease as I rubbed the tingling appendage against my jeans.

He didn't seem insulted. Not that I cared. He now worked for me.

"Do you want to do it here or inside?"

I gaped as images of "doing it" spilled through my head.

"Wh-what?" I blurted.

His grin told me he'd misled me on purpose, just because he could. This trip was not going to be easy, but then I'd never expected it to be.

"You said you'd tell me why you want to meet the *bokor*," he said.

"True." I strolled toward the door. "But I didn't say when."

4

I figured Murphy would argue semantics. Instead he murmured, "Touché," and followed me into the tavern.

"When can we leave?" I asked.

"As soon as I buy supplies."

"I'm supposed to hand over the cash and believe you'll come back?"

Anger flashed across his face. "I agree to do a job, I do it; otherwise I wouldn't live very long in a place like this."

Third-world countries such as Haiti did possess a "hang the horse thief" mentality. I couldn't say I blamed them. People had very little; they protected what they did have with a vengeance. Literally.

"All right." I reached under my shirt to extract money from the belly bag where I kept it. Murphy's gray-blue eyes followed every move.

"When can we leave?" I repeated.

"Sunup."

My watch read well past midnight. He obviously wasn't going to patronize any of the retail establishments in town.

"Are you hiring bearers?

"No one would come." His eyes met mine. "You still want to go?"

"Nothing could make me stop."

He continued to stare into my face for several seconds more, as if trying to figure me out. Good luck.

"All right then, I'll see you at sunrise."

I returned to the Hotel Olafsson, stopped in the lobby, and roused the manager. Edward had made certain I'd be able to draw funds whenever I might need them. I obtained a money order for the agreed-upon amount, then headed to my room.

As soon as I flicked on the light, I knew someone had been inside. Not the maid, either. They usually didn't draw symbols on the wall over the bed.

Bright red. Could be blood.

I crossed the floor and swiped my index finger against the plaster, then stared at the glistening residue. Probably was.

I didn't plan to wait around for an analysis. I didn't plan to call the authorities and tell them about it. I had to meet Murphy, and the police would not be amenable to letting me leave once they saw this.

In Haiti, everyone and their grandchild knew that drawing the icons of a coffin and a cross called the *loa* Baron Samedi, Lord of Death, gatekeeper to the other world.

Loas are the immortal spirits of voodoo. A bridge between God, known as the Gran Met, and humankind, they resemble the saints, angels, and devils of Catholicism.

And in a coincidence that probably wasn't, Baron Samedi also oversees the process of changing the dead into zombies and the shape-shifting of animals.

I wasn't sure what this meant, but I *was* sure I wanted to get out of here before I found out. I turned away from the wall and something crunched under my shoe.

Dirt lay strewn from the doorway to the bed. I'd been dancing in the stuff since I walked in.

The whisper of a thousand voices surrounded me. I staggered, feverish and dizzy. Someone had sent the dead.

Not just any someone. Only a *bokor* can perform this most feared of all black magic spells.

The sorcerer gathers a handful of graveyard dirt for every spirit sent to enter the body of his victim. The amount spilled on the floor of my room explained why I heard so many voices, why I felt innumerable hands pushing, pulling, and pinching me, the pressure in my head as the spirits attempted to invade my mind.

If they succeeded, I'd go insane and then I'd die. The only way to end such a spell was by the interference of a powerful voodoo practitioner.

Wait! That was me.

Struggling to think past the pain, the voices, the confusion, I searched for an answer and thought of a plan.

Each *loa* has a light and a dark side, Rada and Petro,

respectively. To call the dark side requires blood, usually of a large animal, often a pig.

My gaze went to the drawings on the wall. I bet the owner of that blood had oinked at one time.

Baron Samedi is a Gede, a spirit of death. To send him away, I needed to summon a spirit of life, and there was none stronger than Aida-Wedo, goddess of fertility. Conveniently she was also the wife of my guardian spirit, Danballah. I had never had a problem summoning either one of them, sometimes even when I didn't want to.

Muttering a prayer that tonight would be no different from any other, I thrust my hand into my bag, sighing with relief when my fingers closed around the tiny piece of chalk I kept there.

Gasping and grunting against the pain, fighting the insane images of blood, darkness, and isolation that flickered through my mind, on the floor I drew a rainbow—the symbol of Aida-Wedo, who rules the realm of new life.

"Help me," I murmured.

The spirits howled inside my head until my eardrums ached. For an instant I thought I'd only pissed them off; then light fell over my face.

A rainbow spilled into the room, the colors so bright I could see nothing else. Soft music drowned out the grating voices as peace surrounded me. Aida-Wedo's rainbow was the calm that followed every storm.

The whispers and the pain faded. When the colors went away, so had the bloody symbols on my wall.

As soon as I stopped shaking, as soon as I could breathe normally again, I called Edward. Though he preferred e-mail for updates—the old man had a powerful fixation with the Internet—I'd put my foot down at taking a laptop to Haiti. What was I going to do with it while I was trekking up a mountain?

Since I hadn't brought a cell phone, either—as if one would work here—I placed the call from my room.

"Mandenauer," he barked. Edward never bothered with "hello" or "good-bye."

"Sir." I resisted the urge to stand up straight and click my heels. Edward always had that effect on me.

"Have you found the answer?"

I very nearly said, *What was the question?* but Edward had a serious humor deficit.

No doubt being a spy in WW II had cured him of the urge to laugh long ago, and fighting monsters for the past sixty years hadn't improved his disposition. I'd been told he'd lightened up lately, but I found that hard to believe.

"I haven't even been here a day," I muttered.

"What *have* you discovered?"

"There's a man who knows how to raise the dead."

I didn't need to tell Edward the guy could be evil personified, at the least slightly insane, or that I was headed into the mountains with an opportunist to find him. I also didn't need to tell Edward I'd been threatened. What was he going to do about it?

"Has something happened?" he murmured.

How did he always know everything? Perhaps it was

just the wisdom of age, though I doubted it. Sometimes I wondered if Edward was human himself.

"I'm fine," I said, though that wasn't what he'd asked.

"Tell me, Cassandra."

Something in his voice made my eyes prickle. Before I burst into tears and lost my *Jäger-Sucher* membership card, I blurted out what I'd found in my room, and what I'd done about it.

"You're sure you didn't imagine the symbol? You've had a long trip, a difficult life."

I stilled. No one was supposed to know about my life. "What did you say?"

"You think I would allow just anyone to work for me? That I would not investigate your background before you appeared in New Orleans?"

"They promised—"

"They always promise."

Though only the U.S. marshal who'd relocated me, and maybe his boss, was supposed to know who I really was, where I now lived, Edward had powerful connections. There was little he couldn't do or discover. So why was I surprised he'd been able to discover me?

"Trust no one, Cassandra. You will live longer."

I frowned. His warning seemed prophetic, but what didn't around here?

"I shouldn't trust you?" I asked.

"That is your choice. Know that I will give anything to destroy the monsters."

"By 'anything,' you mean 'anyone.' "

"Of course."

At least he was honest. I couldn't throw stones. I'd give anything, and anyone, to have my daughter back.

"Returning to the bringing of the dead," Edward continued, "what does this mean?"

"Either there's a very powerful *bokor* who isn't too happy with me or I'm nuts."

"Which do you choose?"

I drew the toe of my shoe through the dirt on the floor, then lifted my index finger. Blood had dried on my skin.

"Bokor," I said.

"That would be my choice, as well. But how does this man even know you are there?"

Yeah, how did he?

"What is his name?" Edward asked, and it hit me.

Renee had refused to speak Mezareau's name. I had a feeling her reticence was not just because she disliked him.

When Murphy had spoken the *bokor*'s name aloud, a bizarre sensation of being watched had come over me. I didn't think that had been merely a goose walking over my grave but rather Mezareau opening his eyes, wherever he was, and seeing me.

"Cassandra," Edward said. "How does he know?"

Quickly I told him my thoughts, being careful not to utter the word *Mezareau*.

"This man sounds more like a legend than a reality."

My heart stuttered. I needed Mezareau, and all that I'd heard about him, to be real.

"Isn't dealing with legends turned to reality the main

thrust of the *Jäger-Sucher* job description?" I pointed out.

"Ja. Which is why you are in Haiti."

Touché, I thought, the word bringing Devon Murphy to mind. I glanced at the window. The eastern horizon was growing lighter, as was my mood at a new realization.

"Bringing the dead is serious voodoo," I murmured.

Someone who could perform such magic, at such a distance, was very powerful indeed.

"In other words," Edward said, "if he can bring the dead, he can also raise them."

"I'd say yes." My voice came out so chipper, you'd think we were discussing a surprise party.

"Where is he?"

"The mountains."

"Remote?"

"So I hear."

"Dangerous?"

"I've camped before." In a state park.

"That isn't what I asked."

"The mountains are remote, but I hired a guide who knows where to take me." Or so he said. "I'll be there and back before you know it."

I could tell by Edward's silence he didn't like the idea, which was why I hadn't planned on telling him. Until being possessed by the spirits of the dead had made me far too chatty.

"The man is powerful and evil," Edward said. "I should send someone to kill him instead."

"No!" I blurted.

I could almost see Edward lift his brow at my insolence, but I didn't need him sending one of his minions down here. I'd only met a few, but they'd all scared the crap out of me.

"I wasn't going to do it," Edward murmured. "I've had to cut back."

I didn't know what he meant, and I didn't want to.

"Are you certain that raising the voodoo queen is the sole way to end the curse of the crescent moon?" Edward asked.

"According to all the legends, as well as your pal Renee, yes."

"Legends are made to be broken. Once I believed only silver would end a werewolf's existence, but I learned differently."

"Since I have a lead on this particular method, I don't think I should waste time searching for an alternative."

"Fine. I'll expect a full report the instant you return to Port-au-Prince."

"Yes, sir."

Silence drifted over the line. I'd have thought Edward had hung up without a good-bye, again, except I hadn't heard a click and I still heard him breathing.

"You spoke with Renee?"

His voice was different. No longer brusque, there was a softness, and a wariness, which hinted that his question was not merely chitchat. As if Edward ever made chitchat.

"I spoke with her," I said.

"She was helpful?"

"Very."

Since he was asking questions, I decided to ask one of my own. "How do you know Renee?"

"She was in the resistance."

"In France?" My voice went up in pitch and volume.

"Where else?"

I couldn't get my mind around the idea that Renee, a black woman familiar with voodoo, had been a member of the French Resistance. But was that any more bizarre than werewolves, zombies, and bringing the dead?

5

"Did you two have something going?" I blurted.

"We had a war going," he said stiffly.

"Is that what you called it?"

"That is what everyone called it."

I felt bad about teasing him. Especially since Edward didn't seem to get my joke. Not a big shock since I'd never been all that funny. Even before my life went to hell ahead of me.

"That is in the past," he muttered. "Over."

I wasn't sure if he was referring to the war or to him and Renee. Probably both.

"You will discover what we need to know," he ordered. "Then report to me."

I opened my mouth to agree, but he'd already hung up.

Shaking my head, I went into the bathroom. The old man was strange, but he had good reason to be.

I washed my hands, my face, brushed my teeth, and left. I could have used a shower, but I wasn't willing to remain any longer in a place where the dead had swirled through the air, as well as my head. The symbol of Baron Samedi might be gone, but I wasn't taking any chances.

I checked out of the hotel. If Renee's *houngan* came, he wouldn't waste time searching for me, and if Renee tattled to Edward about where I'd gone, it wouldn't matter. I'd already tattled on myself.

The tavern was open, Murphy nowhere to be seen. A few stragglers lounged in dark corners, nursing the hair of the dog. A smattering of Creole filled the air. I understood a little of the language, but not enough to keep up in a normal conversation.

The bartender appeared to be the same one on duty as before. Maybe he was the only one they had, or even the owner. "I'm looking for Devon Murphy."

The man shrugged.

Swell. I'd given Murphy enough money to buy supplies, figuring he wouldn't disappear if there was the promise of much more. Maybe I'd figured wrong.

"I talked to him last night," I pressed. "In the alley?"

"Koboy?"

"What?"

He made the motion of shooting with both hands. *Bang-bang.* "John Wayne. Roy Rogers. Koboy."

"You call him Cowboy? Hell." That could not be good.

"He like to fight. More fists than gun. He very good at the fighting." The bartender grinned, revealing only a few working teeth.

"Where is he?"

The bartender pointed at the ceiling.

I stomped upstairs, the force of my steps an attempt to assuage my annoyance that I'd hired a man called Cowboy to take me into a remote wilderness. Why couldn't his nickname be Helpful Harry or Gentle George? Of course a man like that would probably not be very useful out where the wild things roamed. Perhaps Murphy's penchant for using his fists would come in handy—as long as he didn't use them on me.

He didn't seem the type. Of course, they never did.

I stroked my knife. If Murphy got pushy, punchy, or even too friendly, he'd discover just how talented with the weapon I was.

Several doors lined the second floor; only one was open. I headed there first and wished I hadn't. If I'd pounded on a few, Murphy would have heard me coming and had time to put on some clothes. As it was, I got an eyeful.

He was just pulling up his pants, more loose-fitting khakis, except these covered him from hip to heel. Underneath he wore nothing but skin. I should have known Murphy would be the type to go commando. I should also have figured he'd be the same bronze shade all over, and that his ass would be as incredible as his arms.

I *should* have known, probably did, so why was I standing in the doorway staring as if I'd never seen a naked man? Because I'd never seen one like him and I hadn't seen any for a very long time.

He wore no shirt, and my eyes were drawn to the rippling muscles of his back. Long, sinuous, defined—he'd gotten those from reps, not weight. The way he moved reminded me of the jungle cats Sarah had always loved at the zoo. Lions, tigers, leopards, jaguars, they all flowed with the same loose, muscular grace.

He slipped a faded green T-shirt over his head; his palm skated over his ribs, his belly, his hip, just ahead of the cloth, and the image of that hand touching me in just that way, of my mouth replacing his fingers, made me bite my lip before a moan escaped. I should have gotten laid before I'd come down here.

The floor creaked, and Murphy glanced back, eyebrows lifting at the sight of me just inside the doorway. "Ready?"

He had no idea.

Or maybe he did. The expression in his eyes, the twist to his mouth, said he knew exactly what he was doing and he liked it. Had he known I was there all along?

I remembered stomping on the steps and wondered for an instant if he'd pulled his pants down just so he could pull them up when I got to the doorway. But why?

I might have been pretty once, but anguish and guilt had put lines where they hadn't ought to be. And my body . . . well, it got me where I was going. But my sharp edges far outweighed my curves—in more ways than one. There was nothing about me that would entice a man like Devon Murphy to seduction.

I forced the foolish thoughts away. Murphy was a

game player. He liked to have the upper hand, and since he was working for me, he had to get it some way. No doubt he'd figured out, in the way of scam artists and opportunists everywhere, that I hadn't gotten naked in a helluva long time.

"Are *you* ready?" I asked.

"Born, baby."

"Gack." I pantomimed gagging; it wasn't that hard. "Spare me the infantile endearments."

He sat on the bed and began to put on his socks—heavy, white, athletic, as if he planned to do some jogging. Maybe he did.

"I'd call you Mrs. Whatever, but you won't tell me your last name."

"How do you know I'm a Mrs.?"

"You've got that look."

Murphy stuffed his right foot into a worn hiking boot. The boot soothed my nerves more than anything else had. He'd hiked before. I only hoped he'd done it here.

I lifted my gaze from his foot to his face and found him watching me.

"What look?" I asked.

"The 'some man done me wrong look.' I'm betting you're divorced. He screwed around. You after the *bokor* to kill him?"

I merely smiled. If I'd wanted Karl dead I could have killed him myself, many times. But death would have been too easy.

"I'll tell you why I need to see the *bokor* when you get me to the *bokor*," I said.

Murphy shrugged and finished with his left boot. "Can't blame a man for trying."

Trying what? To seduce me, or to find out what I was after? Either way, he'd failed, and he'd continue to fail until I decided he wouldn't.

I frowned. I meant I wouldn't let him discover my secrets until the time was right. I was never going to decide he could seduce me. Sleeping with a self-serving cheat of a liar once in my lifetime was quite enough, thank you.

Murphy leaned over and snagged two large packs from behind the bed. He handed one to me and swung the other onto his back. I occupied myself taking the things I needed out of my travel bag and stuffing them into the new backpack.

"I rented a Jeep," he said. "Today we drive; tomorrow we're on foot."

I nodded, struggling to hoist the heavy pack. Murphy studied me while he secured the straps over his shoulders and around his waist. Then he plucked the thing out of my hands and whirled me around.

His fingers brushed my arms, and even through the cotton of my blouse I felt the calluses. He stood too close; his hip brushed mine, and I caught the scent of rainwater. Was he bathing in the stuff?

"I can do it," I protested, inching away.

He yanked on the straps, and I stumbled backward, my rear end bumping his crotch. He grunted, the sound more interest than annoyance or pain, and I resisted the urge to stomp on his foot. Though he might act laid-back, even lazy, there was a latent violence in Murphy that made me think stomping on his toes would be like poking a panther with a stick: I wouldn't like what happened next.

With quick, clever fingers he secured the backpack, then gave me a little shove. I spun around too fast and the weight of the pack kept swinging. I nearly toppled over, but he caught my elbows and steadied me.

"You've hiked before?" he asked.

I shrugged, hoping he'd let that go.

"Cassandra. Have you hiked before?"

"I'll keep up. Don't worry about me."

His fingers tightened. "You've never been in the mountains, have you?"

"No."

"What about a forest, a hill, even a dale? Anywhere besides a shopping mall?"

My lips tightened. "I've been places you couldn't imagine."

They just weren't the wilderness. More like hell on earth.

Murphy said something in a language I didn't recognize, but a curse sounds like a curse, regardless. "The mountains are dangerous," he said. "You need to know what you're about up there."

"If I knew what I was doing, I wouldn't need you."

Murphy stared at me for several seconds. "Just do what I say when I say it."

Like that was going to happen, but I managed to nod anyway.

"How many days until we reach the *bokor*?" I asked.

"Depends."

"On what?"

"If he wants us to find him."

"And if he doesn't?"

Murphy brushed past me and headed for the stairs. "Then we're dead."

6

I let the comment pass. Maybe he was trying to scare me. Maybe he wasn't. Didn't matter.

I followed Murphy into the hall. "I hear you're called Cowboy."

He flinched, shoulders drawing in, backpack shifting. "Nicknames like that get people killed."

"Not John Wayne," I muttered. "He never died. In his movies anyway."

"Sure he did. *The Cowboys*. How's that for irony? I think he died in one of his war movies, too. *Green Berets* maybe. Or *Sands of Iwo Jima*."

"You're a John Wayne fan?"

"Isn't everyone?"

"I thought John Wayne was an *American* icon. Don't the Europeans consider him a sad commentary on our cowboy nation?"

Now *I* was fishing—trying to get Murphy to admit

where he was from. He merely shrugged, and I was forced to try harder.

"Why do they call you Cowboy?"

"They call me Koboy." He gave the name a Creole twist.

"Whatever," I snapped. "Why?"

"They call all Americans that."

Aha! I thought. What I said was: "Not me."

Murphy let his gaze wander from the tips of my brand-new hiking boots to the top of my bare head. I'd have to dig out my hat before too long or risk sunstroke. See, I knew a few things about the tropics.

"You don't look like a Cowboy," he said.

I eyed him down and up, the way he'd eyed me. With the feathers in his long hair and the earring in his ear, he looked more like an Indian—even if he was nearly blond. He'd taken off his arm bracelets, but not his silver thumb ring. After the bartender's comments about fighting, I wondered if that was more a brass knuckle than an adornment.

"So you're American?" I pressed.

He gave me a cocky smile. "You're thinkin' so?"

The brogue was back, thicker than ever. God, he was annoying.

Without waiting for my answer, Murphy started downstairs. I followed, bumping into his backpack when he paused only a few steps down.

"What—?" I began.

He lifted a hand, silencing me. His head tilted as he

listened to something, or someone, below. From the tension in his body I knew enough to shut up.

"Upstairs," the bartender said. "But he is with a woman."

I made a face, which Murphy, when he whirled and practically shoved me onto the landing, ignored.

"Let's go."

He pushed past me, grabbing my hand as he went, then dragged me after him down the back stairs, which were narrow, creaky, and dangerous. We burst out of the tavern and into the alley where a battered Jeep waited.

Murphy let go of me and jumped into the driver's seat. I scooted around the hood and barely managed to dive in before he floored it, scraping the passenger door against the chain-link fence.

We spilled onto the street. He flicked a glance into the rearview mirror. "Duck," he said, the tone so casual I could only stare at him dumbly.

He reached over and shoved my head into his lap, dipping his own just as gunfire erupted. He didn't stop, didn't flinch, just kept driving, and in a moment we'd left our pursuers behind.

His thigh pressed against my cheek; his zipper scraped the back of my head. We'd jumped into the car still wearing our backpacks and mine was twisted awkwardly between my shoulders and the seat. His had to be shoving him practically into the steering wheel.

I sat up; he let me. I removed the pack and tossed it backward, then helped him do the same. Silence settled between us, a silence I couldn't let stand. "Friends of yours?"

"They didn't seem very friendly."

"What did they want?"

"Me dead, I think."

"I can understand the sentiment, but what did you do?"

He gave a short bark of laughter and cast me a speculative glance. "You want me dead, sweet thing?"

Southern accent this time.

"Maybe not dead," I allowed.

He was, after all, the only one willing, or perhaps able, to take me to the *bokor*.

"If not dead, then what?" he asked.

"Truthful."

Did he really know how to find the *bokor*? Or was he taking me into the mountains with nefarious designs, if not on my person, then on my money or my life?

My fingers crept to the knife at my waist. I really wished I could trust him, but I didn't.

"The instant you're truthful with me, sugar, I'll be truthful with you."

I scowled. He had a point; however, I wasn't going to tell him what I was really after until we were too far away from Port-au-Prince for him to take me back and dump me at the nearest insane asylum.

"The way you switch accents gives me a damn headache," I muttered.

"A damn headache?" *Southern.* "Well, we cannot have that." *English.* "Which accent should I use?" *American.*

I didn't answer. I wanted to slug him.

"I'll pick one," he said. "American seems to get me the farthest around here. Can't imagine why, since you people invaded the place not too long ago."

Over ten years ago, but who was counting? Probably the Haitians.

"We do that," I said drily. "Invade. But we're only trying to help."

Murphy snorted.

His words—*you people*—made me rethink his nationality. I wasn't sure what he was all over again.

He stared into the rearview mirror and frowned. I turned around so fast my neck crackled, but the road behind us was empty.

"I didn't know them," he murmured.

"Then why did we run?"

"I owe some money. I planned to pay as soon as we got back."

"Sure you did."

"Stiffing people is not healthy in these parts."

I thought of my drug-dealing husband and the enforcers he'd employed. "It's not healthy in *any* parts."

He cast me a quick glance. *Oops.* Must have let too much emotion shine through. A mistake I rarely made anymore. I schooled my face into the polite mask I'd perfected since I'd become Priestess Cassandra. But I doubted the expression fooled Murphy.

"Anyone who comes to Chwal Lanme asking for me is usually someone I owe."

"Until I showed up."

"Which was a refreshing change of pace."

"I bet. Let's get back to the goons with guns. Who were they if not the people you owe or their minions?"

"Minions?" His quick grin was infectious. I very nearly smiled back. "Gotta love that word."

"Unless you're a minion."

"Mmm." He concentrated on making a tight turn and avoiding a stray dog taking a nap in the middle of the road. "They could have been after you."

"Except they asked for you."

"Perhaps because you were asking for me. All over town from what I gathered."

Could the men who'd come to the tavern have been Karl's? It had been so many years since I'd changed lives, with not a hint that anyone had found me, I'd begun to feel safe, and maybe I'd made a stupid mistake.

My coming to Haiti was an invitation for them to dispose of me. No one would ever figure out what had happened. Or at least that was what the assassins thought. I doubted they knew about Edward and his own army of minions.

Still, it wouldn't do me a whole helluva lot of good if Edward figured out I'd been killed for my previous life rather than my current one. I'd still be dead. And so would my little girl.

"No one's after me," I lied. "I'm just Priestess Cassandra, your friendly New Orleans voodoo practitioner."

"Your *what*?"

"Did I neglect to mention that?"

He shot me a glare.

"Sorry." Funny, I didn't sound sorry at all. "It's just my job. No worries."

His jaw worked as he ground his teeth together. I'd finally annoyed him, and I wasn't even trying.

"You come to Haiti," he said in a voice gone deep with fury, "and ask me to take you into the mountains to meet an evil voodoo sorcerer, but you *forget* to tell me that you're a voodoo priestess, and I'm supposed to think nothing of it?"

"I'm not paying you to think anything of it."

"That's the problem with some people; they can't help but think. Even if they aren't being paid for it." He slid a glance my way. "You don't look like a voodoo priestess."

"Yeah, I get that a lot."

We left Port-au-Prince behind, driving north along the coast, before turning inland toward more distant mountains.

No further shots were fired; no one tried to stop us. Of course Haiti had only two main roads. The one we were on eventually led to Cap Haitien. Le Cap, the former capital, was the main launching place to the nearby beaches of the Labadie Peninsula. Sun, sand, and surf—too bad we didn't have the time.

A second road curved southwest, ending at Les Cayes. All other thoroughfares required a Jeep or a truck or one's feet to traverse.

As the day wore on, my jaw ached from clenching it to avoid biting off my tongue as we lurched over every bump and rut in the country. When dusk approached, Murphy wheeled onto a hard-packed dirt track.

We stopped at the base of a tree-covered mountain, the foliage such an unusual sight I could do little but stare. My skin tingled at the loss of sensation and my ears rang at the loss of sound.

"We'll camp here," Murphy said.

"Already?"

He glanced at me, no doubt trying to figure out if I was being sarcastic. I wasn't sure myself. The trip had been long, but we hadn't been walking. We still had about an hour before dark.

"No point in going on tonight," he answered, taking my question at face value. "Better to get a fresh start in the morning."

"Trees," I murmured.

His brow creased. "You OK?"

"It's just . . . there aren't that many trees here and suddenly—" I pointed.

"This is the south side of a national park near Citadelle La Ferriere."

"The fortress?" I stared at the midnight blue mountain rising above us.

In the early nineteenth century, King Henri Christophe built the largest fortress in the Western Hemisphere three thousand feet above sea level. The 12-foot-thick walls and 140-foot-high ramparts had to have impressed everyone who'd managed to climb high enough to see them.

"The *bokor* lives in a national park?" I found that hard to believe.

"Not exactly," Murphy said, and grabbed his backpack.

I stepped out of the Jeep and promptly fell on my face.

Murphy hunkered down next to me. "You OK?"

"My legs are asleep."

"We didn't stop to eat. That was a mistake."

"I didn't notice." Ever since there'd been no one to worry about but me, food had lost its allure.

Murphy helped me to my feet, but he didn't let go. "You want to die, sweetie pie?"

His blue-gray gaze remained steady on mine. If I wasn't careful, he'd wrest every secret from my head, and there were some in there I didn't ever want to examine again.

"Rhyming now?" I kept my voice light as I inched out of his grip. "Please stop."

"Only if you start. Eating."

"Skipping meals has never bothered me before. I'm not sure why it did now."

"The heat."

"This isn't heat. Try living in New Orleans."

"You don't sound like you're from New Orleans."

"Because sounding like you're from somewhere means that you are?"

"Point taken," he said. "But not eating, combined

with the adrenaline rush of being chased and shot at, means dizziness and eventual fainting."

"Then I should be just dandy from now on."

"How you figure?"

"We lost those guys. So we shouldn't be chased or shot at again."

"From your mouth to God's ears," he muttered.

"What's that supposed to mean?"

"Once we get out there," he pointed to the trees, "it'll be open season for anything."

"You're kidding."

"Why do you think no one else would take you where you want to go?"

"They didn't know where the *bokor* was?"

He shook his head, and his earring sparked orange in the light of the setting sun. "The locals know better than to come to this place. They call it Montagne sans retour. Mountain of No Return."

"Why do they call it that?"

"Because people have a nasty habit of disappearing whenever they go looking for Mezareau."

That didn't sound good, but I refused to be intimidated by rumors and a nickname. Nevertheless, I cast a wary glance at the steadily darkening shadows. "We should probably stop using his name."

"Why?"

"He's a *bokor*, a sorcerer. Speaking his name out loud could allow him to see us, maybe hear us. He'll know we're coming before we even get there."

"Right."

"How else do you explain the disappearing people?"

"Oh, I don't know. . . ." He spread his hands. "Great big guards who dispose of any and all trespassers?"

"Maybe."

But I didn't think so. I'd felt watched from the moment Murphy had said the *bokor*'s name. I might be paranoid, but that didn't mean someone wasn't spying on me.

7

Night settled over us like a cool, velvet curtain. I'd never slept under the stars. I wasn't sleeping now. Despite my exhaustion, oblivion would not come.

Murphy wasn't having any problem. After we'd partaken of cold sandwiches and warm water—no campfire in this heat—he'd rolled into his sleeping bag, and I hadn't heard another word out of him. At least he didn't snore.

In the years since I'd lost everything, I'd had trouble sleeping. Every time I closed my eyes I saw my daughter the way I'd seen her last.

In a coffin. No mother should have to see that.

I tried to count stars. There had to be a trillion. If assigning them a number didn't bore me into unconsciousness, what would?

I'd reached 810 when a rustle from the foliage made me tense and lose track.

I held my breath, strained my ears, waited. Then

I waited some more. Just when I'd begun to relax, figuring I'd heard nothing, or if something only a snake
or a rodent, the sound came again—closer this time—
much bigger than any rodent, much heavier than any
snake.

My knife was on the ground next to me, but only a
few feet away lay Murphy's rifle. He had a pistol somewhere, too. I'd seen him take it out of a cavernous
pocket in his cargo pants, making me wonder what else
he kept in them.

I was thinking far too often and too fondly of what
Murphy kept in his pants. I wished I'd never seen his ass.

I wasn't wishing all that hard. A girl had to have
some fantasies.

The rustle continued, slow and stealthy, from the far
side of the camp. I had an intense desire to turn and
look, except I doubted I'd be able to see. Only a faint
sliver of a moon shone so despite the trillion stars,
there wasn't much light.

Nevertheless, I walked my fingers across the ground
until my hand closed over the rifle, then drew it toward
me, wincing at the scratch of metal against dirt.

Sleeping Beauty slept on. I felt so safe.

My other hand crept toward the flashlight I'd com-
mandeered in case I had to hit the outdoor bidet some-
time in the night. However, considering the sound of
what was out there, I'd do better to hold it until morning.

Slowly I turned my head, just as a faint rumble broke
the night. Distant thunder? Or the growl of a predator
much closer than that?

Considering the number of stars in the clear night sky, I was pretty sure I was in trouble.

I hit the button on the flashlight. A bright yellow beam brushed the trees and the foliage, highlighting a single pair of eyes.

"Shit!" I exclaimed, sitting up, fumbling with the gun. I hadn't really expected to *see* anything!

"What the—?"

Murphy had awoken at last, but I didn't have time to explain. The bushes shook, the eyes never blinked, as whatever waited there crouched and crept closer. I dropped the flashlight, and the glare splashed across the ground.

There came a rush of movement, the crack of twigs, the crunching of rocks. Though I knew it was foolish, I fired.

The report was obscenely loud, the silence that followed even more so.

"What the fuck?" Murphy yanked the rifle from my hands.

I scrambled to my feet, figuring I'd have less chance of getting my throat ripped out if I was standing.

"There. There." I couldn't seem to do anything but point and repeat myself.

Murphy got my meaning immediately and spun toward the threat, lifting the rifle to his shoulder. I was impressed with his speed, his agility, his fearlessness, as he stalked toward the shadowed trees.

I expected something large and fierce to erupt. Something I'd really pissed off by shooting at it.

Nothing happened. Maybe I'd hit the thing.

I snatched the flashlight off the ground and hurried after Murphy.

"Stay," he ordered.

I ignored him, shining the light on the area where I'd seen the eyes. Murphy reached out and shoved back the foliage.

I yelped, and the beam of light jiggled, revealing grass, dirt, a lot more trees, but little else.

He shot me a disgusted look. "You sure you didn't have a bad dream?"

"I wasn't even asleep, which is more than I can say for you."

"Sleeping is what we're supposed to be doing in the middle of the night."

"You were supposed to be protecting me."

"I don't recall protection as part of the deal. I'm taking you to the *bokor*."

"You can't take me if I'm dead!"

Well, he could, but that would be kind of sick.

"I woke up," he muttered.

"After I took care of things."

Murphy continued to frown into the night. "You sure you weren't dreaming?"

I scanned the shadowy darkness, traced the flashlight across the ground. No blood, no paw prints. Hell. Maybe I *had* been dreaming.

But I didn't think so.

"You shouldn't shoot at people," Murphy said. "It gets you in trouble, especially when you hit them."

"Who said anything about people?"

"What else would be creeping up on us?"

"Something that growled, with shiny eyes—yellow, maybe green, hard to say in the dark. About so big." I leveled my hand near my waist.

Murphy stared at me as if I were crazy. "You think you saw an animal out here?"

"I know I did. I'm not nuts." *Lately*. "And I wasn't dreaming."

He shook his head and returned to his sleeping bag, placing the gun nearby.

I followed. "Aren't you going to stand guard?"

"Against what?"

"The . . . um . . ." I frowned.

"Exactly," he said, and put his hands behind his head, closing his eyes.

"Wolf?"

His lips twitched, but he kept his eyes closed. "In Haiti?"

Wolves did tend to hang around cooler climates. Unless they were werewolves.

I glanced at the trees again. If a werewolf had been out there, it would have run toward me rather than away. They were funny like that.

I turned back. "Jaguar?

"Nope."

"Cougar. Leopard. Coyote."

"Not here."

"What *do* they have?"

He opened one eye. "Flamingos are pretty common."

"That was *not* a flamingo."

Unless it was a very, very big one. In this new world I'd discovered a few months ago, such a thing was actually possible. Still, no matter how huge flamingos got, I didn't think they growled.

"Anything furry?" I pressed.

"Most of the wildlife was hunted into extinction centuries ago, but even before that, Haiti had no large mammals."

That's what they all say. Then there's the death and the bodies and the werewolves.

Take the situation in New Orleans—a place where wolves had been extinct for about a century. Yet— surprise!—there'd been some, but only when the moon rose.

But in defiance of popular legend, the New Orleans werewolf was a loup-garou, cursed to run as a wolf beneath the crescent moon instead of the full. This made for twice the bloodshed, since that particular phase waxed and waned on both sides of full.

According to Edward, the werewolves were evolving—using magic of many kinds to become more numerous, more powerful, more deadly. Perhaps they'd begun to use voodoo here.

"Go to sleep," Murphy murmured. "From now on it's just you, me, and our feet."

My gaze was drawn to the mountains rising above us.

Somehow I doubted that.

8

I didn't go back to sleep that night. How could I?

I did lie down, after scooting my sleeping bag closer to Murphy's. Not because I wanted to be nearer to him, but I had developed a sudden fondness for his gun.

As soon as the sun peeked over the eastern horizon, Murphy awoke. "We need to get a move on."

The guy had a decent work ethic, despite his laid-back, beach bum persona.

"The earlier we disappear into the mountains," he said, "the easier it'll be to stay ahead of whoever's chasing us."

"I thought we lost them."

"Maybe. Maybe not. Better to get out of here before we find out, *oui*?"

"Oui," I said, then scowled. "I thought you were going to stick to a nationality."

"That I was," he said with a touch of the Irish.

The more I was with Murphy, the more curious

I became about him, which was probably not a good thing considering the length of my sexual deprivation. While I should have been rolling my sleeping bag tightly and cinching it onto my backpack, instead I watched him move, fascinated with the long, lithe length of him, the way the sun cast golden streaks through his hair and sparked shiny flames off his earring.

The feathers were still there, but tangled from the night, and that image gave me all sorts of other ones. His hands flexed as he filled his backpack, the long, agile fingers making me shiver despite the early heat of the day. How would that silver thumb ring feel if he ran it all over my body?

Pretty damn good.

I forced myself to turn away from the intriguing sight of Devon Murphy bending over and got busy. I had no business fantasizing about the man. I had no business fantasizing about any man. Sex was part of a life that was dead to me.

So why did I keep thinking about it?

"Ready?" Murphy asked.

We'd loaded our packs and partaken of gourmet granola bars and some exquisitely warm water.

"You just going to leave that there?" I indicated the Jeep with a lift of my chin.

"I can't figure out a way to take it along."

To me, leaving the vehicle behind was like a big arrow pointing where we'd gone.

"This is a crossroad," he said more seriously. "I'm sure you know what that means."

I nodded my understanding.

Crossroads and cemeteries were where black magic lived. No self-respecting Haitian would come anywhere near here.

Murphy and I traveled steadily, the slight incline causing my legs to grumble. The tropical heat made sweat drip from beneath my New Orleans Saints cap onto my pricey new hiking boots.

Though most of Haiti had been cleared for farming, then farmed often and badly, so that the land was dying, I saw no indication of it here. As we moved farther and farther above sea level, the trees grew closer and closer together, with sections of foliage so dense Murphy had to hack a path with his machete.

By midafternoon, my sense of direction was shot. The sun would have helped, but only a few sparkles of light managed to penetrate the dense cover. By my calculations, we should have walked off a cliff several miles back.

"How do you know where to go?" I asked.

"Do you think I'd have taken the job as your guide if I didn't know what I was doing?"

For money I figured he'd do anything, and I had to wonder why. He'd been educated . . . somewhere. He obviously had a gift for languages. Without the feathers and the beads, he could work at the UN. So what was he doing here?

"Why not here?" Murphy asked.

Whoops. Guess I'd said that out loud.

"Living above a tavern in a slum, hacking your way

up a mountain, dodging creditors and bullets, there has to be something more."

He glanced over his shoulder. "Seems exciting enough to me."

"You're looking for excitement?"

"I'm looking for something," he muttered.

For the rest of the afternoon the heat, the pace, the strangely omnipresent jungle, made conversation minimal. As dusk threatened, I smelled water.

At first I thought it was Murphy's maddening scent combined with my continual thirst. We'd been drinking steadily but sparingly. On a trip like this we couldn't carry as much water as we should.

When I realized the aroma was actual water and not his skin—thank God; I'd begun to have fantasies of licking his flesh and tasting a crystal-clear lake—then I had to struggle against the urge to shove Murphy to the ground and run right over his back.

He gave a last mighty hack with his machete, and the vines fell away to reveal a secluded pond surrounded by ferns. The gentle lap of the water against the banks, the scent of mist, the pleasant chill in the air, caused me to wonder again if we'd stumbled onto a place out of time.

I took several quick steps forward and Murphy flung out an arm to stop me.

"Move that or die," I snapped.

"Might be snakes."

"I've got a pet python. Snakes I can handle."

He gave a long, slow blink, the movement only

emphasizing the dark length of his lashes. "You have a what?"

I suppose that did sound weird to the uninitiated.

"I'm a voodoo priestess," I said. "I need a snake."

"If you say so."

Actually, I hadn't *needed* a snake; I'd wanted one.

Lazarus wasn't cuddly, but after my husband's betrayal and my daughter's death, being touched had made me twitchy. A snake companion seemed like good idea at the time. Lazarus was loyal, and he rarely peed on the rug.

"Just be careful around the water." Murphy lifted his arm.

"There aren't any poisonous snakes in Haiti."

"So they say." Murphy didn't appear convinced.

I lifted the amazingly cool, clear water to my mouth and drank for several long, wondrous moments, then dunked my head, splashed my neck, and let my wrists dangle beneath the surface until the heat melted away.

When I felt almost human again, I glanced around, figuring Murphy was doing the same, or making camp. Instead I found him staring at me.

Droplets of water sparkled in his hair, ran down his neck, and dampened the collar of his shirt. I wiped the back of my hand across my mouth and his eyes, gone misty green as if they'd taken on the hue of the trees, followed the gesture.

"You don't know, do you?" he murmured.

"Know what?"

He walked toward me, his gait easy, his manner

calm, yet he seemed edgier than ever before. "How goddamn sexy you are with your skin all hot, and your mouth all cool."

My cool mouth fell open. "I didn't; I'm not—"

"Maybe you don't," he said, "but you are."

"Huh?"

Who's sexy now? my mind mocked.

Not that I wanted to be sexy. I had no time for dates, for men, for anything but my mission to save Sarah.

Except this man made me think of sex all the time. Wild jungle sex, on the ground, in the water, against a tree. Hell, anywhere, everywhere, any way that he wanted.

He came so close I felt heat rise off of him like steam. His gaze wandered away from my face, and I followed it.

My ablutions had soaked the front of my shirt. My bra, nothing more than a wisp of cotton meant to keep my nipples from thrusting obscenely against my tank top, was not doing its job. No wonder Murphy couldn't stop looking at me. At them. They were practically begging to be looked at. And touched.

I tried to turn away, but he stopped me with just a brush of his fingertips on my arm. "What are you searching for, Cassandra?"

The question was so out of place, I very nearly answered him. Why was he so interested in what I was doing in the jungle?

"Nice try," I said, and inched back.

Instead of letting go, he yanked me into his arms.

Maybe his show of interest wasn't just an act after all. *Probably,* if the force of his kiss and the thrust of his erection were any indication.

I knew next to nothing about men, but I'd heard they could become aroused with very little encouragement. Like "hello," or perhaps a single glimpse of a woman's hardened nipples.

I was certain Murphy wanted me, but he also wanted the truth. Too bad I wasn't going to give it to him. Although I might give him something else.

Because he could kiss like the devil himself. Or how I imagined the devil would kiss if he ever bothered to do so.

And why wouldn't he, if he could kiss like this? Satan would rack up a huge tally of souls if he traded kisses instead of wishes, or whatever it was he traded for souls nowadays.

Murphy didn't bother at finesse; he had no reason to convince me of anything. Within seconds his mouth devoured mine; I clung to his shoulders, my breasts pressed against his chest, my hips cradling his erection as his hands explored my backside.

He tasted of the water and, amazingly, the night, despite the sun and the sweat and the heat. His tongue was as clever kissing as it had been speaking, and I traced the length of it with my own.

His teeth grazed my lower lip, sharp, almost painful, but the sensation only enticed me more. I bit him back and he growled. Or at least I thought he did.

The sound did not vibrate against my mouth. I did

not feel its echo in his chest, and I should have, considering that chest's proximity to my own.

The low rumble sounded again, and I was reminded of the beast in the jungle last night. The one Murphy had insisted was nothing but a dream.

I tore my mouth from his and glanced toward the trees.

Looked like my dream had followed us here.

9

"Get down!" I shouted.

Murphy hit the dirt and so did I. The thing coming out of the trees stumbled over us and slammed into the ground.

Not a wolf or a bear or a cat but a man. That didn't mean he wasn't a beast—or that he hadn't been one last night.

Why did I think our attacker not quite human? Must have been the growling that continued to emanate from his mouth.

He also moved a helluva lot faster than the average Haitian. By the time Murphy and I regained our feet, and neither of us was slow about it, the guy was already coming back for a second pass.

In his dark face his eyes shone eerily light—gray, green, or a faded blue; it was hard to tell when I was riveted by the way they rolled and twitched, as if he was hopped on something, or perhaps just insane.

Murphy shoved me behind him. If I hadn't been focused on the strange, snarling Haitian, I might have been impressed with his chivalry.

Considering Murphy had no weapon, having left the machete and his guns by the pond when he decided to kiss me, I was irritated. At least I had a knife.

Lowering my hand to my waist, I cursed. The sheath was empty.

Before I could wonder how or why or where, the man launched himself at Murphy and the two tumbled to the ground. The attacker was big, bulky, but Murphy held his own. Lucky he'd been to bar fight school, because the other guy did not play fair—if there was "fair" in a fistfight.

The two men grappled for dominance, locked in a struggle of will and strength. Then the Haitian began snapping his teeth directly in front of Murphy's nose, as if he was trying to bite it off.

"What in hell is the matter with you?" Murphy exclaimed.

I had a pretty good idea. Certain zombies of legend had a craving for live human flesh.

I scrambled toward the pond.

Instead of grabbing one of Murphy's guns, which wouldn't be loaded with silver or salt or anything that could work on what that man might be, I tore through my backpack until I found a zombie-revealing powder I'd made myself.

Not that it had ever worked before.

"But those were werewolves," I muttered, yanking open the bag and pouring some into my hand.

"Cassandra!" Murphy shouted. "You mind?"

I ran, lifting my palm, positioning my lips at my wrist, so I could blow the powder into the attacker's face. Just as I did, Murphy threw the man off with an impressive heave and got a snoot-full of zombie-revealing powder for his heroics.

Dust coated his skin. He blinked and particles tumbled from his eyelashes. He coughed.

"Oops?" I said sheepishly.

"Duck!" he shouted.

I did, and a fist whooshed through the air above my head. Murphy shoved me aside and leaped to his feet, tackling the man and driving him into the ground once more.

"The gun!" Murphy yelled.

I took one step in that direction and paused as the Haitian flipped Murphy onto his back and started snapping at his nose again. I yanked my silver crucifix over my head and jammed the end into the Haitian's neck.

He howled and I thought, *Uh-oh. Werewolf.*

Except he didn't explode. He backhanded me, and I flew several feet to land on my ass with a teeth-jarring thud.

"Quit screwing around and get the gun!" Murphy repeated.

I shook my head, wincing as pain shot through my

cheek. I was going to have a shiner, but it wouldn't be the first time.

I crawled to Murphy's pack, yanked out his pistol. I wasn't sure it would work, but I didn't have much choice. Then something sparkly at the water's edge caught my eye.

My knife.

I grabbed it, and headed back the way I'd come.

The Haitian was centimeters away from chewing off Murphy's nose. I wasn't going to reach them in time.

Without thought, I drew back my arm and threw the knife. The weapon thunked into the attacker's back, right between the shoulder blades. Once again—no flames, no smoke, no werewolf. Oh well.

The guy made a horrible sound—I couldn't blame him—and began to claw for the knife. He yanked it out, and I realized my mistake. Now he had the knife *and* Murphy.

"Cassandra!" Murphy roared as the man rose above him, the blade flashing red with both blood and the setting sun.

The report of the gun was obscenely loud in the stillness of the partially shrouded glade.

The attacker jerked once. The knife fell; so did he. Right on top of Murphy.

"Ooof," Murphy said, then scrambled frantically out from under the body.

The attacker didn't move; he wasn't breathing. Either bullets worked on zombies or maybe he wasn't a zombie.

Nausea rolled over me. If he wasn't already dead, then—

I stared at the first person I'd ever killed and felt . . . not good. I'd had to do it, but that didn't stop me from shaking as if I'd suddenly caught jungle fever.

"What were you doing?" Murphy stalked toward me, yanking the pistol from my hand and stuffing it into his pants. "He was going to kill me."

Murphy didn't notice my near catatonia or my shivering. He was too wound up.

"Guy had to be on something," he muttered, turning away and throwing his arms up theatrically. "Trying to chew off my nose. What's with that?"

I thumped to the ground, my legs suddenly too shaky to hold me upright. I couldn't take my eyes off the dead man.

The thud made Murphy face me; then he fell to his knees at my side. "You OK?"

I started to laugh, and the sound wasn't quite sane. How could I be OK after this?

"Shit," Murphy muttered. "You're shivering. Hold on."

He crossed to the backpacks, yanked his sleeping bag free, and tossed it around my shoulders.

"I'm, I'm—" I wasn't sure what, so I stopped talking and sat there—shuddering and staring at the body.

Murphy sat, too, directly in my line of vision. "Hey." He touched my already sore cheek. "You had to do it."

Which didn't make what I'd done any less awful.

My eyes burned, and Murphy cursed again, then pulled me into his arms.

He was as good at giving comfort as he'd been at kissing, and I was surprised, considering the source. Murmuring nonsense, he rubbed my back, then held me tightly until the shivers faded away. Even when they were gone he didn't let me go, and I found I didn't want him to.

Twilight descended as I sat there, feeling unreasonably safe in Murphy's arms. The scent of rain in his hair, the strength of his hands, the shape of his shoulders, became as familiar as the shadow of the trees above our heads.

Minutes, hours, days later, he started to draw back and I clung. I glanced into his face, appalled at my weakness, and he smiled, then pressed his lips to my brow right where my hair grew white.

He didn't speak, and for that I was grateful. I wasn't ready to talk. I wasn't ready for much except . . .

Oblivion.

Reaching up, I wrapped my hand around the back of his neck, my knuckles brushing beads and feathers, my thumb striking his earring and making it swing. Murphy frowned, opened his mouth as if to protest, and I kissed him.

He shut up, although I doubted he'd have been able to say much with my tongue down his throat.

I give the man credit; he was certainly adaptable. One moment the embrace was all soft murmurs and comfort, the next pure sex.

Mouth hot, wet, hands hard, roving. He made me forget . . . everything. Which was the whole idea, wasn't it?

The sleeping bag slithered from my shoulders. I no longer cared; I wasn't cold. My fingers crept beneath his shirt, palms grazing the smooth skin, grasping his hips, drawing him near. His fingers were equally clever, finding pressure points that both relaxed and revived me.

His mouth left mine, scoring the line of my jaw, the vein in my neck, teeth scraping my collarbone, then tugging at the collar of my tank top before moving lower. He mouthed my breast through my shirt and I arched, wanting more, wanting everything. I was empty inside—had been for so long. All I wanted was to fill that hollow, aching space.

I tugged at the waistband of his khakis, and the button gave way. With nothing beneath but skin, it was easy for me to cup him, stroke him, make him want the same thing. Judging by what I found there, he already did.

"Wait—," he muttered.

I drew my fingernail gently up the underside of his erection, then ran my thumb over the tip. Waiting was not an option.

His jaw worked; he seemed to be struggling for control. "Wait," he repeated, and grabbed my wrist.

Leaning his forehead against mine, he sighed. His hair drifted over my cheek, and I winced at the memory of being hit. Then I winced at the memory of who had done the hitting.

"What is wrong with me?"

Murphy lifted his head; his gaze was still a little unfo-cused, his mouth wet and swollen from mine. "What?"

"I can't do this. Not here. Not now. With . . . him right there."

I couldn't look in the direction of the dead Haitian. Instead I closed my eyes, gritted my teeth, and hated myself.

Murphy shifted, then stilled. "I don't think that's going to be a problem."

Something in his voice made me open my eyes.

The body was gone.

10

We practically threw each other aside as we leaped to our feet. Any softness, any sex, forgotten, we crossed to the trampled, bloody grass and gaped.

"What the hell?" Murphy's gaze flitted nervously to the surrounding trees. "If he wasn't dead, why didn't he try and kill us again?"

"I think he was dead. Probably from the beginning."

Silence was the first clue that I'd spoken my thoughts out loud. Murphy's guarded expression was the next.

"What did you say?"

I shouldn't tell him, but he'd risked his life for me. He had a right to know what we were dealing with.

"Our friend was already dead, which was why it was so damn hard to kill him. Again."

"Already dead," he repeated. "Which means?"

"Silver didn't cause fire, so not a werewolf." I frowned. "I don't think. Could be something new. And the crucifix—"

Hell, he'd run off with my necklace still stuck in his neck. I doubted I'd be able to find another out here.

"Didn't work, either," I continued, "so not a vampire. Probably a zombie, though I can't be sure since the zombie-revealing powder got blown into your face." I brushed a last bit from his eyebrow. "At least you're not one."

Murphy put his palm against my forehead, just as I used to do with Sarah. I jerked away. "I'm not sick!"

"Not physically." He lowered his arm. "If I'd known you were nuts I wouldn't have been seduced by your sad eyes and that lovely tight ass."

"Don't bullshit me, Murphy. You were seduced by the money."

"I guess you haven't seen your ass lately," he muttered.

I made a derisive sound. I knew what I was and what I wasn't. I also knew what he was and wasn't.

Great comfort and the promise of excellent sex aside, Murphy was an adventurer to say the most, an opportunist to say the least, and I really shouldn't trust him. But he was all I had.

"The guy could have walked off." Murphy hunkered down and peered at the ground.

Unfortunately, night had fallen and the ground was hard to see. I couldn't discern any tracks. From the tightening of Murphy's lips, he couldn't, either.

Which screwed up my theory. A zombie would walk off; only other things disappeared. I'd even heard tales of invisible werewolves.

I glanced at the steadily darkening forest. I just hoped there weren't any here.

Murphy straightened. "Just because I can't see footprints doesn't mean they aren't there."

"How do you explain his resistance to stabbing and shooting?"

"Killing people isn't as easy as you think."

"I'll take your word on it," I said, my mood much lighter now that *I* hadn't killed someone.

"Guy looked awful good for a zombie," Murphy said.

My mood lightened even more. He *had* looked good, which gave weight to the rumor that Mezareau was a very talented man.

"That's why you have to meet the *bokor*," Murphy blurted. "You want to learn how to raise the dead."

I guess Murphy had picked up a little knowledge of voodoo and the nature of a *bokor* while living in Haiti, then put two and two together.

I shrugged and didn't answer.

"Why?"

That I wasn't telling him.

"Why wouldn't I want to raise the dead?" I asked. "Seems like a handy talent to have."

"You aren't the type who'd do anything for money."

"Who said anything about money?"

"Why else would you want to raise the dead? Can you imagine the kind of cash you could rake in on that scam?"

Only Murphy would make the leap from raising the dead to making money on the practice.

"It isn't a scam," I said.

His eyes narrowed. "You don't actually believe the dead can be raised."

"You don't actually believe the man who attacked us was just a man?"

Murphy didn't seem to have anything to say to that.

"Haven't you seen things in your life for which there's no explanation?" I asked.

"Never."

"Where have you been?"

"Everywhere."

Which kind of explained the accents.

However, his answer surprised me. If Murphy hadn't seen anything amazing anywhere that he'd been, then Edward and crew were doing their jobs better than I imagined.

"You don't believe in magic?" I asked.

"Sweetie, there's no such thing. I believe in what I can touch. Wine, women, and cash."

His opinion disturbed me; I have no idea why. I knew there was magic; I'd seen it. So what did I care if Devon Murphy had no hope, no faith, no soul?

Maybe because I'd kissed him, nearly let him try to fill the great big empty inside of me. Discovering that Murphy was more empty than I was . . . why *wouldn't* that be disturbing?

"You believe in monsters?" Murphy asked. "Evil beasties that go bump in the night?"

"Yes."

"Which explains why you were shooting up the trees."

How could I have forgotten our visitor of the night before? The memory brought a measure of relief. Not an animal stalking us but a person.

If a zombie could be called a person.

My relief was short-lived, however. The man who'd stalked, then attacked us had never spoken, only growled, which didn't bode well for the completely human zombie I was interested in. Although he was moving pretty well for a dead guy—no shuffling and stumbling—and he'd appeared as alive as anyone else.

"We'll go back to Port-au-Prince in the morning," Murphy said.

My gaze snapped to his. "We will not!"

He sighed. "There aren't any zombies, Cassandra. If I'd known that's what you were after I never would have—"

He broke off and looked away.

"What? Tried to screw me?"

His gaze snapped back. "I didn't."

"Then whose tongue was down my throat ten minutes ago?"

He shoved his fingers through his hair, lips tightening when they tangled in the feathers and the beads. "I meant I wouldn't have taken the job if I knew you were . . ."

"Wacko?" I suggested, and he shrugged. "You said you'd do anything for money."

"I wouldn't do you."

"I'm not part of the deal."

"Seemed like you were ten minutes ago."

"Then why did you say 'wait'?"

My question brought him up short. "What?"

"You told me to wait. I find it hard to believe you suddenly had an attack of the Good Samaritans."

"More like a panic attack." His smile was rueful. "No condom."

Now I was the one in a panic. The very thought of having unprotected sex made me dizzy. Not only from the very real possibility of contracting AIDS in this country but also from the thought of birthing another child, the chance of losing him or her . . . I didn't think I could ever do it again. Which only strengthened my resolve to bring Sarah back.

The one thing I'd been good at was being a mom. I'd loved caring for Sarah, sharing her life, teaching her things. I liked to play Barbies, read books, watch her dance. I was the secretary of the PTA, chairperson of the annual bake and book sale. I'd been prime candidate for mother of the year—until I'd fucked up and let Sarah die.

"You OK?"

Murphy stared at me with an odd expression—wary, as if he thought *I* might flip out and try to chew his nose. I guess I'd zoned off too long into the land of guilt and recrimination. What else was new?

"Let's make camp," he said gently.

I got the feeling he was planning something. Like how to trick me into following him back to Port-au-Prince, where he'd turn me over to a psychiatrist.

I went through the motions of unpacking for the night, even helped with dinner, but all the while I was thinking. I couldn't trust Murphy anymore, if I'd ever trusted him at all.

We had to be close to Mezareau's village, hence the zombie henchman. I'd do better to strike out on my own rather than follow Murphy blindly back to a little white room. But how could I get away without his seeing me?

Simple.

Voodoo sleeping powder.

11

The powder was really an herbal remedy I'd been using since Sarah's death. If it put me to sleep with all my issues, Murphy shouldn't be any trouble at all.

Once he crashed, I'd slip away. When he awoke, he wouldn't bother to follow me, since I'd leave his money where he'd be sure to find it.

Having a plan made me downright jolly, and I had to tone down my exuberance lest Murphy think I'd lost more marbles than he already did.

I needn't have bothered, since he was preoccupied, staring into the trees, not speaking to me at all. It wasn't even a challenge to slip the sleeping powder into his applesauce. He ate it out of the disposable container without appearing to know or care what he was consuming.

Night descended. A slightly larger sliver of moon appeared as the sounds of the jungle surrounded us. Murphy lifted his rifle onto his lap. "I'll keep watch."

I doubted he'd be watching much but the inside of his eyelids. I also doubted a gun would be of any use if the Haitian, or some of his friends, decided to come back.

As expected, within fifteen minutes, Murphy's head bobbed, then he mumbled and jerked upright, eyes wide as he searched the darkness. Soon he couldn't fight any longer, and his chin dipped to his chest. I waited fifteen minutes more, just to be sure, then grabbed my things.

I poured a circle of salt around Murphy to protect him until he woke up. No zombie could pass over salt. Interestingly enough, my zombie-revealing powder contained not a hint of it—which might be why it had never worked.

Before I left, I tossed the money order onto the ground in front of Murphy. There'd be no reason for him to come after me now. We were square.

As I headed into the trees, I refused to feel sad about that. I had plenty of other things to be sad about.

Like where the hell I was going. Since we'd been heading steadily up the mountain in a northwesterly direction I continued that way. I experienced a moment's unease that this was too easy—kind of a reverse yellow brick road, leading me away from the wizard rather than to him. But what choice did I have?

Only one: Give up or go on. Which really wasn't a choice at all.

I traveled all night, never once needing to stop and hack at a vine or squeeze through an area of densely grown trees. I was definitely on a trail leading somewhere. Hopefully not off the edge of a cliff.

I heard nothing but insects—no growling, no voices, no paws, no footsteps—until the darkest part of the night, right before sunrise, when the moon and the stars disappeared and the sky went as black as the pits of hell. I hated that time. It was then that my dreams of Sarah came.

"No dreams tonight," I murmured. "Not going to sleep."

I paused because I could no longer see the trail and pulled out my canteen. Leaning against a tree, I drank slowly and watched the sky, waiting for the telltale lightening of the ebony night, which signaled the arrival of the sun, but nothing happened.

"Maybe it takes a little longer here," I whispered, the sound of my own voice not as soothing as I'd hoped.

The rustle from the underbrush was so slight I wouldn't have heard it if I'd been walking. Something light, small, probably furry.

My right hand crept toward my knife, sliding away when a figure stepped through the trees. "Sarah."

I wanted to touch her, but I didn't dare. This couldn't be real, even though I wanted it to be very badly. If I touched her would she disappear in a puff of smoke?

She wore the outfit she'd died in—her private school uniform, all navy blue and white. She'd loathed that skirt. Her dark hair, so very much like mine, was combed, her cheeks flushed with health—with life—

her brown eyes, too much like Karl's, shone. The only oddity was her lack of socks and shoes.

I had to be dreaming, yet here I stood, back against the tree, the damp air of Haiti pressing against my skin.

I shifted and the earth scratched beneath my boots. I slammed my hand against the tree trunk. Pain exploded up my arm.

Mommy? murmured the wind.

Ah, hell, I thought as tears threatened. Was I crazy or wasn't I?

Everything's all right.

Not really. Nothing had been all right since she had gone.

Mommy, she said again, and ran toward me.

I went down on one knee, held out my arms, and she blew through me, like the first chilly wind of autumn.

I closed my eyes, and I could smell her. That particular scent that was Sarah's alone—both sweet and sharp, soft white light and hot pink neon, sunshine, shadow, and the earth. I hadn't smelled it for a very long time.

"You OK?"

My eyes snapped open. I was sitting on the ground, my back against the tree. The sun was up, creating a halo around Murphy's head as he squatted in front of me.

I blinked at the sky. "What time is it?"

"That's all you can say?" He shifted, plopping himself down at my side. "You drugged me."

"Did not."

"You did something."

I'd fallen asleep and dreamed of Sarah. I wasn't sure

why that thought caused a shaft of disappointment so deep I ached with it. If she hadn't been a dream, she'd been a ghost. Which was the entire reason I was in Haiti—or at least one of them.

I'd also lost several hours of travel time and allowed Murphy to catch up to me.

"Why are you here?" I asked.

"I'm taking you to the *bokor*, remember?"

"No, you were taking me to the funny farm."

I startled a laugh out of him. "I haven't heard that expression since me poor sainted mother died."

His brogue was back. Instead of being irritated, I was intrigued. I knew so little about him. "I'm sorry about your mother."

His expression became shuttered. "That was long ago and far away, my wee colleen, no reason to have your sad eyes grow sadder on my account."

My irritation returned. "If you pat me on the head, I'll slug you."

He smiled. "That's better. Now, tell me what you drugged me with and why?"

"Sleeping powder. Herbal. Obviously it didn't work very well."

"I was asleep until dawn, which I believe is what you had in mind."

I glanced at the sky again. From the position of the sun it was midafternoon. I couldn't believe I'd zoned out that long.

"I didn't think you'd care," I said. "I paid you. Why did you come after me?"

"I'm a lot of things, but a murderer isn't one of them."

"Murder? Am I missing something?"

"You think I'd take your money and trot back to Port-au-Prince, leaving you to wander the enchanted forest until you die?"

"Aren't you being a little melodramatic?"

"No."

Oooo-K.

"Why did you call it the enchanted forest?"

"I was trying to be funny. How come you never laugh?"

"I laugh."

"Must be silent laughter. I've never heard you."

"I don't see much to laugh about in this world."

Murphy tilted his head, then touched my cheek. "I'm sorry for that."

"Isn't your fault."

"I'd still like to kick that guy's ass for hitting you."

I realized then that he wasn't apologizing for my lack of laughter but my black eye.

"Damn near impossible to kick a zombie's ass," I said.

He sighed. "We're back to that?"

"Did we ever leave it?"

"How can I convince you there's no such thing as a zombie?"

"You can't, because there is."

"Cassandra—"

"Did you know there was a Harvard ethnobotanist who proved the zombie phenomena is real?"

"I doubt that."

"Seriously. In the early eighties there were two documented cases of people who showed up alive here in Haiti years after they were declared dead. Wade Davis, the ethnobotanist, discovered a poison derived from the blowfish which caused the victim to appear dead."

"I've heard about this," Murphy said slowly. "The victim 'died,' then was called from the grave by the *bokor* and sold into slavery far away from home."

"So when he returned he was labeled a zombie."

"Except he'd never truly been dead," Murphy pointed out, "which means he wasn't a zombie."

"Exactly. But I'm not interested in the zombie poison."

"Then why are we having this conversation?"

"You said there was no such thing as zombies, but there is."

"And I suppose those werewolves and vampires you mentioned—"

"Exist, too. There's a whole world out there most people don't even know about."

"Maybe that's because it doesn't exist outside your own head." My lips tightened, and he lifted one hand to forestall my tirade. "Cassandra, you worry me. Mezareau is not a nice man."

I winced at his use of the *bokor*'s name, waited for the telltale chill and the sensation of being watched. I didn't feel it. Of course that didn't mean Mezareau wasn't snooping.

"He won't have any patience for your fairy tales," Murphy continued. "I don't want you to disappear like all those others did."

"The man is a *bokor*," I said. "The very word means my request won't cause him to bat an eye."

"He's already sent a man to kill us." Murphy frowned. "And the more I think about those guys in Port-au-Prince, the more I wonder if he sent them, too."

I'd figured they were hired guns, but I'd kind of thought my ex-husband had hired them. Either way, guns were guns and dead was dead.

Sometimes.

"He doesn't know what I want from him," I pointed out. "Why get his knickers in a twist already?"

"According to you, just saying his name gives him power. He knows who we are, where we are, and exactly what we want."

"Oh, yeah."

"Yeah," Murphy said. "But if you care to take the saner point of view, the man has people everywhere and every one of them would love to get on his good side."

That still didn't explain why someone had tried to kill me three times. I thought of the bringing of the dead to my hotel room. Make that kill me twice, drive me insane once.

I glanced around the small clearing. Or maybe drive me insane twice.

Had Mezareau sent Sarah? How could he know about her? Was he able to read minds?

If the *bokor* was that powerful there was no telling what he could do. I was both excited and terrified.

"He doesn't want us to find him," I said.

"You think?" Murphy muttered.

"All I need is a little knowledge. Is that so much to ask?"

"Maybe he doesn't want to share."

I hadn't considered that Mezareau wouldn't want to teach me. The religion of voodoo was inclusive—full of gentleness, love, and sharing. But a voodoo sorcerer probably didn't follow the rules.

I got to my feet. Murphy held out a hand and without thought I took it, leaning back as he levered himself upward. I tried to release him, but he held on tight. I glanced into his face, confused.

"Who's Sarah?" he asked.

Suddenly I couldn't breathe. I thought about her all the time. I called out for her in the night. But no one had spoken Sarah's name in my presence for so long the word tore at my heart.

"Where did you hear that?"

My voice was hoarse, harsh. Murphy frowned. "You were mumbling it when I got here."

Oh, right. The dream. Vision. Visitation.

"Who is she?" he pressed.

"My daughter."

His fingers tightened on mine until I winced, but he didn't let go. "Where is she?"

"California."

Bellehaven Cemetery, true. But that was in California.

He turned over my left hand, passed a thumb over my bare ring finger. "Husband?"

"Not anymore."

"Well, that's a relief."

"Relief?" I peered into his face as he continued to rub my knuckles.

"I try not to put my tongue in the mouths of married women."

I winced at the reminder of how I'd practically begged him to take me. "You don't seem the type to care."

His eyes narrowed. "You have no idea what type I am."

He was right. I was angry with myself, not Murphy. I didn't want to want him, but I couldn't seem to stop.

I withdrew my hand from his and he let me. Turning away, I bent to grab my backpack, and my gaze was caught by a mark on the ground, half-obscured beneath a low-lying bush. I reached out and swept back the foliage, just as thunder rumbled from above.

"Storm's coming," Murphy said. "We should probably stay here until it passes. Shouldn't be long. They never last."

The sun was gone; shadows flickered. I could do nothing but stare at the footprint that seemed to waver first closer, then farther away the longer I stared at it. Very small, tiny, perfect toes and a teeny round heel.

Slowly I got to my feet, took a step into the trees, and I saw another one, then another.

I was running. Murphy was shouting. He let me get pretty far before he came after me. By then I'd seen ten footprints, all leading up the same trail I'd been following all night.

"Cassandra!" Murphy shouted.

I didn't stop. I couldn't. Not even when the sky opened and the rain came tumbling down—hard, harsh, chilling needles that soaked us in minutes.

I skidded in the mud, and Murphy caught me before I fell. "What are you doing?"

"Footprints."

He shook the rain from his eyes. "What footprints?"

"I'll show you."

Murphy followed me back in the direction we'd come. I squinted at the dirt, went down on my knees in the mud.

There were no footprints. Not anymore. Had there ever been any at all?

What did it matter since they were now as gone as Sarah herself?

I became aware of another sound, louder than the whoosh of rain and the distant rumble of thunder. Water rushing—a lot of it.

Hell. We were on a mountain and the rain was coming down in sheets.

"Flash flood," I shouted above the storm, but Murphy shook his head.

Instead of running, which would have been my vote, he kept hold of my hand and dragged me toward the sound.

I struggled, not ready to die before I'd tried everything I could to get my life back, but Murphy was strong and for some reason determined.

He shoved me through a tall sheaf of what appeared to be palm fronds, and I stumbled to the other side, bracing myself, expecting a wall of water to sweep from on high and end everything.

Instead, I gaped at the hugest waterfall I'd ever seen.

12

"This is it," Murphy murmured. "The *bokor* lives here."

I glanced around. "Where?"

"Legend says there's a cave behind the waterfall and on the other side of the cave . . . the *bokor*."

"Legends begin in reality," I murmured.

I'd known that even before I'd joined the *Jäger-Suchers*.

There *was* a *bokor* with enough power to bring the dead, to send Sarah's ghost or, considering the footprints, something a little more corporeal, which made one part of the tale a reality. Why wouldn't the part about where he lived be true, too?

"Thanks for bringing me," I said. "I'll be OK now."

"I've come this far; I'm going, too."

"Why risk your life?"

"Why risk yours?"

I met his gaze, refusing to look away.

"Oh." His eyes widened, then narrowed. "You didn't tell me your daughter was dead."

I should have known a man like Murphy was adept at reading faces, putting together a few bits of info, and guessing the truth. He wouldn't have survived as long as he had otherwise.

I turned away. The rain continued to beat down, as if it were trying to compete with the force of the waterfall.

"Why would you think that?" I asked, my voice too high and falsely bright.

"A better question would be why I didn't think it before."

He put his hands on my shoulders. Despite the rain, the warmth of his skin seeped into mine, and I had to force myself not to lean on him. Murphy was still a stranger, and now he knew my deepest, darkest secret.

"It won't work, Cassandra."

I curled my fingers into my palms so tightly my nails bit crescent moons into my flesh. "It will."

"Death is the end; there's no coming back."

"You're wrong. Death is a beginning."

"If that's the case, it's the beginning of something else. Something she won't want to come back from."

I heard the echo of Renee's words but ignored them now as I had then.

"Of course she will."

"Even if it were possible to raise the dead, is a zombie existence one you'd wish on anyone?"

I spun around. "This *bokor* can raise the dead to live again. Just as they were before."

Murphy shook his head, the storm—or maybe just concern for my sanity—darkening his eyes nearly to black. "That's impossible."

"I won't believe that. I can't."

"I'm sure losing a child is a terrible thing, but what you're doing isn't going to fix it."

"You're wrong. Raising Sarah will fix everything."

Including me.

"The *bokor* is a dangerous man. He's up to something out here."

"Exactly."

"I meant drugs. Gunrunning." He frowned. "Maybe slavery. Which would explain the disappearing visitors."

"Slavery. Are we still in the same century?"

"You've never heard of white slavery?"

"Of course, but I don't think there are too many white people out here."

"There's us."

I bit my lip. *Whoops*.

"*White slavery* doesn't actually refer to race anyway," Murphy said. "It's sexual slavery—all races."

"You've lost your mind," I muttered.

"No, that would be you."

I lost my patience. "If you're so worried about what the *bokor* will do to me, why did you bring me here at all?"

Murphy glanced away.

Hmm. He was hiding something, too. But what?

I had a moment's unease. Perhaps Murphy was in league with Mezareau in his white slavery scheme, which meant I might find myself locked in a foreign brothel come next week.

My fingers stroked my knife. Or not. Either way, it wouldn't hurt to make Murphy nervous.

"I work for the government," I blurted. "They know I'm here."

Not here, here, but Haiti here. However, Murphy didn't need to know that.

I had no doubt Edward would find me if I disappeared—or at least send someone to try. If he let his agents get sold into white slavery how would that look?

I was grasping at straws, but right now straws were all I had.

"What exactly do you do for the government?"

"I'm a *Jäger-Sucher*. Monster-hunting society. Very hush-hush."

Murphy stared at me for several seconds; then he laughed. "You had me going there."

"I'm serious."

His laughter died; his eyes had gone gray in the misty half-light that preceded dusk. "You don't have to make up stories. I'm not going to kill you and toss you over a cliff, or keep you alive and sell you to the highest bidder."

I'd never convince Murphy the *Jäger-Suchers* existed until I convinced him the monsters did. I had a feeling that wouldn't be too much of a problem once we reached the other side of the waterfall. I waded into the pond.

"Where are you going?"

"Where do you think?"

I heard a loud, annoyed sigh, followed by a splash; then Murphy was at my side.

"Are these backpacks waterproof?" I asked.

"A little late to be asking that, but yes."

About a hundred yards later we reached the falling water; I braced myself to dive through.

"Hold on." Murphy grabbed my hand. "Let's do this together."

I was touched by the gesture. I should insist he stay behind; we could be going to our deaths. Instead, I tightened my fingers, and we went into the waterfall.

By all rights, we should have been driven to the bottom of the pond by the force of the cascading water, or at least pummeled hard enough to get a headache. But I popped out on the other side with nothing more than a momentary lapse in breathing.

I still held Murphy's hand, but he seemed to be stuck. I tugged; nothing happened. The spray from the falling water made it hard for me to see; the wetness made it hard to hold on. If I lost my grip, what would happen? I didn't want to find out.

I couldn't touch bottom, so I had no leverage. Was he on the other side, or stuck in between? If it was the latter, I didn't have much time before he drowned.

Was the waterfall a trial by faith? Like the Indiana Jones movie where Indy had to step into the abyss and then the bridge appears? If so, how would I ever get Murphy through—oh, he of little faith?

My own would have to be enough.

Reaching forward, I clasped my hands around his. "Please," I whispered, and yanked with both my mind and my body.

Murphy erupted, landing on top of me, dunking me in midgasp. My mouth filled with brackish water and I struggled, kicked, then shot to the surface choking and spitting. I could swear I had a minnow in my mouth.

"You OK?" Murphy asked.

"No thanks to you. What happened?"

He started to cough as if he'd swallowed half an ocean. I eased my frustration by whacking him on the back. After a few good ones, he grabbed my wrist and made me stop. Spoilsport.

"You went through," he said, "but I was stuck in between. My mouth kept filling up; I had to swallow or drown."

"Why didn't you drop my hand?"

He stared at me as if I were nuts. "I couldn't let you go on alone."

Murphy had risked drowning for me? He was almost like a hero.

"Then I heard you say, 'Please,' " he continued, "and suddenly I was flying."

His wet hair kept falling in his eyes, and the feathers hung limply by his cheek. Murphy snatched them out and tossed them aside. The beads were still braided firmly in place.

"I didn't know you were that strong," he said.

"Neither did I." I contemplated the water. "It was like . . . magic."

He snorted. "That was adrenaline, sweet thing, pure and simple."

Some hero. I don't know why I bothered to confide in him at all.

Murphy slogged toward the rocky rim of the pond. We'd landed in a cave, just as he'd predicted. Very dark, the only light came from the fading sun beyond the waterfall. A single tunnel led onward—a black gaping maw that promised answers, or perhaps more questions.

I was momentarily distracted by the flex of Murphy's biceps against the sleeves of his T-shirt, the ripple of muscle appearing particularly fetching beneath wet skin as he hoisted his body upward.

Remember, I admonished. *You're in the land that condom forgot.*

Then I dunked myself.

When I resurfaced, Murphy helped me out of the water without mentioning my sudden penchant for it. He lifted me up as if I weighed no more than a twig, and my foolish heart went pitter-pat.

As soon as my feet touched the cave floor, complete darkness descended along with utter silence. That silence bothered me more than the darkness ever could.

Murphy slid off his backpack, rustled around. Then

a click was followed by a white beam of light splashing from one rock face to the next.

"No such thing as magic, huh?" I murmured.

Murphy continued to flash the light from wall to wall and back again, but he couldn't change the truth.

The waterfall was gone.

"There has to be a logical explanation," he said.

"For water morphing into rock? If you can find one, I'd love to hear it."

My voice was annoyingly cheerful. I couldn't help myself. If the entrance to the cave was magic, there had to be a lot more magic to come.

Murphy shot me a glare. "I wouldn't be so all-fired happy about it if I were you. How the hell are we going to get out of here?"

"We'll worry about that when the time comes."

"We'll worry about it now."

He took a step toward the water, and I grabbed his arm. The flashlight plunked into the pond, and the cave went black again.

"I don't suppose *that* was waterproof?" I asked.

Murphy's answer was a curse.

"Got another one?"

"No."

"Maybe I do." I shifted my pack.

"You don't."

"Well, that wasn't very good planning, was it?"

"I didn't think you'd throw mine into the drink."

"I didn't throw it."

"I may throw you," he muttered.

I laughed. It felt good.

"You don't think I will?" His voice was dangerously low.

I stopped laughing. "What happened to 'full speed ahead, damn the torpedoes Murphy'?"

"He drowned."

"You don't like small, dark, enclosed spaces, do you?"

"Does anyone?"

I reached out, smacking him in the chest. He was closer than I'd thought.

"Oomph," he said. "Watch it."

I ran my hand over his shoulder, down his arm, then entwined our fingers. "Follow me."

He held back. I tugged, but he wouldn't budge.

"We should wait here," he murmured.

"In case the waterfall magically reappears?"

"It could."

"This is probably how all those people disappeared. They're stuck. Somewhere."

"Oh, that makes me feel a whole lot better."

"Come on." I tugged again. "There's a tunnel."

"Tunnel?" His voice—at first hoarse and low—went higher.

"Relax. It's big enough to drive a car through. You'll be fine." This time Murphy let me lead him away from the water.

The dark had never bothered me. I'd always been able to find my way. Unless it was theoretical darkness of the soul, of course; then I was lost.

Free hand in front of me, I walked forward until I reached the far wall, then trailed my fingers across it until my arm fell into space. "Here we go."

"Maybe we should use some matches."

"Save them. You never know when we might need a fire."

"Why would we need a fire?"

"To scare something away."

"Still not helping," he muttered.

I smiled into the darkness. He was sounding more like himself and less like a scared little boy. Although I'd begun to find that little boy just as appealing as the muscley man. My smile faded. I needed to get a grip.

Together we went on.

And on. And on.

Hours, days, weeks later, Murphy paused. "This is ridiculous, Cassandra. For all we know we could be walking in circles."

He was right, but I couldn't go back.

"A little farther," I pleaded.

"All right." His hand tightened on mine. "A little."

Onward I went, both tired and exhilarated; the combination caused a buzzing in my ears. A buzzing I ignored until it started to remind me of something.

I stopped and Murphy bumped into me. "What—"

"*Shh,*" I breathed.

My ears were still buzzing. In the darkness I was disoriented; I couldn't tell if the sound was coming from inside of me or not.

"Look," Murphy whispered, and I saw them.

Just eyes, nothing else. They seemed to be floating in the air about fifty feet away. There was something off about them, but I didn't have time to figure out what.

An unmistakable growl rumbled through the cave—more animal than human, though the echo made it hard to tell for sure.

In a distant corner of my mind I remembered Murphy telling me there were no large mammals on the island. He'd told me that after I'd seen the last pair of eyes, which had turned out to be human after all—or as human as zombies get.

"Your knife," Murphy whispered.

I almost said, *What about your gun?* But he didn't dare fire inside the cave for fear of a deadly ricochet. Not that a gun had done any good the last time.

My hand lowered to my waist and hesitated. The silver blade hadn't been any help, either. I needed the zombie-revealing powder, which, if it worked, should turn any zombie back to the dust from which it came.

My fingers traveled to the bag I'd concealed in my pants. I winced as I encountered my soaked jeans and prayed what was in my pocket wasn't as ruined as I was.

I shook some powder into my palm, sighing in relief when the granules scratched against my skin. "Get a match. Don't strike it until I say so."

I didn't need whatever was there to get spooked by the flare before I was close enough to toss the zombie-revealing powder in its face. Zombies didn't much care for fire, either.

One hand out, one on the hilt of my knife, I inched forward, Murphy at my side. Before we'd moved five feet, the eyes blinked once and disappeared.

I was so startled I dropped the powder. Cursing, I thrust my hand forward and felt fur. I immediately yanked it back, afraid I'd get my fingers ripped off.

"Match," I said.

A snick was immediately followed by a faint glowing light. My eyes, unaccustomed to it, struggled to focus. Something slid around the next curve, and without thinking, I ran.

I came around the bend just as the match went out. Tense, I waited for a sound, a movement, an attack.

"What did you see?" Murphy lit another match.

The wavering, golden glow illuminated rock, dirt, and nothing else. My gaze met his.

"A tail."

13

"You're sure?"

The darkness could have been playing with my mind when I'd heard the growl, felt the fur, but it hadn't been dark when I'd seen the tail.

"I'm sure." I tilted my head. "You aren't going to explain why I couldn't have? Check me for fever again?"

"Maybe later." He hissed and dropped the match. Eternal night descended once more. "What kind of a tail?"

"Black."

"Bushy or thin?"

I thought hard. "I don't know."

"Long or short?"

"I only saw the tip. Maybe it was nothing." I wanted it to be nothing.

"We both heard the growl."

"You did?"

"Uh-huh."

I took a deep breath, then let it out. "I felt fur."

Several beats of silence followed my statement, then: "The guy could have been wearing fur, or what felt like fur."

Gotta love a logical mind.

"Was he wearing a tail, too?" I asked.

"You said you weren't sure about the tail, and who knows—" He made a movement that was most likely a shrug. "Maybe he was."

"So we're talking crazy guy, zombie, or a big furry growling thing where one isn't supposed to be."

"Why is it whenever you talk I get a headache?"

"I have that effect on a lot of people."

Silence fell between us for several minutes, and then: "Did you find anything strange about those eyes?"

I had, but I'd brushed off my unease, and now I couldn't quite recall why I'd felt it. I hadn't been able to distinguish a color beyond light—blue, green, gray, maybe yellow. But that wasn't what had bothered me about them.

"They had whites," Murphy said.

That was.

Because only people have whites around their irises; animals don't. Unless you're talking werewolf.

Hell.

"What do human eyes mean to you?" he asked.

The man wasn't slow. Even without seeing my face he sensed I was hiding something.

"Human," I said. Some of the time.

"There's more to it than that."

Murphy had already fit me for a straitjacket. One more bit of insanity wouldn't change that. "In wolf form, werewolves retain their human eyes."

"There aren't any wolves on this island."

"There never are." I grabbed Murphy's hand and started forward again.

He hung back. "Hold on. You want to chase the scary unknown being?"

"You don't believe in it."

"Just because I don't think there's a werewolf in Haiti doesn't mean there isn't something here I'm not wild about facing. I certainly don't plan on chasing it."

"Not chase. Follow."

"What's the difference?"

"Chasing involves running; following is . . . slower." I tugged. He still didn't move. "Murphy, we need to go on. Behind us is nothing but a dead end."

"Unless the waterfall came back." His voice was wistful.

"You want to spend hours finding out?"

"No," he muttered. "I guess I'd rather fight the unknown creepy thing than stay in the small enclosed dark place until the end of time."

"Aren't you the cheery fellow?"

"That's me. Regular Mr. Chuckles I am."

I was still smiling as I turned, amused now by his British accent rather than annoyed, and I saw it. A light at the end of a tunnel. Literally.

I began to run again.

"That's chasing!" Murphy shouted. "There wasn't going to be any chasing." Except he was running, too.

I burst out of the cave and into a clearing shadowed by a crescent moon. Moist heat slapped me in the face, startling after hours of cool darkness. The scent of greenery, of flowers, surrounded me. The moon's glow caused the trees, the shrubs, to glisten with an ethereal light, and the blossoms shone with colors both muted and vivid.

On this side of the cave lay a true jungle, dense and damp; I'd never seen anything quite like it. Uneasily I wondered where we'd popped out.

I wasn't like Murphy. I believed in magic—white, black, and everything in between. I had to. And if magic existed, hell, we could have come out of that cave anywhere.

He reached my side, his grunt of surprise revealing the differences were as obvious to him as they had been to me.

A rustle drew my attention to the dense underbrush. Slowly I removed my knife from its sheath. At the slight rasp, Murphy reached for his rifle. I only hoped it worked after being doused in the waterfall. Though his gun was loaded with lead, he might be able to slow something down and give me a chance to use the silver blade before the thing ripped out my throat or Murphy's.

Out of the jungle stepped a man. I give Murphy credit; he didn't put away his gun. Maybe he was learning.

There'd been a growling furry beast in the cave a few moments ago. In my world, that beast might be right here, minus only the fur and the growls.

He was tall, very thin, dark skin, light eyes, wearing ancient loose khaki trousers and little else. Because of the heat, the destitution, or the need to dress quickly after shifting from one form to the next?

"Ki jan ou ye?" Murphy gave the traditional Haitian greeting. *How are you?*

"M'pa pi mal," returned the man. *I'm not worse.*

Also the traditional answer. In a land where poverty was a given, *I'm not worse* was often the best that could be hoped for.

The man's voice was strong and clear. Not a zombie. Or at least not a typical zombie who could do little but mumble and shuffle. Which was good.

Or maybe bad, because then he might be—

I stepped forward and before the stranger knew what I was about pressed the silver knife against his bare arm.

He didn't react, which was odd in itself. Wouldn't a normal person be disturbed by my behavior? Murphy was. I sensed his tension, his disapproval, but he kept the gun steady. Just because the guy wasn't a shuffling zombie or a snarling werewolf didn't mean he wasn't dangerous.

"Pardon me." I stepped away from the man. "Did you see an animal?"

He tilted his head, a chillingly canine gesture. "Animal?"

At least he spoke English. "About so high." I set my hand at my waist. "Dog? Coyote? Wolf?"

His smile flashed, a bit condescending but still a

nice smile—even if he was missing a few teeth. "There are no coyotes or wolves here."

"Where's here?"

Confusion flickered. "Haiti."

I had my doubts. "Someone got a big dog?"

"No, Priestess."

I blinked, then glanced at Murphy, who shrugged.

"How do you know who I am?" The man turned away without answering. "Where are you going?"

He paused. "You wish to meet the *bokor,* you must come with me."

"OK."

Murphy caught my elbow. "You're just going to follow a stranger into the jungle?"

"I followed you."

"That was different."

"Really? How so?"

He scowled. "I don't think we should."

"I do." I tugged on my arm; Murphy only held tighter. "What else should I do, Murphy? Wander around wherever the hell we are shouting Mezareau's name?"

"I thought you weren't supposed to *say* his name."

"I think he knows we're here."

"I think he's known from the beginning."

"I'm going."

Murphy released me, then stared over my shoulder at the stranger, eyes narrowed, jaw working. I discovered I was nervous at the thought of going into this new, denser jungle without Murphy. I didn't like the feeling.

"All right," he said. "Let's go."

I let out the breath I'd been holding and together we followed our new friend into the trees.

"You think this guy's a werewolf?" Murphy asked.

I glanced at our guide, but he didn't appear to hear our murmured words, just kept shoving aside fronds and low-hanging tree branches, moving in the direction of the moon with a determination that comforted me. At least one of us knew where we were going.

I wiggled my knife, then put it away. "Not anymore."

"I can't believe I'm asking this," Murphy muttered. "But why would you think that? The moon isn't full."

Since we appeared to be following the Haitian for longer than a minute and the terrain wasn't too rugged to walk and talk, I gave Murphy the lowdown as I knew it.

"Werewolves can change at dusk, any day of the month."

"So the full-moon thing is a myth."

"Yes and no. Under the full moon, they're compelled to change—and to kill. Under any other moon, it's their choice. Though most choose to shift and to hunt whenever they can."

"Why?"

"They like it."

"Again I'll be askin' why?"

His Irish was back. Murphy must be really worried, and he hadn't even heard the best—make that the worst—part yet.

"The way it was explained to me, the lycanthropy virus destroys a person's humanity. They look like people, but deep down there's a demon panting to get out."

"Demon?" He stopped walking and I did, too. "You can't be serious."

"Do you want to hear this or not?"

"Do."

I swept out my arm in a "be my guest" gesture, and he began to walk again. Our Haitian friend was now farther ahead of us, since he'd continued on when we'd paused.

"The demon is pure selfishness—even in human form. Me first, screw the other guy."

"But, Gepetto, how then can you tell a werewolf from a real boy?"

He was catching on. "Exactly. The world as it is now is a perfect breeding ground for evil. People behave like psychopaths and we call it ambition."

Just look at my husband.

"So you're saying there are werewolves in every walk of life, masquerading as people."

"They *are* people, most of the time. Just not people you want to hang out with. Unless you like to turn furry and murder the innocent."

"Not really."

"Then you should start wearing silver."

He lifted one hand. "Like this?"

His thumb ring gleamed blue in the moonlight.

"That'll work."

14

"Where'd he go?"

I followed Murphy's gaze. We were alone in the dense, silver-tinged wilderness.

My knife slid from its sheath with a slick whisper. Murphy's hands tightened on his gun. We moved forward, shoulder to shoulder through the foliage.

I half-expected to confront a slavering, human-eyed beast. Instead, our Haitian friend waited patiently at the outskirts of a picturesque village.

With no evidence of the sickness or poverty Murphy and I had viewed in all the others we'd passed on our way to the mountain, the structures were solid, many new. Cook fires had been banked in front of most; I caught the scent of meat. Most Haitians did not have the means to eat meat.

"Since when is there a village?" I murmured.

"Got me."

Despite the lateness of the hour, villagers bustled

about. Women kneaded bread on flat rocks; men repaired tools; some whittled. The only concession to the clock was the lack of children, who must be in bed. At our appearance, several people stopped what they were doing and came toward us.

"Pierre," they murmured with eerie harmony.

Our guide dipped his head. "Take the priestess to her quarters."

Two extremely tall, equally stout women stepped forward. They were alike enough to be sisters, if not twins, right down to the bracelet of colorful beads that encircled the somewhat manly wrist of each— blue for the woman on the left, red for the one on the right.

Together they reached for my hands. I still held the knife, but they didn't seem to care, Red Bracelet grasping my fingers with the blade still clutched tightly within.

"Hold on." I reared back, crowding closer to Murphy.

No one seemed disturbed by our weapons. No one asked us to give them up or even put them down. Which was just weird if you ask me.

I glanced at Pierre. "We're searching for a man named Mezareau."

"You may see him when he returns."

Murphy and I exchanged glances.

"He lives here?" I asked.

"*Oui*. This is his village."

I don't know why I'd thought we'd find the *bokor* alone. Once initiated, a voodoo priest creates his own community, functioning as a counselor, a healer, a social worker, as well as a religious leader. His followers come to him for advice on everything.

A *houngan* existed to guide his people. Mezareau's trip to the dark side wouldn't negate his leading them.

I let my gaze wander over the villagers and got that chilly, creepy feeling again. But into what was he leading them?

"Where is he?" I asked.

"Not here."

"What time will he return?"

"When he does."

My teeth ground together, and a low ache began behind my left eye. That kind of talk always made my blood pressure spike toward migraine.

"Rest, Priestess. The trials could not have been easy."

My headache intensified. "What trials?"

"Did you think you could just walk into our village?"

"We did."

"No." He smiled as if I were a foolish child; maybe I was. "You were prevented, but you prevailed. Only the worthy may pass beyond the falling water."

"Worthy of what?"

"You shall see when the master arrives."

The master? Oh, brother.

"How do you know she's a priestess?" Murphy demanded.

"The master knows all because he sees all."

I glanced at Murphy, tempted to say, *I told you so,* but he just rolled his eyes. I had to admit that "know all

and see all" stuff sounded hokey, but that didn't mean
it wasn't true.

"May we show you to your hut?" Pierre asked.

Since I wasn't going to leave without talking to
Mezareau, why not? Besides, I was tired.

Sensing my acquiescence, the women reached for
my hands again. I quickly sheathed my knife and let
them lead me. Since either one of them could have
picked me up and carried me, my letting them was
merely a formality.

I looked for Murphy. Two very large men were taking him elsewhere.

"No." I paused, and my handmaidens paused with
me. "We stay together."

Pierre shook his head. "Priestess, you cannot stay in
the same hut with a man to whom you are not wed."

A sinking sensation caused me to demand, "What
century is this?"

Murphy snorted, but I ignored him. For all we knew
the cave could have been a time warp—and wouldn't
that just be special?

"The twenty-first," Pierre answered, with his usual
calm. "However, we have chosen to live a certain way.
Purity of body leads to purity of mind and the granting
of every desire."

I certainly liked the sound of that, but I still wasn't
sure if being separated from Murphy was the best idea.

"We could get married," Murphy suggested with a
quirk of his brow.

"Dream on, pal."

"Sweetie, you have no idea what I dream."

I cast him a quick suspicious glance and he smirked. Would the man never be serious? Did I really want him to? He made me laugh, or at least think about it.

"Fine. We'll stay in separate huts." I needed some sleep anyway.

Not that I planned to sleep with Murphy. At least not now, not here. Probably not ever. My eyes wandered over him, and I gave a silent sigh of disappointment. He really was hot, and I was so deprived.

I was led to a hut on the far end of the village. Murphy was led to one on the opposite side. I guess they weren't going to take any chances. Not that the village was all that big, not that I couldn't sneak over there any time I wanted to.

I just didn't want to.

And if you believe that, I have a very expensive love charm to sell you.

"All is for you, Priestess." The woman swept back the curtain that covered the doorway.

I stepped inside. The curtain fell behind me and I was alone.

A candle sat on the table, so I lit the wick. The room was small enough for the golden glow to penetrate every corner. Table, candle, pallet with a blanket and pillow. I guess all wasn't very much.

I didn't care. I stripped off my wet, dirty, torn clothes and crawled beneath the covers. The world went black as soon as I closed my eyes.

Deep in the dark of the night the furious snarl of a

wild animal sounded. I shifted—uneasy, uncertain. Something was off about the sound; something didn't make sense. But in the morning I couldn't recall what I'd heard, why it had bothered me, or if the sound had even been real.

Besides, in the morning I had better things to worry about. Like where were my clothes?

Sunlight streamed through the hole in the hut that passed for a window. I was naked beneath the blanket and my clothes had been removed from the building. So had my backpack and my knife.

"Hello?" I hoped someone was close enough to hear. I really didn't want to leave the relative safety of my bed and venture out wrapped in nothing but a blanket sari.

Who knows, the sight of my naked shoulders might be an offense worthy of immediate execution. If memory served, the boniness of my collarbone was not at all attractive.

The door was swept aside, and the women who'd escorted me last night appeared. One held a colorful skirt and white cotton blouse common to Haiti. The other carried a bowl of water and dry cloths. They placed everything on the table, smiled, bowed, and left without a word.

I wasted no time washing my face, rinsing my teeth, and donning new clothes. Wrapped inside the skirt was a pair of underwear, but no matter how many times I shook it, the outfit did not yield a bra.

Oh well.

In the village, people hurried to and fro, fetching, carrying, building, sewing, fixing, cooking, so industrious I wondered if they were preparing for something special. Perhaps they were being watched and judged, though I saw no one resembling an overseer or the equivalent.

For an instant, I could have sworn I glimpsed the nose-eating zombie man lurking at the edge of the trees. But when I blinked he was gone, and since I didn't think anyone, especially a zombie, could move that fast, I figured I was mistaken. But it wouldn't hurt to ask.

My ladies-in-waiting awaited me near the cook fire in front of my hut. Breakfast—fried plantains and warm flat bread—had been set on a low, table-like rock.

"Is there a guard for the village?"

The twin wearing the red bracelet glanced up from the fire. "Pierre is the guardian."

"Not him. Big guy, likes noses. He attacked us on the other side of the waterfall."

She shook her head. "Anyone on the other side is of the other world, Priestess. He would not be of this one."

I guess that answered that. Or not.

"What happened to my things?" I asked.

"Your clothes are being washed."

"My bag?" I continued. "My knife?"

"In a safe place."

"But—"

"All will be returned."

I snapped my mouth shut. I couldn't blame them for

taking my weapon. It's what I would have done, although I would have done it sooner.

My gaze was drawn to the hut where Murphy had slept. Nothing moved beyond the window; the place appeared deserted. Trust him to snooze away half the day.

I ate quickly, happy to partake of cooked food after several days of camp rations. But the bread was as bland as baby crackers and the plantains equally flavorless. Perhaps sugar and spice had also been placed on the list of village no-nos.

My request for tea was met with a wrinkled nose and shake of the head. "Not allowed, Priestess. Such things are for the *loas* only."

Since when? Sure, coffee and tobacco were left for the *loas,* but I'd never heard of tea being offered. Even if it were, that didn't preclude the living partaking as well—or at least it didn't anywhere else but here.

I couldn't complain; this wasn't my community. There is no supreme ruler of the voodoo church to tell us we aren't doing it right. Each *houngan* makes his own rules and rituals.

In the slave days of Haiti, every African society contributed a bit of their religion to the new one evolving among those held in chains. They couldn't all become Nigerian, they hadn't all been born in the Congo, but they *could* all become voodoo practitioners.

When the slaves had been forced to convert to Catholicism, they'd shrugged and adopted some of those practices along with the rest. Therefore, voodoo wasn't one thing but everything.

Considering all the rules here, Mezareau ran a tight and slightly anal ship, which was his business and not mine. I needed to do what I'd come for, then get out. Back to the land of coffee, tea, and condoms.

I cursed beneath my breath. I also had to stop thinking like that.

"Will Mezareau be back today?"

The handmaiden closest to me winced. "He is the *master*."

There was no way I was calling him master.

"Right. Can I see him?"

"He will send for you when he is ready."

I was gritting my teeth again. I had to stop that, too, or I'd have nothing but stubs by the time we left.

I strode across the center of the village in the direction of Murphy's hut. The women scurried after me. I couldn't decide if they were guards or assistants. Either way, they were getting on my nerves.

"Get up!" I swept the curtain aside.

I didn't realize how much I'd been hoping to catch him naked and tousled in bed—or perhaps naked and tousled out of bed—until my stomach fell at the sight of the empty room.

The place appeared as if it hadn't been inhabited for months. Either the bed hadn't been slept in or someone had remade it already, then redeposited a fine layer of dust over everything.

"Where is he?"

The handmaidens exchanged confused glances. "Who?"

"Murphy?" More confusion ensued, and I made an impatient, nearly obscene gesture. "The man I came with."

"But, Priestess," said the one who seemed to do all the talking. "You came alone."

15

"Did he put you up to this?" I asked. "Ha-ha. Very funny. Murphy! You can come out now."

The two women stared at me as if I were crazy—which was nothing new. However, this time, I was certain I wasn't.

I turned in a slow circle, expecting Murphy to pop out of the trees, earring swinging, grin flashing. But he didn't.

"I'm starting to get annoyed," I muttered.

"Priestess."

I turned so fast the woman flinched, and I realized my hands were clenched into fists. "Sorry," I said, and forced myself to relax. "Just show me where he is."

"I do not know of whom you speak."

"Murphy. Tall, white, and—" I stopped short of saying "handsome." "Pirate earring? Blondish with beads in his hair. Kind of hard to miss."

She spread her hands helplessly.

I had *not* imagined traveling through the mountains with Devon Murphy. That was as impossible as . . .

Zombies? Werewolves? Disappearing waterfalls?

I began to glance inside every hut and beat the bushes surrounding the village. Murphy was here someplace. But was he hiding from me or were they hiding me from him?

The handmaidens followed, speaking softly in Creole to the villagers who peered at me with varying degrees of pity.

I made a complete circle with no sign of him. Then I stared, stumped, into a dense jungle that really wasn't supposed to be here. Did I dare go walking around without him?

"Priestess, you came alone."

I met the dark eyes of my talkative guard. Either she was an accomplished liar or she really believed what she was saying, and that just didn't make sense. Unless they were all brainwashed.

"What's your name?" I asked.

"I am called Helen."

"Helen. I did not imagine Murphy."

"Are you certain?"

Her question made me think. Some very strange things had been happening since I'd come to Haiti. What was real and what was not? I was pretty sure Murphy had been a flesh-and-blood man—or at least I hoped he was, for more reasons than one.

"I'm sure," I said firmly. "I couldn't have gotten here without him."

"But you could not have gotten here with him."

My head was starting to hurt and it was only . . . I glanced at my watch, which had stopped. That figured.

"I want to see Mezareau."

"You will." She and her evil twin turned and walked back to my hut.

I spent the rest of the day searching for Murphy. I even stepped into the trees, thinking I'd take a walk on a trail. But there was no trail, which was going to make it damn difficult to get out of here. Especially if I had to go alone. My sense of direction was shit.

By suppertime I was worried—about Murphy, about myself and my sanity. I picked at the food—someone really needed to teach Helen how to cook—then faked a huge yawn as an excuse to retire before the sun.

I had to think. To plan . . . something. But several days passed, and I was still there—no Murphy, no Mezareau, no plan.

I'd gone into the mountains and disappeared like so many others. Edward would try to find me, but I doubted he'd have much luck. With Murphy I'd believed I had a chance of getting out. Now I wasn't so sure.

What if Mezareau never came back? What if he was a myth? What if I couldn't learn what I needed to know? What if I could, but I was unable to escape and return to California and Sarah?

Wouldn't that be the ultimate torment? Knowing how to bring her back but being unable to do so? Perhaps we'd entered hell instead of an enchanted land.

Another night passed, and I was getting desperate.

The village quieted but not completely. When I glanced out my window, people still moved about. Was there really that much to do? Their industriousness bordered on obsession.

Along with that oddity, I'd discovered everyone in the village was young and strapping. The children I'd thought asleep the night we'd arrived did not exist, nor did the elderly. I started to have visions of a Stepford Village—created solely for a single purpose, though I couldn't figure out what that purpose might be.

I lay on my pallet at a loss. If I couldn't search the jungle in the daylight I certainly wasn't going to do it under the light of a gibbous moon. I had little choice but to wait until Mezareau deigned to speak with me or my imaginary friend showed up.

"Help," I whispered. The single word sounded frightened, lonely, lost.

I must have dozed, because I awoke and knew I was no longer alone. A slight hiss made me turn my head, and I came face-to-face with a snake.

Most women would freak, but even before the pet python, snakes had never bothered me. I'd been fascinated by them. This one appeared to be some kind of vine variety—skinny, green, and very long.

The snake was the symbol of the *loa* Danballah, my *met tet,* a term meaning "master of the head." Like the guardian angels of Christianity, a person's *met tet* watched over them for life.

I eyed the snake in front of me. I guess I *had* asked for help.

Slowly I sat up, and the reptile slithered toward the door, pausing at the threshold as if waiting. I got to my feet and followed.

The village was quieter, emptier than before, though not completely deserted. I waited for an outcry at my appearance. Where *were* my handmaidens? But no one seemed to notice me following the snake into the trees.

Though no path had magically appeared, the serpent knew where he was going, winding across sticks and stones, beneath bushes, and out the other side. He moved slowly so I was able to follow without too much difficulty.

I wondered momentarily if I were still asleep, which would explain the lack of interest in my leaving, as well as the ease of my travels through a previously impenetrable jungle. Then I stepped on a stone, right in the center of my foot. As pain exploded up my leg and I had to bite my tongue to keep from sniveling, I knew I was as awake as I'd ever be.

We continued on, into the night, the dark, the unknown. Perhaps this was punishment for my recent lack of attentiveness to my *met tet*. I'd been a little busy with the werewolves to leave offerings of food, rum, and shiny things. I'd definitely forgotten to wear Danballah's color, white, on his day of days, Thursday.

Loas could become extremely snarky when ignored. It would serve me right to be led into the wilderness and abandoned.

Just when I thought that was exactly what he had in mind, the trees parted and a hut appeared so suddenly I stumbled over my own feet.

"What the hell?" I said aloud.

The snake didn't answer. Looking down, I discovered the snake was gone.

"Swell," I muttered. "I get to reflect on my sins in the middle of a great big nowhere." I guess I should be thankful I'd have a roof over my head, if no food in my stomach.

Shoving back the curtain across the door, I stepped inside. The hut was occupied; however, the body near the far wall wasn't moving.

I peered into the jungle. Maybe I wasn't supposed to be in here. Maybe this was the home of some hermit, a crazy man who would chop me into a million pieces for trespassing. Hey, it could happen.

Uneasy, I glanced at the shadowy figure again, even took a step inside, I'm not sure why, and the change in angle allowed the moonlight to illuminate the beads woven into sun-streaked hair.

"Murphy!" I shouted, rushing forward, falling to my knees, reaching out. As soon as my fingers touched his skin, I jerked back.

He was cold, stiff, and—

Dead?

16

"No," I said firmly. Murphy could not be dead. I wouldn't let him be.

I rolled him onto his back, put my fingertips to the pulse point just beneath his chin. His hair, soft and free, drifted across my wrist. I closed my eyes, concentrated, and felt the featherlight flutter of a pulse.

"Hallelujah," I whispered, leaning down to press my cheek against his chest. He wore no shirt and his skin was slightly clammy.

Though I'd felt a pulse, I couldn't hear a heartbeat, maybe because my own was beating far too loud and fast in my ears.

I sat back. His chest rose and fell with slow, shallow breaths. Perhaps too slow and too shallow; he seemed almost drugged.

"Murphy!" I slapped his cheeks lightly.

Nothing.

I glanced around for some water to toss in his face.

Again, nothing.

How had he gotten here? Why had he stayed? Unless he'd been drugged from the beginning.

I shook him, pinched his arm, smacked the bottom of his feet, everything I'd ever heard of to wake someone up, but he didn't and I began to get scared. What if he was dying?

"Help," I muttered.

Leaning over, I lifted one of his eyelids, trying to see if his pupils were fixed, but it was too dark to tell. I sighed and let my head droop until we were nose to nose.

"Come on, Murphy," I murmured, and his eyes opened, staring directly into mine.

I yelped and straightened so fast my spine cracked. I tried to skitter backward, but he sat up as if he'd been jabbed with a cattle prod, then grabbed me by the arms, dragging me across his lap.

"What—?" was all I managed before he kissed me.

Since I was damn glad to see him, too, I didn't struggle; I didn't want to. He was real, he was alive, and man, could he kiss.

He tasted like licorice, sweet and dark, as his tongue teased my lips, then dipped inside to explore. Sighing, I let him, wrapping my arms around his neck and holding on.

His skin was still cool, but his hands warmed as he trailed them up my arms, then back down, settling at my waist and shifting me so I rolled over his erection. Together we moaned, the sound vibrating against our joined lips, making mine tingle.

My fingers tangled in the hair at his nape, pressing him closer, angling his head so I could experience every nuance of his mouth.

The broad, bare expanse of his chest gave off a chill, and I ran my hands across it, rubbing back and forth, trying to warm him. My thumbs were drawn to his hardened nipples, brushing over them once, twice, three times.

As if in answer his palms swept from my hips, up my ribs, to my breasts, unfettered beneath the loose cotton blouse. His thumbs ran over the peaks in the same stroking rhythm.

"Cassandra," he murmured against my mouth. "I thought you were dead."

We'd both been under the same misconception, which only made what we were doing more a celebration of life than usual. I'd been so frightened, so alone; I had to be with him right now; then I could put every fear and loneliness behind.

I wiggled, uncomfortable. Our angle was all wrong. I attempted to swing my leg across his and straddle him, but my skirt got tangled with my knees. Cursing impatiently, I yanked the thing above my waist and settled across his lap, pressing us intimately together.

He leaned against the outer wall, eyes closed, hair tangled. I ran my hands across his chest again, down his arms, tracing a fingertip below the waistband of his pants.

His lips quirked; one eye opened. Reaching out, he

took a fistful of my blouse and yanked me forward, pressing our mouths together again.

I was draped all over him, lips nibbling, teeth nipping, hands exploring. Then we slowed things down and, in doing so, only served to rev things up.

The less he gave, the more I wanted. What had seemed like a bad idea once seemed like a great idea now. My body was afire, drawn to the lingering chill of his.

His icy fingers felt exquisite on the heated skin of my stomach, tracing a delicious pattern across my rib cage. When he cupped my breasts I shivered, leaning back and lifting my blouse over my head, tossing it aside without thought, baring myself to him and the moonlight slanting through the tiny window.

I didn't stop to think that I was behaving out of character because right now I seemed to be more *me* than I'd ever been before. Or perhaps this was the new me, a woman born from the ashes of the old.

His tongue did an innovative swirl around my nipple, as our bodies rocked together in a way that was ordained long before we'd been born.

My legs spread wide, knees clutching his hips, I rode his erection, our clothes at first creating a delicious friction and then an unacceptable barrier. I was on the verge of something spectacular, and I existed only to find it.

I fumbled with his zipper. He shoved my hands aside, performing an acrobatic maneuver that freed him, even as I performed similar feats to remove one leg from my panties so he could plunge inside.

My skirt fell in a curtain around us as I clutched his shoulders; he grasped my hips, and we strove toward the conclusion of what we'd begun all the way back in that alley in Port-au-Prince.

My spine arched, body straining; he tugged on one nipple with his teeth, the sharp sensation causing me to gasp, clench, then shudder as the release broke over me, then he suckled to the gentle rhythm of the pulse deep inside.

He tugged me forward, my cheek against his hair, his face cradled between my breasts. His lingering chill seeped into me, and I groped for a blanket, tossing it over us, creating a cocoon that soon filled with our warmth. We stayed that way, arms around each other, bodies still joined, as our breathing evened out and we slowly came back to the earth.

But we couldn't stay that way forever. Eventually I had to climb off him, sit next to him, and ask questions. "You went into that hut in the village; then the next morning you were gone and everyone told me—"

"That I was dead? They told me the same thing about you."

"Actually, they told me you didn't exist. That I'd come into the village alone."

"That makes no sense."

"Does anything around here?" I asked. "Like how did you wind up in a hut in the middle of nowhere?"

"I'm not sure. I woke up here the morning after we arrived—or at least I think it was the morning after. I was dizzy, had the shivers. Pierre was here. He said I needed to stay away from the village. I had a fever. Then he told me you'd already died of it."

He pulled me into his arms again, and I was touched.

"How did you find me?"

I ignored the question, not wanting to get into the snake being my guardian and so on. We had more pressing concerns.

"Why didn't they leave any water? Medicine? Food? Did you see a doctor?"

"I doubt they have one. Pierre told me to fast. Only when I was purified would I be healed."

They were big on purification around here—no tea, no spices, no water, no food.

"That's bullshit if I ever heard it," I muttered.

"I didn't care for it much myself. But every time I tried to stand, I ended up on my ass. So I decided to sleep as much as I could and maybe I'd get stronger."

"Without food or water?"

He shrugged. "I didn't have much choice."

Something wasn't right. I could understand isolating Murphy, but dehydrating and starving him? That sounded like they were trying to kill him. Why not just kill him? I guess there was only one way to find out.

"Let's go back to the village."

17

I expected an argument from Murphy, a demand to get the hell out of Dodge, but as usual he surprised me.

"Let's," he said, and started to get dressed. "Have you seen the *bokor*?"

"No. They keep saying he'll arrive when he does."

"God, that's annoying," he muttered, and my lips curved.

Murphy stood, swaying a little. "Whoa. Head rush."

"I wish I'd brought some food and water."

"I'll be fine."

We stepped out of the hut and I scanned the area. No snake; I guessed we were on our own. I started off in the direction I'd come.

Murphy fell in beside me. I slowed my pace. He was paler than I liked. Several days in the heat without food or water—whether he'd had a fever or not—would make anyone woozy. If he passed out, I wouldn't be able to drag him.

"Maybe I should go back and bring help," I said.

"Because the people who left me here, the same ones who told you I didn't exist, have been so helpful?"

I hated it when he was right.

"Just tell me if you're faint," I ordered.

"If I can satisfy a woman, I can certainly walk back to the village."

"Oh, hell," I muttered.

We were still in the land that condom forgot, and I'd forgotten one.

"I thought heaven m'self."

Irish accent. I wasn't charmed.

"Condom," I said.

"Hell," he repeated, and stopped walking.

"Too late." I tugged on his hand. "Spilled milk."

"Not milk, more's the pity."

England had returned. Poor guy. He looked a little green. I squeezed his fingers. "Timing-wise, we're good."

"When you say 'good,' you mean—"

"For getting pregnant."

He started to hyperventilate.

"Breathe!" I ordered. "I meant for *not* getting pregnant. We're good for not getting pregnant."

He nodded, taking a few more seconds before speaking. "A baby isn't the only issue. But you shouldn't worry . . . I mean, I've never done this before."

I choked on surprised laughter. "You were *not* a virgin, Murphy. Even you can't expect me to believe such blarney."

"I'll take that as a compliment. I meant, I'd never had sex without a condom before."

"In your entire life?" I also found that hard to believe.

"I swear." He held up one hand.

"What got into you tonight?"

"You did."

"I think it was the other way around."

"I wasn't thinking," he admitted. "And usually I am. I'm sorry."

I wasn't, but I didn't plan on telling him so. We were being adults here, I couldn't admit that I'd needed him so badly I hadn't been thinking, either. That was the quickest way to a broken heart, and I didn't have much heart left to break.

"No harm, no foul," I quipped.

"Mmm. It's common courtesy to return the favor, sweet thing."

"Huh?"

"I tell you my sexual history and then—"

"Oh!" Obviously I was no good at this; my grand total of men in my bed now stood at a whopping two. "I . . . uh . . . haven't been with anyone since . . ." My voice trailed off. He could figure it out.

"Your husband," Murphy said. "What happened to him?"

I started to walk again, fast, any consideration of Murphy's weakness forgotten. He caught up easily, though, grabbed my arm, and held on tight. "I think I deserve to know, Cassandra."

He did, but that didn't mean I had to be nice about telling him.

"Karl betrayed me, got our daughter killed, and is now in prison. May he rot in pieces."

Murphy kept pace at my side. "What did he do?"

I didn't want to talk about this. However, I'd just shared my body with this man; why couldn't I share my past?

"He lied."

"About what?"

"Who he was, what he did."

Murphy didn't answer at first. When I looked up, he looked away. "I don't understand."

"Karl was a businessman. I never asked what kind of business. He was successful. We had money—a lot of it. He paid the bills; I ran the house and took care of Sarah."

My voice wavered and my steps slowed. Murphy took my hand. I'd never have figured him one for comfort, but I'd have figured wrong. I'd figured a lot wrong in my life.

"He wasn't a businessman?" Murphy rubbed his thumb back and forth across my palm.

"He was the biggest drug dealer on the West Coast." Murphy's eyes widened. "I don't know how I didn't see it. I guess I just didn't want to."

"And Sarah?"

"Karl got in a dispute with a supplier. They took her and they killed her."

"And then?"

Then I spent a lot of time in a quiet place drugged out of my gourd, but I wasn't going to mention that. Instead I skipped ahead several months. "Then the Feds came, and they wanted to know things."

Murphy frowned. "But you didn't know anything."

"Not then. But I found out."

"How?"

I shuddered, and his fingers tightened. "I pretended to forgive him."

"And then?" he repeated.

"I learned all I could, then testified and put him away forever." *I hope.*

Prolonged silence made me glance at Murphy. I couldn't read his expression.

"You're amazing," he said.

"Don't you mean vindictive?"

"I'll think twice before crossing you."

Though the words were flippant, his expression wasn't. I couldn't say I blamed him for being worried, but what did a guy like Murphy have to hide?

"How did you get involved in voodoo?" he asked.

"I dreamed of a snake, over and over and over again." At his blank expression, I continued, "Dreaming of a snake, of Danballah, means you're destined for the priesthood."

"In Haiti!"

"Actually, anywhere if you're studying to be a priestess. Danballah is a very powerful *loa*. My teacher was impressed."

At first I'd gone through the motions, wanting something from my new religion without giving anything back. Believing in voodoo hadn't been easy for a rich Catholic white girl from the land of sun and surf.

After Danballah had appeared often enough I'd come to believe I was doing the right thing, the only thing that I could do.

"I was lost," I explained. "Confused, uncertain, alone. I went searching, and I found something to hold on to. I'll discover a way to bring Sarah back. I know it."

"Cassandra, that's insane."

"Is it? I guess we'll see." I took a deep breath. "At the least, I needed a new identity, and Priestess Cassandra was a doozy."

Murphy shot me a quick glance. "You're in witness protection?"

"Did I say that?"

Even if I had just taken this man into my body and done things with him I'd never done with anyone else, I wasn't supposed to tell anyone about witness protection.

I'd been drilled in the rules. The only way to disappear was to leave my past behind. Of course I wasn't completely able to do that because of Sarah.

But I could follow every other rule—namely, never tell anyone I was a witness, never share my real name. Not even with the people I dated, not even with my new husband, should I remarry. Since I didn't plan on doing either, it had been easy to agree to those conditions.

"What's your real name?" Murphy pressed.

"Nothing half as wonderful as Cassandra."

"I don't like sleeping with a woman whose name I don't even know."

"We didn't sleep."

"That's beside the point."

"For a man who wears beads in his hair and a ring in his ear you're very closed-minded." He stared at me without any lightening of his expression. "My name is Cassandra, Murphy, and it always will be."

"Devon," he said.

"What?"

"The name's Devon. You'd think after we did the tongue tango you could at least call me by my given name."

"I'm not sure I can." He cursed in what sounded like French. "How many languages do you know?"

Murphy shrugged. "A few."

I'd bared my soul, or what was left of it; now it was his turn. "Why do you change accents all the time?"

"Because I can."

"And why can you?"

He didn't answer, and he wouldn't meet my eyes.

"You'd think after we did the tongue tango you could at least tell me where you're from," I repeated.

"You'd think, wouldn't you?"

"I'd really like to know," I said quietly.

He remained silent so long, I didn't think he was going to tell me; then the words tumbled out, as if he couldn't say them fast enough. "I was born in Tennessee. The mountains. I'm a gen-u-ine hillbilly."

He said the words just like Jethro Bodine, but something in his eyes kept me from laughing.

"You're American."

"As coal, which is what my daddy mined. Ten kids. We had nothing. Then the mine closed and Momma died."

"How old were you?"

"Fifteen. I left the next day."

"At fifteen?"

"Why not? I was practically on my own already. I wasn't going down in those mines, even if they hadn't closed. I figured I could be a model." His lips quirked. "At home I was considered mighty nice looking."

I could imagine. He was still mighty nice.

"All of my life I'd dreamed of being rich."

"It isn't all it's cracked up to be," I muttered.

"Try being dirt-poor and hungry, then choose."

He was right. I had no idea what it was like to have nothing to eat, no job, very little education.

"Sorry."

I had to wonder if the beads and feathers, the hoop and the thumb ring, were an unconscious rebellion against his childhood. Or perhaps he just liked pretty, shiny things, having had so few of them.

"Never mind." He took a deep breath, let it out. "I get riled up sometimes."

While talking about his past he'd reverted to a soft, country accent that flowed over my skin like warm water. He shifted his shoulders and cleared his throat.

When he spoke again, it was with the flat, unaccented tones of a nightly newscaster.

"I made my way to New York with high hopes, but in the big city I wasn't all that. Pretty faces, dime a million. So I wound up on the streets for a while, did some things I wasn't proud of."

I could imagine that, too.

"I discovered I had an ear for accents and languages; there are plenty of them to be heard in New York City. I found a job and got off the streets, but I was always just one step away from winding up there again."

Considering he'd left home at fifteen, Murphy hadn't turned out so badly. To have picked up so many accents and languages, to be as savvy and articulate as he was, he had to be extremely intelligent.

"How did you wind up in Haiti?"

"The job was construction, and after that last hurricane kicked the crap out of the Caribbean I was asked to come down and help out."

"For free?"

He lifted a brow. "Do I seem the free type? Government subsidized."

"The last hurricane?" I frowned. "That was a year ago."

"Job ended; I stayed."

"Why?"

He glanced into the trees. "I like it here."

For someone who professed to love money, Murphy had come to the wrong place.

Suddenly he stumbled and I reached for him. Luckily he recovered on his own, because otherwise we'd have both ended up on the ground.

"You're weak," I said. "Hungry."

He straightened. "This isn't hungry. I've *been* hungry. Hell, I could run a few miles yet before I pass out."

"Let's just keep walking, skip the running, shall we?"

Murphy's smile made me smile, too. I don't know what it was about him—maybe the great sex—but he made my spirit lighter.

He was honest about who he was, what he wanted. No secrets or hidden agendas with Devon Murphy. For a woman whose life had been ruined by secrets, who now lived in hiding, a man like Murphy was too novel to resist.

Though the snake had led me to the abandoned hut, I was having no problem finding my way back. My feet seemed to be drawn along a path no one else could see. I figured we'd reach the village in a few minutes; then we pushed through a particularly dense band of trees and into a clearing I'd never seen before.

As I'd said, my sense of direction was shit.

The fading moonlight filtered through the trees, turning to silver tiny bits of new growth dotted here and there throughout the recently tilled field. In less than an hour the sun would rise. I couldn't believe I'd been wandering about all night.

"What's that?" Murphy asked.

On the opposite side of the clearing stood a hut.

Murphy took off, skirting the edge of the overturned earth, and I hustled to catch up.

I reached him just as he pulled back the curtain on the door and ducked inside. I tensed in expectation of an outcry. We might be in the boonies, but that didn't mean you just walked into someone's hut uninvited.

When I heard nothing, I crept closer. "Murphy!"

"You'd better get in here."

After glancing around uneasily, I did.

Inside was a bed, furniture—handmade, but a chair was a chair and those were few and far between around here—bookshelves with real books, an altar. The hut must be the property of a very wealthy Haitian.

A leopard skin hung on the wall. Not just a cape but also the head, mouth open and snarling, yellow-green eyes bright, shiny; they looked almost alive.

"What's that for?" Murphy asked, never taking his eyes off the thing.

"Decoration?"

"It's not a voodoo costume?"

"Not one that I've ever seen, although that doesn't mean it couldn't be. Still . . ." I shook my head. "Voodoo symbolism leans more toward inanimate objects—rocks, trees, hearts, crosses. If we really want to go wild, there's thunder, lighting, the rainbow, or a snake. Large, vicious animals—not so much."

However, something he'd said tickled my memory. "Remember when I felt fur and a tail in the cave and you said—"

"Maybe someone was wearing fur."

We both returned our gazes to the leopard skin.

"That's weird," Murphy murmured.

I had to agree. "We should probably get out of here."

If someone was strange enough to wear a leopard skin around for whatever reason, I really didn't want to meet him or her.

"Just a minute." Murphy began to search the place.

"What are you doing?"

"You never know what you might find."

"This is breaking and entering!"

"The place was open."

"It's a *hut*; there is no closed."

He ignored me and continued with his search. I was drawn to the altar. Next to it lay an *ason,* a rattle used in voodoo rituals. Made from a gourd, an *ason* was filled with snake vertebrae and decorated with brightly colored strands of beads.

"What's that?" Murphy reached for the rattle.

"No!" I grabbed Murphy's hand before he could touch it. "An *ason* is only to be touched by the priest or priestess it belongs to. They're the sacred symbol of our service."

"Priest?" Murphy stared over my shoulder with an odd expression, and I suddenly realized what the *ason* meant.

"Mezareau," I said.

"Were you looking for me?"

18

The voice was deep and rich; a touch of France nudged it toward mesmerizing.

I turned. The man in the doorway wasn't what I'd expected.

He was slim and elegant in a linen shirt and trousers, and his erect carriage gave him the illusion of height, though in truth he had to be several inches shy of six feet.

His hair was short, dark, without a hint of gray, though there were lines around his thin lips and green eyes. The café au lait shade of his skin revealed someone on his family tree had arrived here in chains.

"Priestess Cassandra, *oui*?" A sharp tilt of his chin brought me out of my stupor.

"Oui. I mean yes. Sir."

He smiled, his teeth white, straight, and numerous. Or perhaps they just seemed that way because they were so small. He couldn't have more teeth than he should. I was just tired, nervous, embarrassed. He'd caught us going through his home.

"I'm sorry—," I began, and Murphy gave me an elbow in the ribs. I coughed.

"You're Mezareau?" he asked.

"Jacques Mezareau, *oui,* and you are the man who should be dead."

Murphy started but recovered quickly. "And you're the one who's been trying to kill me."

"I'm sure he meant the fever," I interjected.

"No." Mezareau bit off the word with a sharp French twist. I half-expected him to click his heels, but he wasn't wearing any shoes. "Monsieur Murphy is right; I *have* been trying to kill him."

"Told you so." Murphy inched in front of me.

I shouldered him back. We struggled for an instant, but Murphy was stronger and he won.

Mezareau watched the exchange with obvious amusement. "Why are you protecting him, Priestess? He has betrayed you."

Though I knew that was impossible—the tongue tango aside, I barely knew the man, how could he betray me?—nevertheless I stiffened. One betrayal in a lifetime was one too many.

"Cassandra—," Murphy began.

"Silence!" Mezareau thundered.

For such a slim man he had the deepest, loudest voice I'd ever heard. A chill rippled along my skin, making my hair stand on end. That voice was almost surreal.

Mezareau strode forward and grabbed Murphy by the throat, lifting the larger man onto his toes. His fingers were impossibly long, the nails even more so. They pressed into Murphy's neck, drawing blood.

"Stop that!" I protested.

Mezareau ignored me, shoving his hand into one of the voluminous pockets of Murphy's cargo pants and yanking something out. Then he let Murphy go with a shove.

Murphy stumbled, and I caught him before he fell. My gaze went to his neck, where tiny red welts had already sprung up.

"Told you he was a nut," Murphy managed.

"Actually, you said he was dangerous." I glanced toward Mezareau, whose eyes blazed like emeralds. "I think you were right."

"He is a thief and a liar, Priestess. He deserves to die."

Mezareau opened his hand, revealing what he'd removed from Murphy's pocket—a diamond the size of a golf ball.

I couldn't help but gape. I'd never seen anything like it. The jewel was exquisite.

"He came for this," Mezareau spit. "Not you."

I knew Murphy hadn't brought me out of the goodness of his heart; I was paying him. However, I *had* wondered why he'd decided to do so for such a reasonable price.

"He's tried to get through the waterfall before," Mezareau said.

Which explained how he'd known where it was.

"But only the worthy may pass, and he is not one of them."

"Then how did he get through?" I asked.

"Did he hold your hand when you went beneath the water?"

My gaze met Murphy's; his expression was carefully blank. "Yes."

Mezareau gave an elegant yet derisive snort. I felt like an idiot. I'd thought Murphy was being sweet, helpful, heroic. But I'd been wrong about a man before.

"I suppose you let him fuck you."

I flinched—from the language and the truth.

"Fool," Mezareau muttered. "He has been using you from the beginning."

Murphy said nothing in his own defense, so I had to. "But . . . I found him."

Mezareau's lip curled. "You went into the city. You asked about me. Even I heard you were asking way out here."

My ears perked up. How had he heard? With his own magical ears? Or from his own low-life spies?

"You think Murphy didn't get word? That he couldn't send someone to you and have them send you to him?"

As I'd said, I was no good at the cloak-and-dagger stuff. Probably never would be.

"What made me worthy?" I asked.

"You came not for yourself but for another."

Murphy spoke at last, his voice stronger but still

hoarse. "Wouldn't seem like a *bokor* would give a shit about that."

"You have no idea what I give a shit about, monsieur. Now, it is best if you are gone." He snapped his fingers and two burly villagers appeared in the doorway.

"No!" I said, a little too loudly.

"You will protect him after what he has done?" Mezareau asked.

"I don't want him dead."

"I thought that all women who are betrayed wish death on the betrayer."

"Not me."

Liar, my mind whispered. I wanted Karl dead.

But there was betrayal and then there was betrayal. Murphy hadn't done anything other than what I'd asked. Even if he'd been playing me, I'd gotten what I wanted. I'd particularly wanted the sex.

Mezareau said something to his minions in French too complicated to catch, and they grabbed Murphy.

"Wait—," I began, but Murphy interrupted, "He just told them to incarcerate me."

"Until I figure out what to do with you." Mezareau smiled thinly. "You are very hard to kill."

"Cassandra, don't believe what he says." The minions began to drag Murphy away. "He lies more than I do."

Mezareau's smile widened as Murphy disappeared through the door.

"You sent that man to our camp," I murmured.

"Oui."

"He was pretty hard to kill."

"I'm afraid he is not quite right in the head."

"I got that when he tried to chew off Murphy's nose."

Mezareau made a "tsking" sound. "As I said . . ." He twirled his finger near his ear in the universal hand gesture for "crazy." "But he takes orders very well."

"Helen didn't seem to know who he was."

"Helen knows only what I wish her to."

She'd also said the guy couldn't possibly be from here; now Mezareau was saying he was. Someone was lying. Big shock.

"So where is he?" I asked.

"You injured him very badly—knife in the back, gunshot to the shoulder, stabbed in the neck with a crucifix."

"Yet he got up and walked away."

"Amazing what the human body can withstand, is it not?"

I had my doubts he'd been human, but I let it go for now.

Mezareau tossed the diamond into the air; the large, heavy jewel made a *thwack* when he caught it in his palm. "Murphy is a thief, Priestess, and has been for a very long time."

"People in glass houses," I murmured.

"Are you insinuating I stole the diamond?"

"I'm not interested in the diamond."

"Just my knowledge."

"Yes." Why should I lie? "You're a *bokor*?" I pressed.

He dipped his chin.

"Why?"

Confusion flickered in his eerie eyes. "Why not?"

"You enjoy being evil?"

"You've been listening to the wrong people, Priestess. Embracing the dark side doubles your power."

"I bet," I said drily.

"A *houngan,* or a *mambo* like yourself," he said, using the word for "priestess," "who only studies the light side of magic is reaping but half the benefits. There is power beyond your dreams if you embrace all—white, black, and every shade in between. You must know this deep down or you wouldn't have come here."

I hated it when evil sorcerers were right.

Silence descended, broken only by the trill of insects calling to one another outside the hut. I wasn't sure what else to say. How did one ask about raising the dead?

My gaze returned to the leopard skin. "What is that?"

Mezareau crossed the room and stroked the pelt. "A family heirloom. You have heard of the Egbo?"

I remembered what Renee had told me. "The secret society of Old Calabar."

"Very good. The Egbo was the judicial arm of the Efik."

"Who were slave traders."

"An unfortunate truth. The Egbo was known as the leopard society. The leader wore this while he passed judgment on transgressors. Usually horrific and unusual punishment followed, to make the others desist."

"When you've got more slaves than captors, you have to make a statement," I murmured.

"Exactly." Mezareau beamed at me as if I were a prize pupil.

"So you're the leader," I said, and Mezareau dipped his chin. "And these people are your slaves?"

His eyes narrowed. "Why would you ask such a thing?"

"They work day and night, in a place from which there's no escape."

"Those in the village chose to come here, to make a better place than the one they had."

"They call you master."

"It is a courtesy title. I lead them, but they are free to go at any time."

"How?" I asked. "The waterfall disappeared."

His head tilted. "You must have been overtired. I'm sure if you return to the cave, the waterfall will exist right where you wish it to."

We'd see about that.

I lifted my chin to indicate the leopard skin. "Do you wear that like a costume? Walk on all fours? Growl?"

He frowned. "That has been on the wall since I built the place. It is an antique. I would never treat an heirloom with such disrespect."

OK, next question.

"Have any of your people seen a wolf in the night? Maybe heard some howls they can't explain?"

His frown became a smile. "I didn't realize you were a *Jäger-Sucher,* too."

I schooled my face into an expression of curiosity. "What's a *Jäger-Sucher*?"

"Come now, Priestess. Wolves in Haiti? I don't think so. Unless they're werewolves."

"Well, are they?"

"No." He lifted his right hand, palm facing me. "I swear there isn't a wolf—were- or otherwise—on this island."

I wasn't sure I believed him, but I hadn't come here for wolves.

"How do you know about the *Jäger-Sucher* society?"

"I know more than you could ever believe possible."

Hope fluttered to life in my chest. "Do you know how to raise the dead to live again?"

"But of course."

19

"Will you teach me?"

"If you wish."

Oh, I wished.

"You do realize that raising the dead is an act performed only by a *bokor*?" he murmured.

"Yes."

"So if I teach you, and you perform the ritual, you become like me."

I'd known that; I'd just chosen not of think about it for fear I'd chicken out. But now, faced with the end to my quest, the prospect of life after death, hope from the ashes, I knew it didn't matter.

"I'll do anything."

His smile widened. "I was hoping you'd say that."

Unease sparked, a trickle of gooseflesh across my neck, then down my arms. I felt as if I'd agreed to a devil's bargain, and I probably had.

"Can you teach me now?"

"The ritual may only be performed beneath the full moon."

Rats. I didn't want to wait another week until the lopsided moon became round, but I doubted even Mezareau could speed up that process.

"Until then," he snapped his fingers again, "you will be my guest."

The minions returned. They grabbed me by the arms and hauled me to my hut, about three hundred yards away. We *had* been close.

The goons shoved me inside, then stood guard at the door. I guess Mezareau's idea of guest and mine were pretty far apart.

The day passed, the night, too, and then several more. They didn't starve me at least. I wasn't so sure they were being as nice to Murphy. I asked after him, but if my guards understood English, they weren't letting on, going about their duties with silent, stoic precision.

My handmaidens had disappeared. I hoped they weren't being punished for allowing me to escape. Punishment around here was probably not pretty.

At last the moon arose complete, and my guards supplied me with a robe of red. The color was worn only in Petro rituals, when the more violent *loas* were summoned. These never took place in a temple but outside at a crossroad in an open field or a forest.

They led me to the recently tilled field, surrounded by trees. Mezareau stood at the edge garbed in a robe similar to mine, his *ason* in one hand and a knife in the other. Murphy lay gagged and bound at his feet.

"What the hell's going on?" I asked.

"You wanted to learn the ritual." He knelt next to Murphy, whose eyes widened at the sight of the knife. More a dagger really—shiny, jeweled, pretty, if it wasn't going to be used on you. "Let's get started."

"I won't let you kill him."

"But, my dear, you said you'd do anything."

My heart gave a sudden thud and the night turned cold. "I don't understand."

"I think you do. You donned the red robe, which symbolizes the blood sacrifice necessary to appease the Petro spirits."

"A chicken or a pig, not—"

"The goat without horns?" Mezareau suggested, using a common reference to a human sacrifice.

"How about just a goat?"

"You think the raising of the dead is a simple prospect? That it happens just by wishing, without the sacrifice of blood?"

I guess I hadn't thought that far. I shook my head, put my hands out as if to stop him, backed up, and bumped into the minions. They shoved me forward and I stumbled, righting myself just as Mezareau raised the knife.

"No," I whispered, but he didn't hear me, or he didn't care.

With a lightning-fast movement, Mezareau slashed

downward. Black dots danced in front of my eyes. What had I done? Given a life for a life? Murphy for Sarah? I'd said I'd do anything, but had I really done this?

"Lucky for you both," Mezareau murmured, "this ritual requires only blood and not the soul."

The dots parted. Murphy wasn't dead, just bleeding. Mezareau caught the blood dripping from Murphy's forearm in a shallow wooden bowl.

Murphy was pale; I felt sick. Mezareau smirked. He was enjoying himself.

A quick jerk of his head and the guards scooted around me, dragging Murphy away.

"You couldn't use your own blood?" I muttered.

"I could, but where's the fun in that? Besides, Murphy needs to be good for something, or he's good for nothing." His cool, light eyes met mine, and I understood the threat. When Murphy ceased to be worthwhile to him, he'd be dead. We needed to get out of here.

The shadows cast by the moon made the field even more eerie. The place was too quiet—a gathering of ghosts. The tiny shoots dotting the earth looked like fingers reaching for heaven.

Shivering, I turned away only to meet Mezareau's eyes, which appeared greener then ever before. "Get on with it," I said.

His smile was sly. "Mirror my movements; say what I say—exactly."

Mezareau set down the bowl of blood and picked up one of water, then he shook his *ason*.

I spread my empty hands, and he pointed to a second

gourd nearby. I'd never used an *ason* that was not my own; nevertheless, I picked it up and followed Mezareau's lead, shaking the gourd as I followed him around the field.

He sprinkled the water, giving nourishment to the earth. Halfway, he handed the bowl to me. I did as he had, continuing on the same path until we'd closed the circle, the two of us on the inside.

I had so many questions: Why were we here? Did the ritual have to be performed on newly turned ground? How long did this take? Where was the body?

But I kept my mouth shut and concentrated on mirroring Mezareau's every move so I could do this myself when the time came.

He began to chant in English, surprising me a bit. In Haiti the rituals have always been performed in French and Creole, perhaps a little Latin. However, the language wasn't as important as the words, the emotions, and the power of the one reciting them.

"Come back to us now. Come back. Death is not the end. Live again as you once lived. Forget you ever died. Follow me into the world. Come back to us now. Come back."

At Mezareau's urging I repeated the chant as we walked in steadily smaller circles toward the center of the field.

I didn't understand how we could raise the dead when they weren't here. And didn't we need a name? How else would the dead know whom we were calling from the grave?

"Drink."

Mezareau held a cup in each hand; one he extended to me. Where had they come from?

I hesitated, but when he drained his I had no choice but to do the same. I recognized the flavor—*kleren,* raw white rum made in Haiti. A particular favorite of the Gede, it was not a favorite of mine. The stuff tasted like rotten sugar, which was kind of what it was, being made from fermented cane.

Grimacing, I wiped my mouth with the back of my hand. Mezareau tossed the empty cup over his shoulder; so did I. They bounced with a soft, plastic thud.

"Whoops." I giggled. Was I drunk?

The world spun. The moon seemed to grow larger, come closer, and whisper, *Soon. Very soon. You'll do anything.*

Mezareau didn't seem affected. He appeared before me, this time with the bowl of blood.

His robe parted, revealing the diamond strung around his neck. I guess I wouldn't leave that lying around, either.

"One last thing," he murmured, and tipped the bowl.

The air seemed to thicken. Time slowed. The blood fell in a crimson stream toward the earth. The moon glinted off the jewel at the center of his chest.

I knew I shouldn't speak, but I couldn't seem to help myself. "Where's the body?"

My tongue was heavy; the words came out in a voice that wasn't my own. I'd been possessed before, by my *met tet,* but this was different. When Danballah was driving the controls, I spoke in a hiss, not words, a sacred language that had originated in Africa, akin to speaking in tongues, which only the *loa* could understand.

Mezareau didn't answer. In the end, he didn't have to.

The blood splashed against the earth, springing up, then plopping down, turning black beneath the full silver light of the moon just before midnight.

My gaze was drawn to the tiny shoots that looked like fingers sprouting from the ground, and I suddenly understood that the plants didn't *look* like fingers.

They *were* fingers.

20

The earth shook. The ground spilled outward like the Red Sea. Bodies tumbled up and onto the surface.

I stumbled, then fell. A hand shot out of the dirt right next to me; a red beaded bracelet encircled the wrist.

I watched, mesmerized, horrified, as Helen's face emerged from the dirt. On her other side lay her twin. I guess they'd been punished more severely than I thought.

I dragged myself to my feet, glancing around for Mezareau, but he was gone. I stood alone in a grave-yard that was spitting up people all around me.

Concerned they'd start to grab my ankles, or chase me as I ran screaming, I staggered toward the hut. However, no one followed. No one was moving. They still looked pretty dead.

Maybe Mezareau had needed something more to re-animate the corpses. I shoved aside the curtain, caught my feet in the long red robe, and practically pitched headfirst into the room.

Whatever he'd put into my rum kicked in with a vengeance. Swirling colors appeared at the edge of my vision, along with wispy tendrils like smoke. I heard a whisper behind me, spun around, but nothing was there.

My body became coated with a light sheen of sweat. I could hear my own breathing, a labor in my lungs. I was both hot and chilled, uncomfortable. I wanted nothing more than to lie down and sleep until this all went away.

I probably would have, too, except drums began to pulse on the air. I ran outside, but the clearing was empty—except for the bodies.

"Where are they?" I plunged into the jungle, determined to find out.

I wandered to and fro, round and round; I couldn't get a bead on where the sound originated. At times I thought the bone-jarring thuds were merely echoes of my racing heart inside my aching head.

My skin felt too small for my body. My fingernails itched. My nose burned. Perhaps I had a fever.

"Mezareau!" I shouted, my voice barely audible above the beat of the drums. "Come and *get* me!"

I threw out my arms, spun in a circle, my hands smashing against branches, sending leaves cascading every which way. I began to giggle—definitely drunk, if not drugged—then I caught my toe on something and fell to my knees.

The growl reverberated from the ground through my

palms, making my teeth rattle. Slowly I lifted my head and came face-to-face with a leopard, lips drawn back in a snarl, just like the one on the wall of Mezareau's hut.

The wispy smoke swirled across my vision; all of the colors collided. My eyes rolled up; I went down. Face-first into the ground as I fainted.

My dreams were fevered visions of death, blood, and the eyes of a jungle cat. Voices whispered, reciting names I didn't know, the echoes dying away into a swirling, colored midnight.

Corpses rose from the earth and marched across the land like an army, destroying everything in their wake.

Wild animals prowled—wolves, coyotes, lions, tigers, and leopards—all with human eyes. The night came alive with their calls.

The moon pulsed behind my closed eyelids to the beat of the drums in my head. I came awake with a sharp gasp into a night gone still and silver. I lay on the ground; the leopard was gone. Instead I saw Sarah. Far away in the jungle, she beckoned me.

I sprang to my feet and ran, but so did she. The farther I went, the farther away she seemed. Her laughter filled the night; the scent of her skin filled the air; the ache of missing her spurred me onward.

I was almost close enough to touch her when she turned. One look at me and my little girl screamed, and then she wouldn't stop.

Glancing down, I saw that I was a leopard and my fur was covered in blood.

I awoke next in a hut bathed in moonlight. Naked, my body tangled with that of another. I stiffened, prepared to struggle, but the low, throaty murmur made me pause.

I knew the scent of his hair, the slide of his skin, the taste of his mouth against mine. "Murphy."

I doubted he was any more real than Sarah, but right now I needed a better dream. I clung to him as if my life hung in the balance. My sanity certainly did.

The room darkened as the moon fell down. Urgency overcame any unease. I needed the darkness, the total night; I wanted to do things to him that weren't done in the sun.

As I tangled my fingers in his hair, my knuckles brushed the beads, and my thumbs traced the line of his jaw, the curve of his neck. I pressed him backward until my body sprawled over his. His erection brushed my stomach as I explored with my mouth the soft skin stretched taut over his collarbone.

With gentle nips of my teeth and swirls of my tongue, I took my time moving downward; the longer this dream continued the better. He quivered with anticipation as I brushed my cheek over his stomach, then drew my thumbnail along the hollow at his hip.

His penis jerked against my breasts—eager, edgy—and I leaned forward letting my warm, moist breath brush the tip. I put my tongue out slowly, stopping just short of touching him before I leaned back.

He groaned and I took pity, rubbing my thumb over him, then taking him in my palm and stroking him—at first slowly, gently, then harder, faster, replacing my hand with my mouth, relishing the flavor of strength, the power and the heat.

Suddenly I flew onto my back, and his body covered mine. He filled me in a single deep thrust. I arched, bowing off the blanket to meet him.

I wanted him rough, demanding. I couldn't afford to think of anything but this. He lifted my legs, hooked my knees over his hips, and drove into me, the slap of flesh an enticement, reminding me of the beat of the drums in a far-off jungle.

I jerked my mind off that memory, forced myself back to this one. Reaching up, I hooked my hand around his neck and drew him downward.

I wanted to mark him as mine forever. Foolish—he wasn't a forever kind of guy. But this was my dream and I could do as I wished, so I buried my face in his neck as he buried his body in mine, again and again.

My teeth scraped the pulsing vein just above his collarbone; I drew his skin between my lips and tasted life, salt, and man. I could hear the rush of his blood, and for just an instant, I wanted to taste that, too.

He stiffened, stilling inside of me. The release began—his, mine, I wasn't sure, and it didn't matter, because suddenly it was both of us.

Best of all, deep in the thralls of a dream orgasm, I forgot all about the moon and the leopard, but strangely, I still wanted the blood.

21

The sun warmed my face. I stretched, surprised at how achy I felt. Last night had been a dilly for dreams.

I opened my eyes and stared straight into Murphy's.

"Aarck!" I squeaked, and scrambled backward. Realizing I was naked, I yanked the blanket off of him and over me.

"What the hell?" he snapped. "You can suck me off until I nearly explode, I can screw you until you scream, but I can't see you naked?"

"That—that—was a dream."

"Really? Then what's this?" He lifted his hair away from his neck to reveal a whopper of a hickey.

Now that I took inventory of my body, the aches and pains told the tale. I hadn't dreamed of sleeping with Murphy; I'd actually done it.

I groaned and covered my face with my hands. "I don't suppose you bummed a condom off a friendly neighborhood villager."

"The villagers haven't exactly been neighborly," he said. "At least not to me."

I lifted my head. There were worse things to worry about than waking up in Murphy's bed. I'd had more than one dream last night, and if this one had been real, then—

"How did I get here?" I demanded.

"I have no idea. After the bloodletting," he lifted his arm, which sported a disturbingly dirty bandage, "I was a little woozy."

"Sorry."

"I lived. Though with Mezareau around, I can't say how long that condition will continue. I passed out, and next thing I knew you were naked in my arms. Being a guy, I couldn't complain."

"You couldn't stop, either, I suppose."

"I half-thought I dreamed you, too, until I woke up." He rubbed a hand through his hair, and his silver thumb ring flashed gold in the sunlight blaring through the window. "I was pretty out of it."

Drugs or blood loss, either way, we'd both been loopy. We'd behaved stupidly, though not completely of our own accord. What I couldn't understand was why it was suddenly OK for the two of us to inhabit the same hut.

Catching sight of my backpack in the corner, I pounced on it, thrilled to find my extra pair of clothes. Also inside were the remnants of the herbal sleeping draught and my zombie-revealing powder, as well as my knife—why did no one seem to fear sharp and shiny silver around here? However, the salt was suspiciously absent.

I got dressed, stuffed the zombie-revealing powder into my jeans, never could tell when I might need some, then fastened the knife at my waist. I felt much better in my own clothes, with my favorite weapons.

"What did Mezareau tell you about me?"

Murphy was dressed, too, but he sat hunched in a corner, appearing very un-Murphy-like. Since when did he care what people said?

"He said you were a thief, had been for a long time."

"Huh," he muttered. "The truth."

"I thought you were a construction worker."

"I am." He glanced up. "But I *was* a thief—as a kid, after I left home. Sometimes I didn't have a choice."

I saw him as he'd once been—young, alone, starving—stealing was understandable. *Then.*

"I was very good at it."

He appeared to be good at everything he set his mind to. Lucky me.

"I could have gone professional."

"I'm supposed to believe that you haven't?"

"I've been working for a living. Seriously," he said when I lifted my brows. "Look at my hands."

I'd felt his hands. He'd definitely been using them on rougher things than me.

"I came to Haiti and I heard rumors about the diamond."

"I thought no one ever got out of this place?"

"Someone must have, or there'd be no rumors."

Good point.

"So instead of leaving when the job ended, you stayed."

He lifted his shoulder. "I figured . . . one last time. Then I'd never have to worry about money again. I'd never wake up in the night thinking I was back on the street, that someone was going to kill me, or worse. I'd never be so hungry I ached with it. And what's so bad about stealing from a sorcerer anyway?"

"Stealing's stealing, Murphy," I said softly. "You know that."

He lowered his gaze, and his hair shrouded his face.

I went to the window and glanced outside. The number of villagers appeared to have doubled. They were all milling about, socializing. No one was paying any attention to us.

"Come on." I slipped out the door and into the trees. No one raised a hue and cry, even when Murphy followed.

"Where are we going?" he asked.

"Last night Mezareau showed me how to raise the dead."

Murphy stopped. One glance at his face and I knew he planned to argue with me.

"Just look, listen, then decide," I urged.

He nodded and we continued on until we reached the clearing. I stepped into the field, which seemed to have been rototilled recently, or perhaps just excessively jumbled by the newly arisen dead.

Nowhere could I see any signs of growth, not a stray

finger to be had. I went on my knees where Helen's body had sprouted forth, pulled out my knife, and started to dig.

"Cassandra, what are you doing?"

"You remember when we found this place, it looked as if they'd planted something here?"

"Yes."

"They planted bodies."

His jaw clenched, so I quickly told him what had happened. As I spoke I continued to dig, and when I was done, I had a big hole but not a single bone or even a skull.

"There's nothing here," Murphy said in a voice that told me he didn't believe there ever had been.

"I think we raised them. That would explain the sudden increase in villagers."

"And the leopard?"

"Maybe Mezareau does run around with that costume on his head."

"Was the skin still on the wall when you went into his hut last night?"

I couldn't remember. "I was a little dizzy, drunk, drugged—maybe all three."

"Hold on." He stalked across the field and ducked inside the hut. I tensed, expecting an outcry, a gunshot, something. Murphy came back out. "It's there now."

I followed him, glancing inside, discovering that what he said was true; however, that didn't mean what I'd seen wasn't real. Or even that it was.

"Weird things happen in Haiti," Murphy murmured.

"I'll say."

"But raising the dead? That's a little weird even for here."

"How can you stand there and say you don't believe? Your blood was what raised them."

"Just because some psycho cut me open and poured my blood on the ground proves nothing. You need to give up this obsession, Cassandra. Go home. Maybe see someone."

"You think I'm crazy?"

Why did I keep asking that? The answer had always been yes.

"I think you miss your daughter," he said softly. "That's understandable. But you need to let Sarah rest in peace and move on with your life."

"I can't. Without her there is no life."

Something flickered in his eyes. I thought it might have been sorrow, but that was probably just a reflection of my own.

"Make a new one," he said.

"You have no idea what you're talking about. You never had a child."

"Not that I'm aware of."

How could he be flippant at a time like this? Because he was Devon Murphy—rogue, charmer, thief. He'd risked his life and mine for a hunk of rock. He had no right to take the high ground. I doubted he even knew where it was.

"You've obviously never loved anyone," I snapped.

"Right you are, and no one's ever loved me."

Silence settled between us. He was breathing hard; his hands clenched. So did mine. This was getting us nowhere.

"If there's a chance in a million of having her back, I'll find it." I stared at the empty field. "Last night *something* happened."

If only I could remember what.

"You were drugged," Murphy said. "You imagined everything. People don't come back from the dead. It's impossible."

I was furious now, probably because I was a little bit scared that he was right and if he was, then what would I do?

I stalked back to the village, leaving Murphy to follow or not; I didn't care. I had to talk to Mezareau, and since he wasn't here, he must be there, or I'd find someone who knew where he was.

I stepped into the common area between the huts and froze at the sight of my handmaidens. They no longer looked dead. Instead they smiled and chattered in the midst of what appeared to be the Haitian version of a block party.

"I'll show you impossible," I muttered, and reached into the pocket of my jeans for the zombie powder.

I dumped what was left into my palm, creating a tiny hill. Too much, really, but I was in a hurry.

I headed toward the crowd, but before I reached them, the wind whipped in from nowhere, lifting the particles into the air. Like a cartoon cloud, they expanded, flying into the face of every villager milling in the vicinity.

I don't know what I expected. Most likely the nothing that had happened every other time I'd used the stuff. If my powder had been of any worth, why had Mezareau allowed me to keep it?

What I hadn't planned on was two dozen people screaming in agony as they melted like the Wicked Witch of the West.

Their flesh pulled away from their bones as their eyes lost all signs of life. Fingernails lengthened, hair, too. The wounds that had killed them reappeared. I had never seen anything like it, nor did I ever want to again.

"OK," Murphy said. "That I can't explain."

22

"What have you done?"

Mezareau's thunderous voice made both Murphy and me jump, then glance up from the pile of flesh and bones at our feet.

The *bokor* didn't appear happy. Several villagers who hadn't been in the village before now cowered at the edge of the trees as if they planned to run should I produce more powder. Too bad I was all out.

Mezareau stalked toward us. When Murphy stepped in front of me Mezareau backhanded him so hard he was lifted off his feet and flung across the yard.

My eyes widened. That kind of strength wasn't quite human.

Mezareau grabbed me by the throat. Without thinking, I ground my palm against his cheek, leaving the remnants of the powder stuck to his skin. The only reaction was a tightening of his fingers until I saw stars.

I grabbed my knife, but he shook me like a dog with a rope, and the weapon flew from my hand. I probably didn't need it. The way he was behaving, silver wasn't going to kill him, either. And wasn't that a cheery thought?

One more brain-jarring shake, and he dropped me to the ground. "What did you do?" he repeated.

I managed to stay on my feet, barely. A quick glance at Murphy revealed he was unconscious, but I swore I saw him breathing.

"Zombie-revealing powder," I answered, voice hoarse and wispy.

"I tested your powder." He sniffed. "Harmless."

"Tell it to your friends."

His eyes narrowed. "What is the formula?"

"Little of this, a lot of that."

"Any salt?"

"No."

"Then it cannot work."

That's what I'd thought. Until today.

Of course, until today, I don't think I'd tried it on an actual zombie.

Mezareau stared at me with an expression of dawning understanding. "It is not the ingredients that provide the power, but the one who combined them. You are far stronger than I realized."

I rubbed my throat reflectively. "That makes two of us."

Mezareau threw out his arms to indicate the village, the trees, the land. "This place is special. That is why

I chose it. The longer you are here, the more potent you will become."

"Sounds like bullshit to me," Murphy said.

He'd managed to sit up. One eye was already swollen shut. He looked more like a pirate than ever.

Mezareau turned his gaze—hazel in the early-morning light—toward Murphy. The expression reminded me of wild cats I'd seen on Animal Planet—right after they discovered delectable prey.

"You would be the best judge of bullshit, would you not, monsieur?"

"Got that right," Murphy muttered.

The two of them stared at each other like two beasts over a single bone. If they fought, I knew who'd win—and who'd die.

"What's the problem with salt and zombies?" I blurted.

The staring continued for several more ticks of the clock before Mezareau glanced away. "They are mutually exclusive," he said. "A zombie cannot exist if touched by salt; salt cannot exist within a zombie."

"What do you mean, within?"

"It is amazing how much salt is contained in the human body. However, to be raised from the dead, there can be none within. Therefore, the body must be purified—either by years in the grave or through fasting before death." He glanced at Murphy. "The priestess discovered you before we could complete your purification, so there could be no transformation under this full moon."

"You were going to make Murphy a zombie?" I asked.

"Of course."

"Of course," Murphy mocked. "Why the hell not?"

I guess he was feeling better.

"You have qualities I admire," Mezareau said. "Strength, agility, devotion to a goal, even if it is money. Besides, once you were dead, you'd stop trying to steal my diamond."

"Maybe." Murphy's lips tightened. "But I wouldn't count on it."

"When you're a zombie, you'll do anything I ask."

I frowned. "What are you talking about?"

"Zombies are slaves, Priestess. Even centuries cannot change that."

"No," I whispered. "They're human again. As if they'd never been dead at all."

He smiled indulgently. "Yes and no. My zombies appear human. However, they do not die like normal humans."

"All it takes is a little salt," Murphy sneered.

Mezareau and I ignored him.

Not dying was a good thing, wasn't it? I didn't want Sarah to ever die again. All I had to do was keep her out of the ocean. That shouldn't be hard. We'd just move to Topeka.

Despite my rationalization, these revelations were making me uneasy.

"You said the people of the village could leave whenever they wanted to."

Murphy gave a snort of derision. Mezareau cast him a narrow glare before returning his attention to me.

"I may have stretched the truth a bit."

"They can't leave?"

"Once they are raised, they do not want to."

"Do zombies have to be slaves?" I pressed. "Couldn't you release them from bondage?"

"I do not know." Mezareau's forehead creased. "I've never tried."

"How did you plan on zombifying me?" Murphy asked.

"Death becomes life." Mezareau spread his hands. "The ritual."

"But I wasn't dead."

"That would have been easily remedied once you were purified."

"You're killing people in order to raise them?" My voice rose higher and higher with every word.

"How else would I be able to populate my army with the worthy?"

"A zombie army." Murphy gained his feet and only wobbled a little as he returned to my side. "Why?"

"My ancestors ruled here once. I plan to rule again."

"When was this?" I asked.

"The island was called Saint-Domingue. The French were in control. My great-great-many-times-great-grandfather was the governor."

"And he had a mistress."

Mezareau dipped his chin. "The mulatto elite were society's darlings. He would have married her if he could."

"Mmm," I said. What I thought was, *Yeah right*.

"But he was killed in one of the revolts and ever

since there has been chaos. I will turn that around when I reclaim my rightful place on the throne."

Murphy and I exchanged glances. *Throne?*

"So you're going to . . . ?" I let my voice trail off encouragingly.

"Take over the country. It won't be hard."

"Not with an army of people who can't be killed," Murphy said.

We looked down at the pile of flesh and bones. Except by me.

Murphy inched in front of me. "I won't let you kill her."

"Why would I?" Mezareau asked. "She's the most powerful voodoo priestess I've ever known."

"I think you're confusing me with someone else," I protested. "I'm new at this."

Except I *was* kind of good at it, and I seemed to be getting better with each passing day. I had to wonder if Mezareau's claims that his village was "special" were true. Maybe that was how he'd become freakishly strong in both a physical and a metaphysical sense.

The *bokor* contemplated me with continued amusement. "I've never known anyone who didn't run screaming when I sent the dead, let alone dispersed them. How did you do it?"

"I called on Aida-Wedo."

His brows lifted. "The *loas* always come when you call?"

"Shouldn't they?"

"Oh, they should, but that doesn't always mean that they will."

I hadn't realized I'd been doing something extraordinary; I'd only been doing what I'd been taught.

"You are the one I've been waiting for," Mezareau continued. "I asked the Lord of Death to send me a powerful partner. I can't create the army all alone." He frowned. "Especially now that you've disintegrated an entire month's work."

He'd called on the Lord of Death—Baron Samedi, gatekeeper to the otherworld and overseer of zombies. I guess when Mezareau sent the dead I should have known he had an in with Samedi. But there was something about the revelation that bothered me. I just couldn't put my finger on what it was.

"She'll only kill more of your zombies," Murphy pointed out.

"Keep it up," I said. "You'll convince him yet that he's better off killing me."

Mezareau laughed. "She won't be able to make any more of her powder here."

"How do *you* know?" I demanded, then had to refrain from smacking myself in the head. I wasn't any better than Murphy.

"Because if you try anything of the kind, I'll kill your lover, then embalm him with salt so he can never rise again."

"He's not my lover," I felt compelled to explain. There hadn't been any love involved.

Murphy shot me a glance that seemed kind of hurt. What was up with that?

For that matter, what was up with my racing heart and my extreme unease at the idea of loving another man? I wasn't going to, and that was that.

"I'm still certain you wouldn't want his blood on your hands. And it will *be* on your hands, Priestess. Literally."

I flinched, which caused Mezareau to smirk. "Excellent. You will be my guests until I have what I want."

"And then?" Murphy asked.

Mezareau's smirk widened. "Then we shall see."

Murphy and I were dumped back into his hut.

"Amuse yourselves, children," Mezareau said, and tossed me my knife.

I stared at the weapon, which had once struck fear into monsters of the night. Mezareau seemed to have no fear of anything, which scared the crap out of *me*.

I tossed the knife into my backpack. "How come it's all right for us to stay together now? Sudden change of heart on the premarital sex issue?"

"I could care less who you fuck, Priestess. I only wanted you separated so I could kill him."

Ask a stupid question . . .

"Why was I told Murphy didn't exist? Did you actually think I'd believe that?"

"My villagers live only in this new world we've created. Once someone leaves their world, they no longer believe the person exists."

I frowned. That would explain why Helen didn't

remember crazy nose-eating zombie man, even though he had to have been in the village at one time or another. This place was downright bizarre, and so were all the people in it. Like that was news.

Mezareau signaled and two guards appeared. "Keep them inside," he ordered, "or I will feed you a bowl full of salt."

The two men took up positions on either side of the door.

"We've got to get out of here," I said.

"No shit."

I glanced at Murphy. "What's wrong with you?"

"Oh, I don't know—maybe I just saw people become corpses right in front of my eyes. Maybe I had a little Frenchman toss me across the yard, then tell me he was going to kill me and make me into a zombie so I could join his bloody zombie army."

Murphy hadn't resorted to an accent for quite a while. I guess his whole world *had* changed; I should really cut him some slack.

"At least you don't think I'm crazy anymore."

"That depends. Are you still planning to raise your daughter from the dead?"

"Why wouldn't I be? You saw them. We had no idea that most of this village was the risen dead. They were alive again."

"If you don't feed them salt or throw voodoo powder in their faces!"

Murphy's voice was different; so were his eyes, the expression on his face. He seemed to have aged.

I suppose being starved, threatened, and involuntarily giving blood for a zombie-raising ceremony could do that to a guy, especially a guy like him who'd spent his life on the good-time trail. This trip, this place, my problems, had to make him want to run for the hills, or at least the waterfall.

"I'm sorry you got caught up in this, Murphy."

"I knew what I was doing."

"I don't think you did."

His sigh was impatient. "You got what you came for; now it's time to get out of here."

He stalked to the far side of the hut, where he shoved against the corner posts. I followed, hunkering down next to him when he began testing the base of the wall for a weakness.

"What's the rush?" I asked.

"Besides the crazy guy who's threatening to kill me?"

He straightened and so did I. After a quick glance at the door, where the guards continued to stare in the other direction, he turned, shielding me with his body. "Because I think he probably *will* kill me if he finds this."

Murphy reached into his cargo pants and withdrew Mezareau's diamond.

23

I cursed and grabbed the stone, shoving it down the front of my pants. He tried to go in after it, and I slapped his hand. "I don't think so."

The commotion caused the guards to glance inside. All they saw was Murphy trying to get in my pants. Grinning, they turned around again.

"Where did you get that?" I whispered furiously.

"Where do you think?"

I tried to recall when he'd been anywhere near the diamond.

Aha! Earlier that morning he'd ducked into Mezareau's hut to check on the leopard skin.

"Mezareau just leaves it lying around?" I asked. "With you on the loose?"

"Not exactly." His expression was sheepish. "I have some experience unlocking things." Murphy cracked his knuckles.

Of course he did.

"What happened to stealing is stealing no matter who you steal from?" I asked.

"You said that, not me. I didn't come all this way—get kidnapped, drugged, donate blood, and become next on a *bokor*'s hit list—to walk away empty-handed."

"When did you plan on telling me about this?"

"I just did. Now give that back."

"No."

"Cassandra."

"Devon."

"You sound like my mother." He made a face. "Call me Murphy."

"No problem." I didn't want him remembering his mother when he looked at me, either.

Murphy glanced at the door. "I don't think you should keep it."

"And you should? He'll kill you, but he won't kill me."

"Not until he's got his army anyway."

"Mezareau's going to notice his diamond is gone."

"I don't plan to be here when that happens; do you?"

"No. Have any ideas on how we get out of here?"

"Not a one. Even if we can sneak past the guards, half a zombie army, and Mezareau, we're going to have waterfall issues." He paused, considering. "You don't know any spells that would make them all go away? Or even better, one that might transport us back to Port-au-Prince?" He snapped his fingers. "Poof?"

"Suddenly you believe in spells?"

"After this morning, it seems foolish not to. So, you know any?"

"Voodoo is about religion, not magic."

"Turning those zombies to dust seemed like magic to me. Hell, them being alive in the first place is so against any religion I've ever heard of it has to be something outside of it."

"It is," I murmured.

My prattle about religion and magic just wasn't holding up. As Mezareau had said, the longer I was here, the more magic happened. I wasn't sure if that was a result of me or the jungle, perhaps both. Either way, I was getting kind of scared of my power. Though if things got nasty, my power might be all that stood between Murphy and me and eternity.

The day passed with agonizing slowness. We sat and stared at each other, the wall, the floor, out the window. Our meals were brought to us. We were allowed to use the facilities—such that they were—one at a time. When darkness fell, I was no closer to a plan of escape than I'd been when the sun shone.

I fell asleep, and when I awoke the soft glow of a candle illuminated the hut. Murphy sat on the ground, shirtless, his skin gleaming in the heat and the murky light. I'd have been captivated by the sight, if he hadn't gone through my backpack and laid out every one of my things in a tidy row.

I sat up and he glanced at me. "Sorry. I just—" He spread his hands. "All we've got is this. I was trying to figure out how we could use it." He picked up the knife. "Never thought I'd see the day when sharp steel was worthless."

"Silver," I corrected.

Murphy turned the blade, and the flames of the candle sparked off the polished surface. "Fancy."

"Practical. Until recently, silver killed just about anything."

He lifted his gaze. "You've used this to kill things?"

"No," I admitted. "I'm not that kind of *Jäger-Sucher*."

I could tell he wanted to roll his eyes and say something derisive, but he couldn't anymore. "What kind are you?"

"Not much of one, really. I know voodoo, and since the latest werewolf problem involved a voodoo curse, I was asked to help. Most of the *Jäger-Suchers* are fighters." I took a breath. "Honestly, they're killers. They stop at nothing to get the job done, because they know if they don't, people will die."

"Tell me about them," Murphy urged.

I hesitated. The *Jäger-Suchers* were supposed to be a secret, but since I had my doubts Murphy and I would get out of here alive—and really, what else did we have to do?—I told him.

"The *Jäger-Suchers* are a monster-hunting society run by Edward Mandenauer. He was a spy in WW II, sent to discover what Hitler was up to."

"He was up to a lot," Murphy muttered.

"More than anyone ever knew. Hitler was fascinated with wolves and werewolves. Maybe because *Adolf* means 'Noble Wolf'—who knows? He chose the title *führer* because it refers to the leader of a pack of hunting wolves. He even sanctioned a secret terrorist organization known as the werewolves."

"What did they do?"

"Near the end of the war, when things began to go badly for Germany, recruits were taken from the Hitler Youth, the SS, the army, civilians. In the way of a werewolf they would appear to be normal citizens in the daylight, but at night they were charged to wreak death and destruction on their enemy by any means possible."

"And they were really werewolves?"

Huh. I hadn't thought of that.

"Edward never said. I'm not sure if *he* knows."

"What did your boss discover about Hitler?"

"Have you heard of Josef Mengele?" At Murphy's blank expression I elaborated. "The doctor who performed medical experiments on the Jews, the Gypsies, and—well, pretty much anyone he wanted to."

"Nutcake," Murphy muttered.

"Times ten. Hitler ordered Mengele to make a werewolf army, so he did."

"How?"

"A little bit of this, a whole lot of that. No one's really certain, since Herr Doktor destroyed all the records."

"But he didn't destroy the werewolves."

"No. Those he released. They've been multiplying ever since. Along with a lot of other things he devised in his secret lab in the Black Forest. Edward was supposed to eliminate the monsters, but he got there too late. He's been trying to make up for that ever since."

"This all sounds crazy. Until you see a zombie disintegrate before your eyes."

"Try watching a man turn into a wolf and back again. It isn't pretty."

"I can imagine." His lips tightened. "Or maybe I can't. What other things did Mengele release?"

I thought of Edward's answer when I'd asked the very same question.

"Let's deal with one monster at a time."

"Don't you know?"

"Actually, I don't. The werewolves and the zombies have kept me well occupied."

"If Mandenauer was a spy in WW II he must be pretty old."

"He's also," I tried to think of a word to describe Edward, "scary."

"He's got to be eighty."

"He can still fire a gun." And he did so with great regularity. "He runs the *Jäger-Suchers*—all divisions— though his granddaughter helps. They also have a lab—"

I stopped short of mentioning the location, which was supposed to be a *J-S*-only secret. Although someone *had* blown the place to smithereens not too long ago, so it couldn't be *that* big of a secret.

The one they'd built since was supposedly impenetrable, a word that always made me nervous.

"In this lab they concoct monsters of their own?"

"No." Or at least I didn't think so. "They try to find cures to the various mutations. Elise, that's Edward's granddaughter, is a virologist. She's working on a cure for the lycanthropy virus."

"Lycanthropy is like a cold?" He tilted his head. "On steroids?"

"In a way. The curse is passed through the saliva when a victim is bitten, causing changes in the DNA."

"Aren't viruses hard, if not impossible, to cure because they're constantly changing and evolving?"

The lycanthropy virus had changed all right. Mostly because the werewolves had begun to combine their power with magic in an attempt to rule the world.

What is it with ruling the world? Every crazy person wants to.

So far the *Jäger-Suchers* had thwarted every attempt. But sooner or later . . .

"Viruses are tricky," I said. "And lycanthropy even more so. But Elise is pretty tricky herself."

"How did you end up involved with the *Jäger-Suchers*?" Murphy asked.

"There was a loup-garou in New Orleans," I said. "That's *werewolf* in French."

"I know," he said wryly. "My French is pretty good."

"Oh. Right. The loup-garou was created by a voodoo queen around the time of the Civil War."

"And the thing's still running around the city making more werewolves?" He scowled. "Remind me not to visit."

"Henri was captured; then Elise took him back to the lab. Edward sent me here to learn what I could about the curse."

Murphy frowned. "I thought you came here to learn how to raise your daughter."

"Conveniently, what I wanted to know and what they wanted to know coincided. From all I've been able to discover, we need to raise the voodoo queen who placed the curse and have her remove it."

Murphy turned the knife over in his hands again. "Why does that not surprise me?"

"Because it makes sense?"

"In an alternate universe."

"The universe isn't what you thought." I touched his arm. "Which takes some getting used to."

"How long did it take you?"

I smiled. "I'm still not."

"Well, that's a relief," he murmured, and kissed me.

His French *was* really good.

I don't know what it was about this man, but every time he touched me, my mind went blank and my body went wild. I didn't care who he was or what he'd done, as long as he did me.

Maybe I wasn't so much reacting to Murphy as this place, our isolation—we only had each other to depend on; that created a bond—and the very real possibility we wouldn't live to see the other side of the waterfall.

However, even before we were trapped here, I'd wanted him. Before I'd known anything about him beyond his talent for accents and an intense desire for money, I'd fantasized about the shape of his mouth and the taste of his skin. How could I not when he was so damn beautiful?

Now, knowing what I did about his past, having trusted him with my life and him trusting me with his, having shared more with him than I'd shared with anyone for a long time, I'd become attached. Despite the deceptions—both his and my own—I wanted to share an embrace, perhaps more. If we could only get rid of the guards outside the door.

I tore my mouth from Murphy's. He yanked me right back, began to press his lips to my jaw, then my neck, murmuring my name.

"Murphy. I've got an idea."

"Me, too. It kind of goes like this." His palm covered my breast and his thumb caressed my nipple. My body, needy, treacherous as always, responded, the nipple hardening, my head falling back to give him better access to everything.

My gaze went to the door, where the guards were indeed watching. "We aren't alone," I whispered.

He lifted his head, but I tugged it back, shoving his nose into my cleavage. "Mmmph," he said.

"Pretend you're busy."

"I don't have to pretend." His teeth scraped the swell of one breast; his fingers traced beneath my shirt and across my rib cage.

"Listen to me." I nuzzled his hair, put my lips next to his ear, and licked the lobe, tangling the tip of my tongue in his earring, making him shudder. "I have an idea of how we can get out of here."

"Later," he murmured.

I groaned, and he took the sound as encouragement,

dragging me into his lap. The diamond scraped my stomach; something else poked my backside.

"Get a grip, Murphy." I shoved my hands into his hair and gave a sharp tug.

His head lifted, and I pressed our mouths together before he could say anything damning. I meant to give him a quick peck, but when his tongue slipped between my lips, I lost track of my thoughts.

Several moments passed before I found them again and pulled back just enough to whisper, "I've got some of the sleeping powder left."

His brow creased. "You want to put me to sleep?"

"The guards."

I waited for the blood to flow out of his cock and back into his head. His frown deepened the instant he understood. "How are you going to convince them to take it?"

"I haven't gotten that far."

"Once we make it past them there are still a few more zombies, not to mention Mezareau. Will the powder work on zombies?"

"It's all we've got."

"We could do with a lot more powder," Murphy murmured.

"Wait." I stroked his shoulder, rubbed my breasts against his chest.

"You keep that up, waiting isn't going to be an option."

I ignored him. "There's a way to multiply an effect to every like being."

"Lost me again." He nibbled at my collarbone. From the brush of his erection against my hip, he didn't appear to have lost anything at all.

I grasped his wrist before it could creep up my shirt. There was throwing off the guards and there was just copping a feel.

"Let's say a woman came to me for a love charm, but she wanted all the men to love her. By combining this spell with a single love charm on a single man—"

"All men would adore her," Murphy finished. "Sounds like a handy spell to know."

24

"What do you have to do?" Murphy whispered.

"I repeat an incantation while the charm, powder, whatever, is being administered."

"Then poof, it works on everyone."

"Theoretically."

I'd learned the spell while in training, but I'd never actually used it. According to my teacher, only a practitioner of incredible power could make the magic work.

"If that's true," Murphy said, "then we'll fall asleep."

"We're not zombies."

"Oh, right." He shifted, uncomfortable on the hard ground. "What if it puts only the male zombies to sleep?"

"We'll just have to hope it works on all zombies."

"Which would leave the *bokor* wide awake."

At least Murphy had remembered not to say the man's name. He was catching on to how things operated around here.

"He doesn't seem to come to the village much—especially at night. Stays in his hut, lord of the manor."

"So maybe he won't know we've escaped until breakfast."

"By then we should be long gone," I agreed.

"If we can get past the waterfall."

"One problem at a time." I rubbed my forehead against his. "How are we going to get the powder in a guard's mouth?"

"You mean how am *I* going to do it?"

"You could say the incantation instead."

He lifted his head just enough so I could see the glitter of his eyes by candlelight. "I'll pass."

"I thought you might. So how will you do it?"

"Jump on his back and shove some right in."

"Then he smacks you across the island and you land on your head."

"I think I can avoid getting my ass kicked by a single zombie long enough for you to say a few words. Unless we're talking a sonnet."

"A couple of lines. We'll need to separate the two of them."

"I have to take a leak."

"Now?" My voice rose in exasperation. He lifted a brow. "Oh. I get it. But how will I know when to start?"

"Count to one hundred, then begin."

The plan was so simple; it had to work.

Or fail abysmally.

"Ready?" Murphy stood, and swept the bag of

sleeping powder into his hand. He didn't wait for me to answer, just headed for the door.

"Buddy." He tapped the smaller of the two guards on the shoulder. "Gotta drain the snake."

The man obviously knew what he meant, or maybe he just got the idea from Murphy's lewd hand gesture. Murphy glanced back and mouthed, *One, two*.

I began to count silently to myself as I packed. Turning away from the guard, who wasn't watching anyway, I tugged the diamond from my pants and tossed it inside, too, then set the bag by the door.

By the time I reached ninety-eight, cold sweat dribbled down my back. If this didn't work, Murphy and I were stuck here, and I doubted Edward was going to be able to get us out before I ended up Mezareau's zombie-making partner and Murphy became a zombie.

"One hundred," I murmured. "Hear me, Simbi, master magician."

Simbi, the overseer of white magic, was invoked in the making of charms. He was the patron *loa* of all freshwater, his symbol the green snake. Simbi and I got along great.

The guard turned when I spoke. I wished I could have said the words silently, but a spell like this must be spoken aloud.

"Grant me the power!"

A tingling began in my hands, spreading across my skin. Both hot and cold, kind of electric, a surge of strength and energy. My hair stirred in a nonexistent breeze, and the hut seemed to glow with more light than there should be from one tiny candle and a just past full moon.

Thunder rumbled. Simbi's voice. He had heard me, and he'd answered.

The guard had started walking in my direction, but now he began to back up. He sensed it, too. The night belonged to me now, and there was nothing he could do about it. I stepped toward him, and he ran.

Outside thunder still rumbled; the air smelled like sulfur, but the sky was as clear as a pure blue lake. Not a hint of rain.

"Lend strength to my magic," I continued, as I followed the guard. "Send it to all of a kind."

He crashed face-first into the ground like a tree felled by lightning. I skirted his unmoving body. "That had to hurt."

Murphy was on the ground, too, and for a second I feared he was asleep—like the guard snoring nearby—if not dead, which, come to think of it, was also like the guard snoring nearby. But Murphy lifted his head, struggling to get up, and I hurried to help him.

The strange crackling energy I'd experienced in the hut had disappeared the instant I'd finished the incantation. I'd called on Simbi before in the making of charms. The most that had ever happened was a little bit of thunder.

Though the ease with which I'd performed this difficult spell and the surge of power that had come with it made me nervous, I was also intrigued. What more could I do?

I reached Murphy, and my gaze searched his face for bruises. At least there weren't any new ones. Though his black eye looked painful, at least he could see out of it now. The one I'd received from the crazy zombie man had faded fairly quickly.

"You OK?" I asked.

"Yeah." He shook his head, and his beads clacked. "He fell like a ton of bricks, and I flew."

"He didn't hit you?"

"He wanted to, but he didn't have the time before he went nighty-night. Since you're here, sans guard, I'll assume the spell worked."

I put my arm up and pantomimed falling, then hitting, hard.

"You're something else, Cassandra." He stared into my eyes, seemed about to say more, then just grabbed my hand. "Let's make some time."

My stomach did a flip. "My bag. I left it at the hut."

"You need it?"

"My papers—," I began.

"One second. Stay here."

"I can—"

"Believe me, I can better."

Since I knew he was right, I quit arguing. The trip took him more than a second and it seemed like an hour. Waiting alone in the shadowy jungle, I started to hear all sorts of weird things.

Rustles, grumbles, growls—maybe the last was my

stomach. At any rate, when Murphy burst through the trees, I let out a startled shriek, and he winced. "Shh! You want to wake the dead?"

"Are they all asleep?"

"I didn't see anyone milling about like they usually do all night long."

"Shouldn't we check?"

"Does it matter?" He tugged me away from the village in the direction of the cave. "We're still out of here as fast as our happy feet can carry us."

I kept waiting for a hue and cry, but none came. I still had the feeling we were being followed. From the way Murphy kept glancing over his shoulder, he thought so, too.

"Almost there," he murmured.

Then all hell broke loose.

Shadows flew out of the night, screeching so loudly I could do nothing but cover my ears. At first I thought the zombies had found us and they were pissed, but the shades that separated from the trees had the forms of animals, not people.

A cat, a dog, a pig, then a few birds swooped low, brushing the tops of our heads, before flying away. If Mezareau controlled the beasts, that could be a problem, even though, according to everyone, there weren't any large, vicious animals on the island.

Of course such rules didn't hold since I'd met Edward. Usually where there wasn't supposed to be something was exactly where it was found.

The greenery rustled and I tensed, expecting that

large, furry, vicious creature to burst forth. Instead a misshapen dwarf and a twisted troll joined the others, and I understood what they were.

"He's sent the *baka*."

Murphy eyed the troll with distaste. "Don't sound so happy about it."

"They aren't real."

"Look mighty real to me."

"The *baka* are evil spirits that roam the night; they can steal your life if you let them, maybe drive you insane."

"So even if they aren't real, they're still pretty dangerous."

"At least we didn't drop dead at the mere sight of them." I glanced at him and shrugged. "It could happen."

"How do we get rid of them?"

"They grow stronger on fear."

"Terrific," Murphy muttered.

The circle of demons stepped closer. Their eyes began to glow. "Stare them straight in the eye," I said, "and they'll disappear."

"Sure they will," Murphy said. "That always works."

"Do it," I said between gritted teeth.

Though the glowing eyes were hard to meet, I focused on the troll creeping up on me from the right. I thought of Sarah and what would happen if I didn't get out of here. Any fear of the thing Mezareau had sent evaporated; the demon went *poof*.

The others advanced. One of the damn birds smacked into my head. Murphy was right. The thing felt pretty real.

I glanced up, furious, not frightened, and *poof*, poof, poof—the birds were gone. When I lowered my gaze, Murphy and I were alone again.

"That was . . . weird." Murphy's eyes were bright; he could hardly stand still. Jazzed. I could understand the feeling. Thwarting evil spirits really got the juices going.

He kissed me, and I could swear his lips sizzled, like we'd both been struck by lighting. As he lifted his head, his forehead creased. "I thought your eyes were blue."

"They are."

"Huh. In this light they look aqua."

I rolled my aqua eyes. "No time for that now. Let's get out of here before he sends the *diab*."

"I know I'm going to be sorry I asked," Murphy hurried along at my side, "but what's the *diab*?"

"Wild spirits. They resemble gargoyles, except for the protruding red tongues. The only way to get rid of them is with a knife."

"Which we conveniently have, and you seem pretty good with the thing."

"I am. Except I'd have to use the knife on us."

Murphy stumbled, then righted himself. "Us?"

"The only way to get rid of the *diab* is to carve a *gad* in the upper arm."

"What the hell is a *gad*?"

"A guard. The symbols, or tattoo, invoke the *loas* to keep us safe." I frowned. "Though I'm not sure if it will work without the sacrifice of a rooster."

"Let's not find out."

"That would be my vote."

We continued on for what seemed like a very long time.

"We weren't walking this long when we went *to* the village," Murphy grumbled.

"We have to be getting close to the cave."

"Unless it disappeared, too."

"The *bokor* said the waterfall would be right where I wished it to be."

"He said a lot of things, Cassandra. I doubt any of them were true."

My lips tightened. I had to believe that what Mezareau had told me about raising the dead was real. If it wasn't, I wasn't sure what I'd do.

Murphy put his arm around my shoulders. How had he known I'd needed a little comfort? Maybe he'd just needed some, too.

I slipped my arm around his waist and we continued to walk hip to hip.

"You still expecting gargoyles to show up?"

"Don't worry; I'll protect you."

Our gazes met. "Ditto," he said, and I got all warm in places I shouldn't.

What was it about this guy that kept turning me on? His penis? A lot of guys had them. Since Karl, I hadn't been interested in a one.

If we got out of here, I'd probably never see Devon Murphy again. And that was OK. Without the constant threat to life and limb, I probably wouldn't want to.

Murphy stopped walking, and his arm slid from my shoulders. I glanced up and my hand fell back to my side.

We'd found the cave.

Murphy didn't waste a minute before tugging me into the cool, misty gloom. He no longer seemed to care about enclosed, dark spaces. Amazing what a sorcerer with a little zombie army can cure.

When we'd traveled in the opposite direction, we hadn't been able to see two inches in front of our faces, and that had been in the daytime. In the middle of the night, the silvery glow of the almost full moon didn't penetrate the cave for more than a few yards.

Murphy kept one hand in mine and one on the wall. We moved at a pretty good clip. I only hoped we didn't move right into a dead end.

I strained my ears for a hint of falling water. All I detected was the rattle of pebbles.

From behind us.

I tried not to panic. The sound could be anything. Or a lot of things. None of which I wanted to know about.

Murphy didn't appear to notice, or maybe he just realized we had no choice but to move forward. Unless we wanted to face the unknown scary thing that might or might not be following us in the dark.

Suddenly he stopped, and I bumped into him, crunching my nose against his back. "Hear that?" he breathed.

I listened, half-afraid there'd be a snarl, right behind us. Instead I caught the lap of water against a shore. I could even smell it.

We rounded a corner, hustled down a long corridor, and turned the opposite way. Murphy let go of my hand and struck a match, illuminating the cavern and the pond. We were still sans waterfall. Mezareau appeared to be a big fat liar.

"We're fucked," Murphy muttered.

The flicker of the flame threw shadows across his face, highlighting his cheekbones, making him appear both older and younger than he was.

A sweet water-scented brush of a breeze swirled past. The match went out, and in the complete darkness footsteps echoed loudly in the corridor. They made me stop wondering how the breeze had swirled in from a wall.

I took off my backpack, pulled out both my knife and a ruined T-shirt. I shoved the latter into Murphy's hand. "Light this."

Stones scattered in the darkness, closer now, and I tensed. Murphy struck another match and touched it to the shirt, then dropped the flaming material between us and the gaping black maw of the cave.

"Give me the knife," Murphy whispered.

"Not yet."

"When? After he's turned us into zombies?"

"I won't let him." I was the only chance that Sarah had.

"I wish I had my rifle."

Mezareau had returned my things, but not Murphy's.

"Me, too," I said. "But since we don't . . ." I moved nearer to the opening.

A growl drifted down the corridor, followed by the distinct shuffle of a shoe against dirt.

I glanced at Murphy, who appeared as puzzled as I was. The growl was inhuman; shoes, not so much.

My gaze returned to the black hole. Eyes shone, coming closer and closer, bobbing much lower than they should have been if Mezareau were walking upright.

I tightened my grip on the knife as the outline wavered in the light of the flames. Man? Beast? I had no idea.

A snarl erupted, so loud it seemed to ricochet off the walls. I forced myself to meet the disembodied eyes.

Help, I thought; what I said was, "I am not afraid."

If Mezareau was sending bigger and better *baka,* the creature should have disappeared. Instead it shot forward, and I threw the knife.

The weapon struck with a thunk. An unearthly shriek erupted, and Jacques Mezareau fell out of the darkness, my silver knife embedded in his heart.

25

As soon as Mezareau hit the ground, the thunder of falling water filled the cavern. I could do nothing but stare dumbly at the waterfall that had appeared in place of the rock face. Mezareau must have used some sort of shielding spell, which disappeared when he became unconscious—or worse.

"Nice shot," Murphy muttered, and strode to the body.

Going down on one knee, he checked Mezareau's pulse, then yanked my knife out of his chest. After wiping the weapon on Mezareau's shirt, Murphy returned, snatching my backpack as he passed. "Come on."

"Is he—?"

"Yep." He tossed my knife in the bag, adjusted the pack on my shoulders, and shoved me into the pond.

The cool water revived me enough to mount a resistance when he tried to pull me through the waterfall. "Wait."

"No." Murphy lifted me into his arms and dragged me along.

The waterfall clouded my vision, soaking me, soaking us, driving both Murphy and me beneath the water. I couldn't breathe—for an instant I thought I'd drown; then we broke the surface on the other side.

The slightly lopsided moon shone brightly as Murphy helped me out of the water. Together we collapsed onto the bank.

"Do you think the zombies will come after us?" Murphy turned his head; so did I. Our noses brushed.

"No," I said.

"Why not?"

"If he could have sent them, he wouldn't have sent the *baka*. I think the zombies are still asleep."

"What happens when they wake up?"

"Hard to say. With their master dead, they might be a little confused."

"Why did you do it?" Murphy asked quietly.

We were still nose to nose, our breath mingling as the moon cast silvery shadows over both us and the night.

I decided not to mention what I'd seen—the odd height of the eyes, the indistinct shape that had not seemed entirely human. Murphy might not think I was crazy anymore, but that didn't mean he couldn't think so again.

I sat up. "He'd have killed you."

Murphy sat up, too. He lifted his hand, and the diamond appeared between his thumb and forefinger, for all the world as if he'd plucked it from thin air. "You're probably right."

"How did you—?" Last I'd looked the damned diamond had been in my backpack. Of course so had he.

I opened my mouth to admonish him for stealing, for risking our lives, then snapped it shut again. Mezareau had been a killer. He'd murdered all his zombie minions and would no doubt have murdered many more to fashion an army to take over Haiti. Once he had control of the country, the world was next. It always was.

He'd have killed Murphy eventually. The diamond had nothing to do with it.

Murphy brushed his fingers against my hair where it grew white at the temple. "You OK?"

He was a liar, a cheat, a thief, yet my stomach did a weird little dance at his touch. If I wasn't careful, I'd fall for him, and I couldn't allow that to happen. It was time to leave both Haiti and Murphy behind.

Our Jeep was right where we'd left it, just as Murphy had predicted it would be. The sun shone bright and hot as he drove me straight to the airport.

I counted backward. Had I gotten off the plane only two weeks before?

Murphy came around the front of the car, opened my door, held out his hand. "I'll walk you in."

We hadn't taken two steps inside the terminal when three young, buff Haitians dressed in the spiffy uniform of the local police appeared and zeroed in on Murphy.

"Uh-oh," I murmured.

Murphy didn't even get a chance to turn around

before they grabbed him. "You are under arrest for trespassing."

"Trespassing?" I followed as they dragged Murphy toward the door. "Where?"

"Many places."

"I was there, too."

Murphy gave an annoyed sigh. "Cassandra, shut up."

"Well, I was."

"Your fine has been paid, Priestess."

Priestess? How did they know that?

"Who paid it?" I demanded.

"You have friends in high places."

Edward. Figures. Though I wasn't sure how he could have found out about the charges already, still I wasn't surprised that he had.

"I'll pay Murphy's fine," I offered.

"There are other issues."

"There always are," Murphy muttered.

"Wait!" I cried, and they actually stopped dragging him and waited.

"Go home," Murphy said. "I'll meet you there."

"In New Orleans?"

His brow quirked. "Isn't that where you live?"

"I guess."

I was impatient to return to California, but if I didn't return to New Orleans and see to the raising of that voodoo queen, Edward would only follow me west and take me back.

I'd rather test the raising ceremony on someone other than Sarah anyway.

"I'll clear this up and follow you," Murphy continued. "Maybe tonight."

One of the cops snorted.

"Or tomorrow."

"But—"

Leaning forward, Murphy kissed me before either the police or I knew what he was up to. "You didn't think I'd just let you walk out of my life now, did you?"

Actually, I'd thought exactly that.

The cops lifted him from his feet and carted him away.

"See you in the Big Easy," Murphy called as they shoved him through the door.

"I don't know why everyone insists on calling it that," I muttered. "The place may be big, but it certainly ain't easy."

I'd arrived after the last hurricane, which had almost been the last for New Orleans. While California awaits the big one to knock it into the ocean, New Orleans has been waiting for the big one to submerge it in the waters of . . . Take your pick—river, lake, swamp—the place was surrounded.

Katrina had been that big one—a category five—the one all the doomsday predictors had said was coming.

Then it came. New Orleans was devastated. Water, water, water everywhere and not a drop to drink. I used to like that poem.

Lucky for me, I'd still been in voodoo training and hadn't made it to the French Quarter yet. Lucky for everyone, the French Quarter was a bit higher than the city proper, because it fared better against the floods, not so well against the crazies and the looters.

However, with the typical savoir faire of New Orleanians, they picked themselves up, dried themselves off, and were open for business within months. There was even a bar on Bourbon Street that never did close—just served warm beer right through the hurricane. You gotta love that. Cities like New Orleans did not go away.

Because of Katrina I was able to buy my shop rock-bottom cheap. The place was rumored to have belonged once to Marie Laveau—the infamous voodoo queen of New Orleans.

Marie had actually been two women, a mother and a daughter, who had greatly resembled each other. When the first died the second took her place, which led to the rumors that Marie had great power. When you appear to live two lifetimes, that'll happen.

Whether Marie—the first, the second, or both—had been powerful was irrelevant. The locals thought she was, and they believed my place had been hers. Both viewpoints had been very helpful in the success of my voodoo shop.

After the purchase, I'd spent several months fixing the store and the attached living quarters. Just because the building hadn't flooded didn't mean it wasn't a mess.

I was amazed to discover that I missed it, along with Lazarus and Diana, my two best friends in the world.

"Miss Cassandra." Marcel materialized from somewhere, and I didn't even think that was strange. "I am to take you to your plane."

I'd been staring at the door through which Murphy had disappeared, and I forced myself to look away. Murphy was gone, and despite his words, his kiss, I didn't think I'd see him again. "I don't have a ticket."

"Monsieur Mandenauer has taken care of everything." Marcel beckoned, and I followed.

"How did he know I was coming back today?"

"He was not certain you would come back at all. So he had me wait for you here."

"Since I left? Don't you have a job?"

Marcel paused at security and spoke in soft, rapid-fire Creole to the guards. I lifted my backpack from my shoulders in preparation for a search, but they waved us through without comment.

"My true job is to serve the monsieur. He saved my life many moons ago, and this I will never forget." Marcel pushed open a door that led onto the tarmac where a small plane idled.

"How did he save your life?" I asked. "Where?"

"That is a tale of another time, for another day. Monsieur asked me to ascertain that you and anything you have with you was put on this plane without question of the authorities." Marcel pressed a boarding pass into my hand. "And now I have done so. Priestess, may the *loas* bless you all of your days."

"And you." I walked up the metal staircase that led to the plane.

Edward was no dummy. He'd considered I might be bringing back more than myself from the mountains. Most voodoo spells, both white magic and black, were augmented with roots, herbs, even the bones of the dead. Things that would not be allowed through commercial security. Not to mention my solid silver knife.

But all that I needed for the raising of the dead was water, fresh blood, and the incantation. Which didn't seem enough, but then the simplest of rituals were often the most powerful.

26

When I got off the plane at Louis Armstrong International Airport, my friend and fellow *Jäger-Sucher* Diana Malone Ruelle was waiting. Without so much as a howdy-do, she hustled me past customs. No one even glanced our way. Working for Edward was great.

"What did you find out?"

Diana had never been much for small talk, which was one of the things I'd liked about her from the day she'd stepped into my voodoo shop.

"Nice to see you, too," I quipped as I followed her to her car.

"Sorry." She put a hand on my arm and when I stopped, she hugged me. "Welcome back."

"Thanks."

I would have liked to say it was good to be back, but I wasn't all that thrilled. I didn't want to examine too closely why, but it had something to do with Murphy.

I guess after two weeks in his company I'd gotten used to having him around.

I'd just have to get un-used to it.

Diana straightened, a long trip since she was nearly six feet tall, even in low-heeled shoes. She had the lovely pale skin of a true redhead, and her curly hair tumbled past her shoulders, ending just above her waist. She was curvy, sexy, and just funny enough that I didn't have to hate her. She was also the second-best friend I'd ever had.

"How's Lazarus?" I asked.

Diana clicked her key chain and the locks on her SUV thunked open. "How would I know? It's not as if I visited your python and took him for a slither."

My lips twitched. Despite her being a cryptozoologist— with a degree in zoology—Diana did not care for snakes. She and Lazarus had never gotten on, hissing at each other whenever they were in the same room. Lazarus might have been jealous. I'm not sure what Diana's problem was, beyond her uncharacteristically girlie aversion to snakes.

"Adam and Luc?" I asked, referring to her new husband and his son, who was now hers.

"They're both hunky-dory, Cassandra." She started the car with an annoyed flick of her wrist. "Now spill the beans."

I didn't blame her for being impatient. The curse of the crescent moon would ruin Diana's new life if I wasn't able to stop it.

Her husband was one of a long line of cursed men, starting with his several-times-great-grandfather Henri. Not a demon yet, Adam would be eventually, as well as his adorable eight-year-old son, Luc. No one wanted to see him turn furry one night.

"Cassandra, please," Diana murmured. "Do you know how to end the curse?"

"I know how to raise the voodoo queen," I said. "Whether she can end the curse . . ." I spread my hands.

We just didn't know.

Diana parked in front of my combination voodoo shop, living quarters, and voodoo temple on Royal Street. The late-afternoon sun blared hot, despite the calendar insisting we'd reached autumn. In New Orleans, autumn could still be scalding.

"Did you find out where the voodoo queen is buried?" I asked.

"That was fascinating."

Although Edward had hired Adam to be a hunter—he'd been killing the things his *grandpère* had made for years—Diana was a *Jäger-Sucher* more in the searching sense, like me.

"There's a slave cemetery not far from the Ruelle Mansion," she continued. "I found her there."

"Couldn't have been easy."

Most slaves had been buried without benefit of a marker, or if there was one it had been made of wood, which didn't last.

"Easier than a lot of other things lately. Have you ever homeschooled an eight-year-old?"

We were walking down the path that led away from Royal Street toward my shop, set back from all the others. My face turned away from her, thankfully she couldn't see my expression. I hadn't told Diana about Sarah. I hadn't told anyone.

Except Murphy—and why was that?

"Can't say as I have." I set my backpack next to the door and dug out my key.

Sarah had just started first grade when she died, and she'd gone to private school. Homeschooling gave me the willies.

"The kid's too bright for his own good," Diana muttered.

"Aren't they all?" I opened the door.

Cool air brushed my face. I'd hired a local to run the shop while I was away, as well as take care of Lazarus. But it was past closing time, so Diana and I had the place to ourselves.

I led the way through the shop to the kitchen. Everything seemed in order. I'd check more thoroughly later.

"Can you pour us a drink?" I asked, not waiting for her answer as I went to greet Lazarus.

His head was up; he took one look at me and hissed.

"I was only gone a few weeks."

"What's the matter?" Diana stepped through the multicolored beads that hung from ceiling to floor in the doorway between the shop and my apartment. They clattered far too loudly in the silence that followed.

"He hissed at me."

"Probably saw me and got confused."

I cast her an exasperated glance. Diana and I were as unalike physically as two women could be. Nevertheless, I switched on the light and moved closer to the cage.

Lazarus struck, smashing his head into the chicken wire. Shocked, I fell back. He continued to strike so violently I was afraid he'd injure himself.

"What's wrong with him?" Diana asked.

"I don't know." I went to the phone and dialed the number of the kid I'd hired.

He answered on the second ring. "Yo."

"Ben, it's Cassandra."

"You back? Excellent. I can party tonight, you don't need me to open tomorrow."

"No. Fine. Whatever. I was wondering about Lazarus."

"He's OK. For a snake."

"Was he behaving strangely? Hissing, angry, striking at the cage?"

"My boy? Naw. He was excellent."

"Thanks." I hung up and dialed the first veterinarian in the phone book. Unfortunately, he wasn't up on the latest snake psychosis and couldn't help me.

"Your best bet would be to check with a zoologist who specializes in reptiles," he advised.

My gaze met Diana's. She tilted her head, frowning as I hung up. "What did he say?"

"That I should check with a zoologist."

Her eyebrows shot up, and she stared at the cage. Lazarus had slithered into a box in the corner and was now hiding his head. Better than the aggressive behavior but still worrisome.

"What do you think?" I asked.

"You're barking up the wrong zoologist."

"Ha-ha," I said.

Diana's specialty was wolves, which had come in handy recently.

"I don't know anything about reptiles. Except that I don't like them."

"Shh," I murmured.

Lazarus seemed to have a sixth sense for those who were afraid of snakes, and he took great pleasure in tormenting them. Which probably explained his animosity for Diana better than any jealousy over my affections.

"He seems better now," she said. "Maybe he was just expressing his displeasure at your leaving him behind."

"Maybe," I agreed, though I didn't think so. I'd been around Lazarus enough to recognize hate when I saw it. The only thing he'd ever disliked more than Diana had been my neighbor's cat.

"Let's have that drink while you tell me all you know." Diana preceded me to the kitchen table, where she poured us both a glass of thick, ruby red Cabernet.

I stared into the liquid and thought of the blood dripping from the bowl and into the ground, then the bodies shooting up out of the dirt, then—

Nothing.

Frowning, I took a sip. Diana took one, too, watching me over the rim of her glass. I must have looked pretty tired, probably because I was. Hoping to get this over with quickly, I launched into the tale of my trip to Haiti.

She didn't so much as blink when I spoke of the waterfall, the zombies, Mezareau. She'd seen worse.

"The spell sounds too easy," she murmured.

I'd thought the same thing, but what could I do? The spell was what it was.

"It isn't easy if you don't know what it is," I pointed out. "You can't just make this shit up."

Diana leaned forward. "Can we try it tonight?"

I guess I hadn't told her *every* detail. "Have to wait for the full moon."

Her face fell. "You'd think in order to break the crescent moon curse, you'd need a crescent moon."

Which wasn't tonight, either, but why point that out?

"Full moons have great power. Every witch knows that."

"I'm not a witch and neither are you."

"Some would beg to differ on that." Karl had called me far worse than a witch, but then the last time we'd met, I hadn't been calling him darling, either.

Diana smiled as if I'd been kidding. "I guess we've waited this long, we can wait a while longer."

I only hoped that when I raised the voodoo queen she'd be amenable to removing the curse, or at least telling me how. If not, I didn't know what we would do.

I finished my wine in a single gulp. Diana's was already gone.

"Another?" I asked.

"I'd better get back. The new babysitter is great, but I don't want to push it."

As the last sitter had wound up werewolf lunch, I completely understood her point.

At the door she paused. "Have you talked to Edward?"

"Not since I arrived in Haiti. Is he in New Orleans?"

"No. But you'd better get in touch before he shows up. You know how he hates to waste a trip. He'll want to be here when you raise the dead, but not a minute before. Places to go, monsters to kill, you know."

I knew.

"Make sure you tell him what happened to Mezareau. He might want to send someone to check on the zombies."

"Except the village isn't exactly easy to find."

"With the sorcerer dead, it might be a lot easier."

True. The waterfall was at least water and not a wall.

"You remember when we asked the moon goddess, Erzulie, for help, and you sent me to voodoo heaven?" Diana asked.

"Not you, just your mind."

"Yet I brought back a very real piece of the goddess's garden."

That had been kind of hard to explain. It had been my finest hour in the realm of magic.

"You'll be able to do this, too," Diana said. "You'll see."

She was trying to pump me up, give me some confidence. It was working.

Diana continued to hover half in and half out of the shop. "There's something different about you."

Probably the sex. Another thing I hadn't told her about, and I wasn't sure why.

"Can't put my finger on it," she murmured, and left.

I closed and locked the door, then wandered through the shop, touching things as I went. This was the first place I'd ever had that was truly mine.

As I passed the chicken wire cage, Lazarus hissed again. In the sudden silence that had followed Diana's departure, the sound was harsh, almost evil.

If he didn't stop that, I was going to hunt down a vet who knew his snakes, even if I had to search the entire state of Louisiana, then take Lazarus in for a checkup.

I poured another glass of wine, grabbed my backpack, and carried both into the living area on the far side of the kitchen, where I had a bedroom, bath, and sitting room. The kitchen and the office next to it were common areas that separated where I lived from where I worked.

I hadn't done much decorating, saving my time and money for the shop and the voodoo temple. I had a bed with a plain blue bedspread and white sheets, a couch, also blue, a chair in brown, and a TV, but no VCR or DVD player. I did not have the time or the inclination to rent movies.

Before I forgot, as if I could, I placed a call to Edward. His voice mail answered, so I left a message. "I'm in New Orleans, sir. The *bokor* is dead, but I'm not sure about the zombies. Maybe someone could check and get back to me. I'll be able to perform the raising ceremony on the night of the full moon." I hesitated, then ended with a bright and cheery, "See you then!"

Edward would love that. Or maybe not. His funny bone wasn't very well developed. Considering his life, that was understandable.

I planned to take a bath, sip my wine, go to bed. But before I did, I made the mistake of unpacking.

Crumpled, damp clothes. My knife. Empty plastic bags. Everything kind of smelled, and I decided to cut my losses and toss it all, except for the knife.

I reached into the bottom of the pack to make sure I wasn't throwing out anything important, and my fingers brushed cool, slick stone.

I thought of my last sight of Murphy being dragged out of the airport—probably to be handcuffed, booked, and searched, everything on his person confiscated, while I was led directly to the plane and ferried out of the country.

You didn't think I'd just let you walk out of my life now, did you?

Of course not.

I picked up my glass and downed every last drop of bloodred wine.

I had his diamond.

27

I wondered when Murphy would show up. It wouldn't be long.

I wondered why I was so angry, so hurt, such an idiot.

Had I secretly been hoping he'd come here for me? Murphy was a thief and a liar. He cared about no one but himself. However, he'd been very good at making me believe he'd cared about me.

My eyes burned, and that just pissed me off. I'd cried an ocean over Karl. I wouldn't shed a drop for another man just like him.

I would not let Murphy ruin my homecoming, so I poured another glass of wine and got in the tub. But I couldn't relax. I wanted to kick something.

Make that someone.

Had he been romancing me from the beginning in order to get the diamond out of the country? I seemed to remember a movie with a similar plotline. I'm sure it had ended happily. I didn't see how this could.

When I got out of the tub I wavered a bit. The heat, the long plane ride, and three glasses of wine on an empty stomach had made me light-headed. Oh well, I didn't have anything better to do than pass out.

So I tumbled into bed, naked, and fell asleep almost immediately. But in the way of wine-induced slumber, I didn't sleep well.

Hot, sweaty, too big for my own skin, I threw off the covers, leaving myself naked to the night. I was thirsty, oh, so thirsty, but there was no water nearby. In truth, I didn't think water would satisfy the craving. I needed something stronger, thicker, redder even than wine.

I drifted deeper, drawn into dreamland by the whisper of falling water. I was in the cave, in the pond, all alone.

Or was I? I heard a low, rumbling growl from the darkness, but instead of being afraid I was intrigued, and strangely aroused.

The cool water lapped at my breasts, caressing them, making them harden with desire. I walked toward the rocks, toward the eyes that materialized from the night.

I watched, fascinated, as the shape wavered in and out, just as it had when this had been reality and not a dream, never becoming solid enough for my mind to give a name to the shadow.

The snarl echoed off the cave walls, yet still I moved forward, climbing from the pond, walking across the dirt floor as the water streamed down my body. My skin no longer on fire, goose bumps made me tingle.

The sound of my own harsh breathing kept time

with the thud of my heart. "Show yourself," I whispered, and the beast stepped into the light.

Expecting a wolf, at first my mind didn't register what my eyes clearly saw.

A glistening coat, rippling muscles, black spots on an amber background, the teeth and the eyes of a leopard.

The beast stalked forward, growling, the sound, now that it no longer echoed, distinctly that of a big cat. Nevertheless, I wasn't afraid. This was, after all, just a dream.

The cat leaped, hitting me in the chest, driving me to the ground, which in the way of dreams had shifted to soft, sweet grass instead of the hard, rough earth.

There was no pain, only curiosity. Why a leopard and not a wolf?

The answer was simple. The leopard society. The skin on the wall of Mezareau's hut. Those memories in my subconscious had led me to this dream.

The beast sniffed my neck, nuzzled my breast. I closed my eyes and wished myself awake.

Instead a long, lazy cat tongue swirled around my nipple. My eyes shot open, but the cave had gone completely dark. At least I wouldn't have to watch.

The tongue continued, both soft and sharp, teasing my nipples to aching peaks before moving down my body, laving my skin, teeth scraping just below my belly button, over my hip, then down the insides of my thighs. Pleasure, pain, the allure of the forbidden, I could barely breathe past the fear and the excitement.

This had to be a dream. No leopard would lick my neck; such a beast would rip it open.

Neither would a leopard taste gently between my legs, tormenting me to a screaming core of need. Such a thing would drink of my blood and nothing else.

I was trapped by unwelcome desire, caged by a dream that seemed far too real. The animal that lived in the darkness crept closer, and its erection slid along my inner thigh.

I tensed and slammed my legs shut. There was only so far I was willing to go, even in a dream.

The weight lifted and for an instant I thought it was over; then someone kissed me, open mouth, a lot of tongue. Human lips that tasted of me.

Confused, uncertain, at first I didn't respond, but the mouth was so insistent, so skilled, and the hands that now caressed me were the same. With a mental shrug, I wrapped my arms around my dream lover's neck. Tugging him close, I opened my legs to welcome him in. But he wasn't ready, or perhaps he didn't think that I was.

He traced his long, clever fingers over my body, touched me, kissed me, let his tongue and his teeth take me to the edge; then he refused to shove me over.

The cave filled with the sounds of my desire, no words, only whispers, perhaps whimpers. I was on fire, my breasts, my mound, engorged and throbbing.

He urged me to my knees. His hands cupped my hips; his thumbs stroked my back, rubbing the base of my spine, making me arch. I rocked against him, wanting him to fill me, hard and fast, and at last he did in a single fierce thrust.

I moaned as the tip of his penis seemed to nudge my very womb. He leaned over my back, nuzzled my neck, kneaded my breasts with one hand while brushing my exposed center with the other. His long fingers increased the pressure until the orgasm hit, and then his teeth scraped my neck, pain bringing the pleasure into sharp relief.

As the last quivers of desire faded away, he shoved into me one last time, and the deep pulse of his orgasm drew mine on. He sagged against me, nuzzling my cheek, then licking my earlobe once before retreating.

I collapsed to the ground, winded, sated. Reaching out, my fingers brushed fur. Bright animal eyes glowed in the darkness, and a slow rumble swirled through the cave.

The black veil lifted, and I could see again. Next to me lolled a huge leopard, panting as if he'd exerted himself recently. I guess he had.

I glanced down, wondering if I was bleeding from his claws, shredded from his teeth, and I just didn't know it. But I was a leopard, too.

I awoke thrashing, mewling, trying to force a scream past the blockage in my throat that tasted of terror.

Dawn hovered, filling my room with an unearthly gray light. I patted my body. Thank God. Still a woman.

"Shit," I managed, and the weak, frightened sound

of my voice disturbed me. I hadn't been afraid for a very long time.

I didn't have to throw back the covers; I'd already tossed them to the floor. I stepped to the window and threw up the sash.

Fog rolled in from the river, shrouding the buildings, muting the colors. The city appeared to have drifted back in time to a previous century.

Of course the French Quarter always looked like that, if you could ignore the tourists with the hurricane glasses and the T-shirt shops and the strip joints. But at this time of the morning, when the sun was just beginning to rise, that was easy to do.

My body still tingled; my skin still felt too small. The languid aftereffects of an orgasm I wasn't sure I'd had made my knees a little shaky. I rubbed at my eyes. "What the hell *was* that?"

A dream. Nothing more. Nothing less. Though why I'd have a sex dream I had no idea. I'd had more sex over the past two weeks than I'd had in the past five years.

Maybe that was it. I'd opened the floodgates, and now I couldn't stop thinking about it. But sex with a shadowy stranger, sex with a leopard . . .

Pretty weird.

The shower called to me; I wouldn't sleep any more. Strangely, I couldn't bear the hot water and turned it to tepid instead. I let the stream tumble over me like a waterfall, washing away the remnants of the dream along with a sticky sheen of sweat.

When I was finished, I almost felt human again. Since I had to wait until the next full moon before I could raise the voodoo queen, I'd try to find peace in the day-to-day–ness of my life. And if I tensed whenever the bell rang to announce a customer, that was no more than had happened when I'd first come here and daily expected the arrival of Karl's minions. Now I'd just be waiting for Murphy.

I finished brushing my teeth, lifted my head, and froze, staring into the mirror.

When had my eyes turned green?

28

I tilted my chin to the left, to the right. Then I leaned in close, blinked, and gave a little laugh, though it was more uneasy than amused. My eyes were blue. Always had been.

I was just more spooked than I should be by the dream. The shift in color had no doubt been caused by the angle of the light in the bathroom.

The rationalization allowed me to breathe easier. I'd had a dream, nothing more. That decided, I dressed, made myself some tea, and tackled the paperwork in my office.

Two hours later I was caught up and ready to open the store. I walked into the shop, and Lazarus went nuts, hissing and striking at the chicken wire of his cage over and over. There was definitely something wrong with him.

"Trip to the vet for you," I said, and the sound of my voice seemed to infuriate the snake more. He increased the strength and speed of his strikes and only succeeded in bloodying his nose, then knocking himself out.

I reached in and snatched him while he was unconscious. I knew better than to loll around. Lazarus had a habit of waking up and scaring the crap out of people. He was a regular jokester for a snake.

Quickly lifting him from his large cage, I placed him into a portable one, then hustled to the yellow pages and started calling people. Eventually I found a snake doctor.

Half an hour later I took the Crescent City Connection toward Gretna, a historically picturesque suburb across the river from New Orleans. Settled by German emigrants, Gretna had all the amenities of a small town, yet it was within minutes of a major metropolitan area.

Katrina had flooded them, of course; you couldn't have a view of the river and not be flooded. However, they'd come back strong. I could see little evidence of the damage as I drove down the main street and parked in front of the veterinarian's office.

Lazarus was awake if the furious hissing and the rhythmic thuds against the sides of his prison were any indication. Luckily the portable cage was more of a box with a handle and I couldn't see him any more than he could see me. So what was he so mad about?

I stepped into the waiting room, and the three dogs already there began to howl, the sound earsplitting in volume. Their owners tried to shush them, but no luck. All three darted skittish glances in my direction between yowls.

"Cat?" one of the owners shouted above the din, pointing at my box.

"Python," I said.

The man frowned. "He never cared about snakes before."

The woman next to him tugged on the leash of her German shepherd, but he ignored her. "King's never even seen one."

I headed for the desk and the flinching receptionist. I hadn't taken two steps when the dogs crawled under their masters' chairs and their howls turned to whimpers.

The noise brought the vet, an older man with tufts of white hair over his ears but nowhere else, into the room. "What's wrong?"

The dog owners pointed at me. I lifted my free hand. "I didn't do anything."

"She's got a python," the first man said. "The dogs whacked out."

"Come on back," the vet ordered, and I was happy to. He pointed to an open door, and I entered, setting the cage on the exam table.

"Weird," he said, as he joined me. "I've never known dogs to be bothered so much by a snake."

"And here I thought they wouldn't like snakes at all." So few mammals did.

"I didn't say dogs liked snakes; they just don't howl and hide from them. Dogs are usually curious, which is why I end up treating them for snakebites."

"Ah, that makes more sense."

The vet smiled. He was tan in a way that suggested the

outdoors, not a tanning booth, and his eyes were cheery and dark. His hands were gentle as he opened the cage and drew Lazarus out. "What seems to be the trouble?"

"He—"

Lazarus hissed at the sound of my voice and began to thrash. The vet had obviously handled snakes before, because he held mine behind the head, and Lazarus could do nothing more than that. With a muttered curse, the vet set him back inside and slapped the top shut. The thing rattled against the table, then stilled.

"*That's* the trouble," I said. "He won't stop freaking out."

The vet frowned. "He's your pet?"

I didn't think it prudent, or productive, to explain about my *met tet*. This might be New Orleans, but I doubted the local vet would know what one was. Besides, *pet* was as good a description as any, if we weren't using *friend*—also difficult to explain.

"Yes," I replied. "My pet."

The box shook like fury.

The vet looked me up and down. "You don't seem the type for a python."

"Appearances are deceiving." Since I was exactly the type for a python. "I like snakes. Always have."

As a child I'd been fascinated—snake books, snake movies, snake stuffed animals. My mother had drawn the line at a snake pet. So had Karl. One of the best things about becoming a voodoo priestess had been the python.

"How long have you had him?"

"Three years."

Over half as long as I'd had Sarah. No wonder I was so attached.

"Do you know how old he is?"

My heart stuttered. "Pythons live forever in captivity."

"Not forever." The vet's face gentled. "More like forty or fifty years. However, I wasn't worried about his dying, just curious."

"Oh." I took a breath. Why was I so nervous?

Because Lazarus's love had been the one constant thing in my life since I'd become Priestess Cassandra. Until Diana, he'd been the only one who loved me. Now he seemed to loathe me, and if I felt as though I'd lost my best friend that was only because I had.

"I was told he was two years old when I bought him," I answered. "So around five."

"Still young. Might just be snake puberty." At my blank expression, the vet laughed. "Kidding. Though a lady python might help his disposition."

"Know any?"

"A friend of mine has a female. I could ask about breeding."

"You think that's what his trouble is?" I'd never considered lack of nooky a big python problem, but what did I know?

"Hard to say with a snake. Still, it couldn't hurt to set him up."

"I guess." I reached for the cage, and Lazarus hissed again, rattling the container so hard it nearly tipped over.

The man's eternal smile became a frown. "Maybe you should leave him here for a few tests. Parasites. Viruses. If my friend is amenable to breeding, he'll have to be kept isolated at a lower temperature for a few weeks before the big day."

"A few weeks?"

The thought of being without Lazarus that long disturbed me; however, I seemed to disturb him even more.

"OK," I agreed. As I withdrew my hand, the cage stilled.

"What's his name?"

"Lazarus."

The vet's eyebrows shot up. "Because he's going to live so long?"

I shook my head. "He likes to play dead."

The vet stared at me, as if waiting for me to laugh, but I wasn't kidding.

"He thinks it's hysterical when you reach in to check and he suddenly comes back to life."

"I'll have to remember that."

I turned away, eyes burning. "Let me know if you discover anything."

"You'll be the first."

I drove back to Royal Street, and my days returned to normal—or as normal as they get when you made your living as a voodoo priestess.

Most of the people who wandered into my shop were tourists, interested in books, sightseeing expeditions, and recreational gris-gris bags. Of course I was perfectly capable of producing gris-gris of a more potent nature.

Gris-gris were charms or talismans—small cloth bags filled with herbs and other, more secret, items. The term itself came from the French word for "gray" and referred to the black and white nature of the magic.

In New Orleans we referred to good magic as juju and bad as mojo. I had never made a mojo gris-gris, though I had been asked countless times. There was enough evil in the world; I didn't plan on making more of it.

Did I really believe that a little bag of *stuff* could hurt or help people? Yes. I'd seen it happen.

My community was growing slowly, probably because I was a skinny white girl practicing an African religion, but it *was* growing.

I was busy day and night, yet still I was lonely. Diana had called, even brought Luc to visit once. The boy had to be the cutest thing on two feet; I wanted to hug him *and* burst into tears—which just wasn't like me.

Diana had been as near the brink as I was. We were both waiting for the full moon, and there was nothing we could do to make it come any faster.

Murphy didn't show up—he didn't call; he didn't write. I was starting to wonder if he was incarcerated or dead. Those were the only two reasons I could fathom for his not arriving to steal from me the diamond he'd already stolen from Mezareau.

One good thing, my period arrived right on schedule. So my time in the land that condom forgot could be forgotten.

If only I could stop dreaming of Murphy's face I might be less twitchy. At least I hadn't had the leopard dream again. Great mind sex aside, I think a repeat just might have sent me over the edge.

And I was getting mighty edgy. Perhaps because the moon was growing larger every night and would soon be a big round November Frost Moon hanging heavy in the sky. I'd have to raise the dead, and if it worked, by the Cold Moon of December I'd have Sarah back.

You think I'd be happier about it.

Lazarus remained at the vet. The man hadn't been able to find anything wrong with him but had set up a date with the lady python. The vet wanted to supervise the session, which seemed a little pornographic to me, but whatever trips your trigger. So the cage where Lazarus usually spent his days remained empty.

Two nights before the full moon, I sat at the window in my bedroom sipping red wine. Since I had returned from Haiti, I preferred it to white.

Perhaps the weeks in the jungle had made me slightly anemic. That was the only thing I could think of to explain my sudden attachment to red meat, when I'd been more of a fish and chicken girl before.

The fog swirled in again, brushing my face with a cooling mist, reminding me of the jungle and the waterfall. But beyond the fog I heard the hum of Bourbon Street—laughter, music, glasses clinking—then a loud screech that started out sounding like an animal and ended up sounding like a woman.

I shook my head. The fog played tricks, amplifying

noises, enlarging shadows. Nevertheless, in the distance, sirens wailed.

Nothing new in the French Quarter. Something was always going on, which meant something was usually going wrong.

I turned from the window, leaving it open to the breeze and the mist. The night was warm, but not warm enough to bother with the air-conditioning.

I was safe here. Not only was the courtyard surrounding my temple walled and gated, but most people were kind of scared of me. Word had gotten around that I could raise the *loas,* and while that was helpful to some, to others it was downright creepy.

After finishing my wine, I tumbled into bed wearing nothing but my underwear and a thin tank top. The sirens followed me into my dreams.

Basin Street near St. Louis Cemetery Number One, a dicey neighborhood unfit for tourists except in the daytime. I caught the scent of perfume, so strong I fought a sneeze. The click of stiletto heels against the pavement was so loud I twitched with every footstep. The closer I got, the faster she walked, as if she knew I was behind her and she was afraid.

The woman turned right, toward St. Louis Number Two, an even rougher place to be. I tried to call out, to warn her, but for some reason I couldn't speak. Instead, I increased my pace and so did she.

A shadow materialized from the mist—definitely a woman—her breath came fast, a bit panicked. I caught the scent of terror mixed with the perfume. She kept looking over her shoulder, which only slowed her down and allowed me to narrow the gap. I wished I could speak and calm her fears, but I couldn't.

She gave in to her panic and began to run; then I was compelled to run, too, or I'd lose her. Somewhere in the night I smelled food, and my mouth watered almost painfully; my stomach cramped, growling loudly. Dreams are so damn strange.

I'd never been a fast runner, but tonight I was. I had unending stamina and pretty impressive acceleration. I understood the allure of the runner's high as it slammed into me, making my head light and my heart aflutter.

The woman stumbled on the ancient cracked sidewalk and cried out, falling. The mist thickened. I couldn't see any more than a shadow, could only hear terrified gasps, her frantic attempts to stand.

My steps echoed in the fog, but there was something off about them. At first I thought it was just the magnification that happens to sounds in the night, in the fog. Except mine were muffled, as if I were barefoot, and there seemed to be more thuds than two feet would cause. I glanced behind me, but there was nothing and no one.

As I turned back, the fog parted. The woman's eyes went wide, and her scream made me skitter. I opened my mouth to tell her everything would be all right, and a low growl rumbled out instead.

The shock of that sound should have awoken me, if the terrified screams of my prey didn't. Instead power surged, a heady mixture of strength and magic. I gave myself over to the beast, lifting my head, calling to the night.

Hunger throbbed in my belly and my blood. I wanted the woman to run again, and she did. I gave her a few seconds' head start; then I flexed my muscles and followed.

I let her think she might get away, waited for her breathing to even out, her steps to falter. Then I sprang, sailing through the air, hitting her in the center of her back, driving her to the ground beneath me.

I tore out her throat before she could scream; her blood tasted better than wine.

At last, I awoke. Tears had dried on my cheeks. I sat up, staring at my hands, rubbing at the blood I felt but could not see.

Out in the night, in the dark, in the distance, a small animal died shrieking, and I jumped, then glanced at the window.

There was a man standing in my room.

29

I had my knife in my hand before he could speak. The man could be anyone or, lately, anything.

"Jumpy, sweet thing?"

Murphy. I should have known.

"You have no idea," I muttered, and returned the knife to the sheath under my pillow. If he'd wanted to hurt me, he'd have done it a long time ago.

I knew why he'd come; I wasn't going to give him a chance to ask. I'd hand over the diamond and then he'd be out of my life. I'd no longer be waiting for him to show up—every day, every night—and that would be a good thing. Really.

Swinging my legs over the side of the bed, I was surprised when he shifted closer and put his palm to the center of my chest. "Where you off to?"

"To get—"

His mouth descended on mine, and I figured, *Why*

not have one more for the road? I knew the score. He'd come for the diamond and not for me.

Except he could have taken it and left. Sure, I'd put the thing in my safe—I wasn't stupid—however, I didn't think something as simple as a combination lock would stop the man. Maybe it hadn't.

I slid my hands down his chest; he reciprocated. My breasts seemed to swell until they fit perfectly into the palms of his hands. I became distracted by the sensations, his tongue in my mouth, his fingers on my skin, mine flitting everywhere.

I'd missed this; hell, I'd missed him.

But first things first, I wanted to check his pockets. Pretty easy to do in this situation. I frisked him as foreplay, skating my palms over his ass, then up the insides of his thighs, where I found something hard, but it wasn't a diamond.

Maybe he hadn't been able to unlock the safe. Maybe he figured once he screwed me I'd give him anything.

But I'd been screwed before, and it hadn't made me feel very giving. I do believe the last man who'd tried it was doing twenty to life.

My lips curved against Murphy's. He could try to romance the diamond out of me; I didn't have to tell him I'd gladly give him the jewel.

Until after.

He slid his thumb under the elastic band of my panties, stroking the sensitive skin where my leg became my hip. I yanked on his shirt, wanting to feel his skin, and he drew it over his head, tossing it away.

Going to his knees on the floor at my feet, he kissed my thigh, opened my legs, and leaned over, mouthing me through my white cotton underwear. I collapsed backward on the bed as he divested me of all my clothing, which didn't take long.

If I hadn't already planned to give him the diamond, his performance would have convinced me. Clever mouth, teasing tongue, nimble fingers, I was gasping, begging, clutching his shoulders in minutes.

He rose, losing his own clothes, and while he did I found a condom and tossed it his way.

"Isn't this a case of closing the barn door after the horse has escaped?" he asked.

"Time to start all over again."

"Ah." He tore the packet and sheathed himself with a practiced movement. "I'd wondered."

He didn't seem the type to wonder, or care, but then he hadn't seemed the type for a lot of things, and I'd been wrong.

Murphy rejoined me on the bed, filling me so completely, then leaving me so alone—in and out, faster and faster. He was so very good at this. Even better than the leopard in my dream.

I stiffened, and he murmured in my ear, nonsense words that aroused rather than soothed. He thought I was coming a second time, and as I felt him climax I thought, *What the hell?* and did.

He lifted his head, stared into my face. Something

in his expression made me catch my breath, a connection more disturbing than the connection of our bodies.

"Jolis yeux verts," he murmured, and kissed me.

I guess French was the appropriate language at the time. The flowing words, the sexy accent, made my eyes flutter closed so I could concentrate on the sensations: the slick slide of skin against skin, the softness of his hair beneath my fingers, the scent of rain that forever surrounded him, the taste of his mouth, the shape of his lips.

He stilled inside of me, the interlude at an end, but I didn't want him to go. I kept my arms around him, kept his body deep within and my memories close.

"Cassandra," he whispered, lifting his head again, waiting for me to open my eyes, but I couldn't. What had happened between us tonight had been both more and less than the times before, and I wasn't sure what to say, what to do.

After a second he rolled away and went to the bathroom. The light switch clicked; the toilet flushed; then the water ran.

"Turn off the light," I said, not wanting to see his face when he asked me for the diamond, then took it and walked out of my life.

Cool darkness descended, and Murphy walked back into the room. He came directly to the bed, crawled in, flipped the sheet over us both, then drew me against him. "Go to sleep," he whispered.

And though I knew it was a mistake, I relaxed in his arms and let the whole world fall away.

I awoke alone. I don't know why I was surprised. If it hadn't been for the telltale traces of sex on me and the sheets, I'd have thought I dreamed Murphy as I'd dreamed everything else.

After a quick cool shower, I dressed in shorts and a loose gauzy top, then took my cup of tea into the office. My gaze scanned the desk; nothing appeared to have been disturbed.

I twirled the tumbler on the safe, pulled it open, and stared at the empty space where the diamond should be. I'd known it was gone, yet still my stomach dropped.

A sudden pounding at the entrance made me jump and slosh tea onto my bare thigh. Grumbling, I slammed the safe shut and spun the dial, then hurried through the darkened store. Who could be pounding at this hour?

For an instant I imagined Murphy on the doorstep, and my heart lightened pathetically before sense intruded. Why would he knock now when he'd waltzed right in through the open window last night?

Come to think of it, how had he gotten over the wall? It wasn't exactly low, and barbed wire protected the top. For Murphy, that had probably been a two-minute hitch in an otherwise stellar day.

Diana flashed the morning paper up, then down as soon as I opened the door. "Did you see this?"

Without waiting for my answer, she stomped inside, heading for the kitchen. "I don't suppose you've come to your senses and started drinking coffee."

"No."

"You haven't taken pity on your dearest human friend and bought a coffeepot just for me?"

"No."

"Crap. Then I guess I'll have to drink tea."

"Don't sound so happy about it."

"I'm not."

"Someday you'll thank me."

"But it won't be today when I'm nursing a lack-of-caffeine headache."

"Which is why you should stop drinking coffee. What possible good could come from a liquid that causes withdrawal?"

"Oh—bite me," she muttered.

"Wrong side of the bed this morning?"

"Adam's still gone." She sighed. "I can't sleep when he isn't here."

The two of them were so in love it was painful—especially to a woman who'd thought she'd found love and discovered she had nothing. What would it be like to love a man so much you'd do anything?

"You're awfully cheery." Her eyes narrowed, and I turned away to make tea.

I didn't plan on telling her that Murphy had shown up and screwed my brains out in the night. She'd only scold me for letting him. I had to wonder why I had. Was I that lonely?

Duh.

"What's in the paper?" I asked.

"Animal attack."

My heart gave one hard thud, then sped up. "Wolf?"

"They never say."

"I thought Adam got rid of Henri's leavings."

"Not everything stuck around New Orleans, which is why he's gone so much."

She slumped, staring at the paper. Adam spent a lot of his time traveling, searching for the werewolves his *grandpère* had made and released into the world, shooting whatever else he found along the way that didn't belong.

"The woman died in town, not the swamp," Diana continued. "Of course that doesn't mean one of Henri's werewolves couldn't have killed her. They go wherever they like."

I'd been walking toward the table, and my hand shook so violently I sloshed tea onto the floor. Luckily Diana was preoccupied and didn't notice. I swept my foot over the blotch, smoothing it into the vinyl. Setting the tea in front of her, I took a seat on the other side of the table.

"A woman?" I asked, proud when my voice didn't shake.

"Yeah. Near St. Louis Number One. We both know that area's a breeding ground for beasties and ghoulies."

Black spots danced in front of my eyes. I blinked, several times, then took a huge gulp of tea. The pain from scalding my tongue brought me back to reality.

I couldn't have shape-shifted and killed the woman; I'd been here last night. With Murphy.

Besides, I hadn't been bitten by a wolf; I couldn't be a werewolf. Not that biting was the only way to become a lycanthrope these days.

"How do they know it was an animal?" I asked.

"Throat torn. The usual." Diana bit her lip. "I need to call Edward."

"Let's check the site first," I said quickly. "No reason for Edward to come running until we're sure."

"We aren't sure? Since when has there been an animal attack in the French Quarter that didn't involve werewolves?"

"First time for everything," I muttered, and I really hoped this was it.

"I'm up for taking a peek," Diana agreed.

We locked the shop and set off for Basin Street on foot. One nice thing about the French Quarter, you can walk everywhere.

Even before we were close enough to distinguish the yellow crime scene tape, I saw the crowd and had to force myself to keep walking. They were gathered at the exact spot I'd dreamed of last night.

We paused across the street. "We aren't going to be able to find out anything with all these people around," Diana said. "The cops will never let us past the tape."

I caught sight of a familiar blond head. "Unless we can get Sullivan to talk."

We'd had dealings with the homicide detective before. He didn't exactly like us—figured we were up to something but couldn't figure out what. Still, it wouldn't hurt to ask if he knew anything.

"Detective!" I shouted, lifting a hand when he glanced our way. From his scowl, he remembered me.

We'd gotten off on the wrong foot during the loup-garou incident. Bodies had turned up missing, and when that happened the first place to look, at least in New Orleans, was the local voodoo shop—home of zombies, gris-gris, and magic spells.

Talking to a voodoo priestess had made Sullivan—the born and bred Yankee—a tad snarky in his interrogation, which in turn had made me snarky right back. Things had gone downhill from there.

Of course the bodies had turned into werewolves and loped away, but we hadn't known that at the time. Come to think of it, Sullivan still didn't know.

The detective glanced both ways like a good Boy Scout, then crossed the street, his gait quicker and lighter than one might expect for a guy built like an offensive lineman. Sullivan had to be six five, about 250, with large hands, tree-trunk legs, and decent teeth, if he'd ever smile. If he hadn't had a penchant for wearing amusing ties with his dark suits, I'd say he had no sense of humor at all.

Today the accessory sported pumpkins so small I thought they were orange spots, until I squinted. Each one was, in fact, a jack-o'-lantern, complete with a different funny face.

I smiled, then lifted my gaze. My smile died in the chill of his glare. "Priestess," he snapped.

"Detective."

It annoyed Sullivan no end that I refused to acknowledge a last name—as if there were more than one Priestess Cassandra hanging around.

I was certain he'd checked up on me and discovered my false background, along with the stupid last name of Smith, which must have made him more suspicious than *Priestess* had.

However, he'd never be able to prove the lies were anything other than the truth. I had a new Social Security number, a new driver's license, hell, a new everything. Too bad all I wanted was my old daughter back.

"Fancy you two showing up here." He glanced between Diana and me. "What took you so long?"

"We were out for a stroll," I said.

"You just happened to be strolling near St. Louis Number One?" he asked. "Were you perhaps strolling here last night around two A.M.?"

"Sorry."

"Got an alibi?"

"Do I need one?"

"Might."

"Why?"

His lips tightened as he stared at the yellow tape. "Is this body going to disappear, too?"

Diana and I exchanged a glance.

"Why would you think that?" she asked.

He hesitated, then shrugged. "The papers already reported this as an animal attack, which I assume is why you're here."

Neither one of us answered.

"The rabies expert the department hired assured me there was one rabid wolf in the swamp and he killed it.

Although he never did explain how in hell a wolf turned up where there hasn't been a wolf for decades."

Whenever there were reports of unexplained animal attacks, Edward was notified. Then he showed up or he sent someone else, giving the standard *Jäger-Sucher* excuse of rabies run amok.

The werewolves were eliminated, and an explanation was levied for the populace. Didn't sound like Edward had done too great of a job with the details on his last trip.

"You're sure it was a wolf?" Diana asked.

"Not really. We're waiting for a zoologist from—" He stopped and stared at Diana. "You're a zoologist."

"Crypto-," she said.

"You're a wolf expert."

"So?"

"We've got some evidence. I'd like you to take a look."

He started across the street. Since Diana and I had come here to do just that, we practically stumbled over each other to follow.

"Wolf tracks resemble really big dog tracks," Diana said.

"Except we don't have tracks; we've got spoor."

"Spoor?" I asked.

"In layman's terms, they want me to stare at doggie doo-doo."

"You're familiar with wolf feces?" Sullivan asked.

"Far more than I'd like to be."

"Great." He led us past the tarp-covered body, which

I did my best to ignore, without success. Blood marred the sidewalk and a single high heel lay in the gutter. The same high heel I'd seen in my dream.

Dizziness washed over me. How could I have dreamed what happened here last night? Was I finally starting to have the visions I'd longed for when I took this job? Right now I'd like to send them back.

"There." Sullivan pointed to a pile of dung in the center of the sidewalk.

If not for the size, I'd have thought someone walked their dog and forgot a Baggie. Except I'd never seen canine feces that big. Not that I'd studied it or anything. However, Diana had.

"That isn't wolf spoor." Diana hunkered down, staring at the pile of poop. Suddenly I liked my job a whole lot more than usual.

She glanced up, first at me, her expression unfathomable, then at Sullivan. "This is from some kind of cat."

30

Sullivan frowned. "It'd have to be one helluva big kitty."

"When I say 'cat,' I don't mean domestic," Diana said.

"We've got bobcats, but not in the French Quarter."

"Looks like you do now."

"Can rabies pass between a wolf and a bobcat?"

"Rabies can pass between anything." The glance Diana shot my way was concerned, and I couldn't say I blamed her. If I hadn't been trying to keep from hyperventilating since she'd said the word *cat* I'd have been more concerned myself. "Haven't you ever heard of a raccoon infecting a dog?"

Sullivan cursed and stormed off, presumably to notify his superiors that they still had a rabies problem. If Edward hadn't had to return for the raising of the voodoo queen, he'd have to return to kill whatever it was that had killed this woman. I could only hope it wasn't me.

Diana was already striding away, a cell phone attached to her ear. With a last glance at the body, I hurried after.

"Can lycanthropy pass between one species and another?" she asked, lowering her voice.

Obviously she was talking to Edward. Who else?

She glanced at me and shook her head. Guess not.

"We've got a problem," she continued. "Seems to be a big cat. You'll be getting a phone call shortly." She listened, then snapped, "I am not going to shoot the body with silver before God and everyone, Edward. That's the quickest way to jail or a nuthouse."

She paused once more. "OK, fine. See you then." She hung up.

"What did he say?" I asked. Though a lot of it I could guess.

"Since *lycanthropy* by definition refers to a werewolf, he's never heard of it being passed between species. However, that may just be because werewolves like to bite people."

"And he wanted you to shoot the body with silver, just to be sure."

"Doesn't he always?"

Dumb question.

"If this isn't a werewolf, will silver work?"

Diana's expression became contemplative. "Interesting theory. Edward can figure it out when he gets here."

"Which will be . . . ?"

"He's going to make some calls, talk to Elise, then come on down."

"From?"

"Montana."

Which meant he'd probably arrive by tomorrow. I'd better figure out what was going on.

"You think we're dealing with a bobcat?" I asked.

"No."

I cast her a sharp look. "But you said—"

"I said it was cat poop. Sullivan said there are bobcats in the area."

"But you don't think this was one of them?"

"I'm not an expert on large felines, but that seemed like the dung of a much bigger kitty than a bobcat. Say a leopard?"

I winced.

"Something you want to tell me, Cassandra?"

"I have no idea what." My voice sounded as nonchalant as I wanted it to. God, I was good. But Diana wasn't bad. She grabbed my elbow.

"You go to Haiti to meet with an evil sorcerer. One who has the power to bring the dead back to life, who can make a waterfall appear and disappear, a man who lives in a jungle where there hasn't been a jungle for a very long time, and this man is a member of an ancient, secret group called the leopard society."

"So?"

"Did you ever see him shape-shift?"

"No." Of course that didn't mean he hadn't. Still— "Mezareau is dead."

"You're certain of that?"

"Reasonably." Murphy had been the one doing the

checking. "I stabbed him in the heart with a silver knife. That usually works."

"Did he explode?"

"No." I lifted my chin. "So he couldn't have been a shape-shifter."

"You pointed out only a few moments ago that what works for a werewolf might not work for a leopard."

Shit. Why did I have to be so damn smart?

"And even if he is dead," Diana continued, "there's something else to consider. The Egbo is a secret *society*. Definition: more than one."

My eyes widened. "You're saying there might be a pack of leopards wandering around New Orleans?"

"Wouldn't that be wereleopards?"

"Whatever, Diana." I threw up my hands. "I cannot believe we're discussing wereleopards."

"But werewolves, no problem?"

"I believed in them before you did," I pointed out. "But even Edward said he hadn't heard of other shape-shifters."

"No, he said he hadn't heard of lycanthropy being passed between species. There are more things on this earth than we know. Remember Mrs. Favreau?"

Mrs. Favreau had been a sweet little old lady we'd met while trying to find the loup-garou. Sadly, the loup-garou had found her, but not before she'd given us quite a bit of information.

"She told us that the wolf creates the werewolf. Other animals create other monsters."

Mrs. Favreau *had* said that. I hadn't been any happier to hear it then than I was now.

"Fine. So there could be wereleopards, but why would they be here?"

"Good question. Is there something in New Orleans that they might want?"

"People?"

"There are people everywhere," Diana said, "and a lot more in Haiti than Louisiana. I'd think wereleopards would want to stay where there were other leopards, so as not to stand out."

"There aren't any leopards in Haiti. Never have been. Just like there have never been any timber wolves in Louisiana, but that didn't stop the loup-garou. Right there in the swamp he was."

"That was a curse." Diana bit her lip. "But if the leopards appeared because of a curse, too, that probably had something to do with the leopard society. Which originated in Africa, where there *are* leopards."

"OK."

"And that would explain why leopards showed up in Haiti, or even here."

She'd lost me. "Why?"

"Because the Egbo is here, or at least one of them."

"Why?" I repeated.

"Could they be after you?"

"Looks like they were after her." I jerked my thumb over my back in the direction of the crime scene.

"That was just food, or maybe companionship, if she rises."

The very idea made me twitchy. "We should probably do something about that."

Diana cast me a quick, wry glance and began to walk. "What do you suggest?"

"Hell, I don't know."

"Exactly. Let Edward handle it, and let's get back to the problem at hand."

"Which is?"

"What possible reason could the Egbo have for following you? What do you have that they want?"

I couldn't think of anything I'd taken from Haiti but knowledge.

And the diamond.

31

But I didn't have it anymore. Murphy did.

Was I actually buying into this whole wereleopard thing? Not completely. However, something strange was going on, and I appeared to be right in the middle of it.

"Any ideas?" Diana asked as we reached the shop.

She deserved an answer, so I made us more tea, and then I told her what I hadn't.

"Murphy stole the diamond," she murmured.

"Twice."

"Mmm," she said. "It might have magical properties the Egbo needs."

"Or it might just be worth a freaking fortune."

"Or that." She sipped her tea and made a face before swallowing. "You dreamed of the attack as if you were the attacker."

I shuddered, remembering the thrill of the chase, the need for the blood, and the taste of it. "Yes."

"But it couldn't have been you."

"Theoretically, no. At two A.M. I was having sex with a diamond thief."

"Great sex?" She wiggled her eyebrows.

"That seems to be the only kind Murphy has." And I was going to miss it.

"So you think the dream was really a dream?"

"Since I didn't wake up covered in blood, I'm inclined to believe just that."

"You could have changed into a leopard, killed the woman, shifted back, taken a shower, and—"

"Been all cuddled up in bed when Murphy arrived."

Diana shrugged. "Stranger things have happened."

"So I hear."

"There's another explanation. You probably won't like it."

"I don't like much lately."

"You know that when a person is bitten by a werewolf, they change within twenty-four hours—day, night, doesn't matter." I nodded. "But what you probably don't know is during that time they experience a kind of collective consciousness, imagining the coming change, remembering things that have happened to others. They feel the pain, the power, both the terror and the temptation."

Uh-oh. That sounded familiar.

"You think the dream was someone else's memory, and I shared it?"

"Better than it being yours, isn't it?"

I wasn't sure. Because even if I hadn't killed that woman, I'd be killing someone soon.

"Whether it was real or not," Diana continued, "we should keep the dream to ourselves. Edward would want to—"

"Shoot me in the head."

"That *is* his usual method for dealing with problems."

"I used to like that about him."

"Me, too."

We were quiet for a moment, sipping tea and thinking.

"You need to get the diamond back," Diana said.

I snorted. "Yep. That'll happen."

"You don't think Murphy will show up again?"

"He got what he wanted; why would he?"

"Maybe he wanted more than the diamond."

"If that were true, he wouldn't have left when I was still sleeping. What kind of guy sneaks out before dawn?"

"Only a guy who feels too much would bother to sneak out too soon."

"Guys sneak out all the time so they don't have to face the morning after. It's a typical sleazy guy thing."

"I guess I wouldn't know." Diana frowned. "I've only slept with two men in my life, and I was married to both of them. Actually I wasn't married to Adam at first, but—" She shrugged. "I'm probably not qualified to give advice."

"Me, neither."

After a few minutes, the silence made me glance up. Diana stared at me with concern. "I've never pressed you, Cassandra, about your past."

"For which I'm grateful."

"But there's something that haunts you. You lost someone, too."

Diana had lost her first husband, a man she'd loved very much. His mysterious and violent death had set her on a quest that ended here, in New Orleans.

"Was it your husband?" she asked.

I shook my head. I *had* lost him, but not the way she'd lost hers. And while I'd told Murphy about Sarah, I still wasn't sure why, I didn't want to tell Diana. She wasn't a dummy; she'd figure out what I was up to with the zombie raising, and she'd probably try to stop me. If not her, then Edward certainly would.

"I really can't talk about it," I said.

Which was true. I wasn't supposed to tell anyone about my past. WITSEC would have a conniption.

"Sorry. I didn't mean to pry."

I lifted one shoulder, uncomfortable. We were friends; I should tell her.

But I wasn't going to.

Diana called the next morning and woke me out of a comatose sleep. In an effort to prevent another dream, I'd taken some of my sleeping powder. It had knocked me flat.

"Cassandra? You OK?"

I must have sounded loopy, maybe because I was. "Yeah. What time is it?"

"Ten thirty. You're still in bed?"

I sat up, then stood. "No."

Crap, I should have opened the store by now. I went

into the bathroom. A quick glance into the mirror made me frown. I looked like hell.

"What's up?" I asked.

"Edward's here. He wants to know when we should meet tonight."

"Tonight?" I splashed some water into my eyes, not an easy trick when you're holding a phone to your ear.

"Full moon? Raise the dead woman? Ask her how to rid my husband of a curse? Ring any bells?"

"That's tonight?"

"Are you high?"

"Sorry. I took a sleeping powder."

"Bad dreams?" She lowered her voice, ostensibly so the old man wouldn't hear.

"Not when I take the powder." But there was something . . .

I lifted my head, then stared, transfixed, at the mirror. My eyes were bright green.

I dropped the phone; it clattered to the floor and I automatically bent to pick it up. When I straightened, my eyes were blue again. What the hell *was* that?

"You OK?" Diana asked.

"Dropped the phone."

"You better have some coffee."

"I don't drink coffee."

"Start."

I leaned in close, tilted my face this way and that. My eyes weren't green. Although they did seem a lot less blue than I remembered.

"Cassandra?" Diana pressed.

"Um, yeah." I forced myself to turn away from the image. "I'll come to the mansion at dusk. Just after sunset, we'll try the ritual."

"See you then."

I made the appropriate farewell noises and hung up. Returning to the bedroom, I sat on the mattress and rubbed my forehead. I was so damn tired. I shouldn't have used the sleeping powder, because now I couldn't seem to wake up and tonight I'd need all my energy for the zombie raising.

I took Diana's advice and walked to the Café du Monde for chicory coffee. That stuff'll wake the dead. Perhaps I could just pour some on the voodoo queen's grave and forget about the blood.

I finally opened the shop around noon. No one seemed to notice or care that I was late. Midweek in early November was not the height of tourist season.

I used my downtime to call hotels in the area and ask if Devon Murphy was registered. He wasn't.

Not that I'd expected him to be. Knowing Murphy, he was in Oahu by now, his pocket full of cash from the sale of the diamond. He'd lounge on the beach for the rest of his life and seldom think of me.

I needed to get over him. Too bad all I wanted was to be under him.

About an hour before dusk, I closed my shop—not a customer had appeared all day—then packed a small satchel with the items I'd need: a knife, two bowls, my *ason,* a cup, rum, a bottle of water, and bandages. I'd get the blood there.

Diana's home had once been a plantation of great beauty. Most such structures in this part of Louisiana were located on the Great River Road, which ran from New Orleans to Baton Rouge. Why there was one here no one seemed to know.

Diana and Adam planned to restore the mansion to its former state, as soon as they had the money and the time. Right now, the place resembled every haunted house I'd ever seen.

Sagging, listing porch; at least they'd replaced the broken windows and door. The swamp came right up to the yard. I figured she had to keep a close eye on Luc lest an alligator drag him away, although Luc Ruelle could probably best any alligator in Louisiana.

Luc opened the door, crying, "Priestess!" at the sight of me, the formal address negated by his enthusiastic hug.

"I told you to call me Cassandra."

He took my hand and dragged me inside. "But it's so much more fun to call you Priestess."

He grinned. His missing front teeth were just starting to grow in, giving him the appearance of a juvenile jack-o'-lantern.

The mansion looked much better on the inside. The place was spotless; the floors had been refinished. They had furniture now, even a few curtains.

Diana had never been a housewife or a mother until a few months ago. I wondered how she managed. Of course I'd managed to become a completely different person from the one I'd been without too much trouble.

The things we do for love.

My eyes misted, and I blinked several times to make them stop. All I needed was for Edward to see me crying. He'd kick me out of his club.

"Hey, Cassandra, how you been?"

The man leaning against the entryway to the living room gave meaning to the word *sexy*—shoulder-length dark hair, smooth bronzed skin, bright blue eyes, and a body that had been honed to perfection years ago.

"Adam." I cleared my throat, tried not to drool. "I didn't know you were coming."

He shoved away from the wall, then leaned down to brush my cheek with his lips. "I wouldn't miss this for de world."

That Cajun accent always made everything he said sound both lazy and oh, so important at the same time.

"I—uh, well . . ." I wasn't sure how to tell him I didn't think everyone and their sister should be at the cemetery. This was going to be my first zombie raising; I didn't need an audience.

"Relax. I won't be goin' along. Someone has to watch de boy." He winked at Luc, who'd left my side to lean against his father's. They resembled each other so closely it would be creepy if it weren't so cute.

"Oh, right." I wasn't used to worrying about babysitters anymore. How quickly we forget.

Sometimes, lately, I'd had to think really hard to remember the shape of Sarah's face, and that frightened me.

"I thought I'd better get home," Adam continued. "If

you find a way to end de curse, we celebrate. If not . . ."
He shrugged, but his eyes were far from indifferent.

If I didn't find a way to end the curse, I wasn't sure what Adam and Diana would do.

"Don't worry." I straightened with determination. "I'll raise her."

I had to. Because the next stop was Sarah.

"Of course you will." Edward stood at the top of the steps.

As unlikely a leader of an elite monster-hunting unit as could be imagined, Edward Mandenauer was well over six feet tall and cadaverous thin. His once blond hair had faded, as had his blue eyes. However, his mind was as sharp as anyone's.

He joined us in the front hall, throwing a sharp glance in Adam's direction. "Did you do as asked?"

"Yes. She won't rise."

I figured they were talking about the woman I'd dreamed of.

"Silver?" Edward asked.

"Among other things." Adam glanced pointedly at Luc and they let the subject drop.

"Are we ready to go?" Edward asked.

"As soon as Diana is."

Edward frowned. "Why do we need her? You are the voodoo priestess."

"I don't really need *you,* but I have a feeling you're still coming."

He didn't bother to answer.

"And I'm coming, too." Diana hurried down the hall

from the kitchen. "No one else knows the location of the voodoo queen's grave."

"You could tell us," I said.

"Not on your life. This I've gotta see." She turned. "Pizza's in the oven, boys."

Not only did they have furniture, but they had electricity also. Life was looking up at the Ruelles'.

Diana kissed Luc, then Adam, running her fingers along her husband's cheek and staring into his eyes for a long moment. Something passed between them that didn't need words. I practically sighed out loud. How could I miss such a connection when Karl and I had never even had it?

"Enough kissy-face," Edward ordered, and Luc giggled. Edward's stoic blue gaze lowered to the boy. "What is so funny, young man?"

"You said 'kissy-face.' "

"I say a lot of things. For instance, 'go to bed.' "

Luc wrinkled his nose. "It's not even dark yet."

Edward glanced at each of the adults in turn, his expression puzzled. "What does that have to do with anything?"

Obviously Edward had spent very little time with children. Not surprising. He'd been busy with the werewolves for the past sixty years.

A short while later we reached a small, enclosed plot of land set back from the highway. Diana turned onto the dirt road, and we made our way to the gate, then climbed out of the car.

The sun had fallen, though there was still a thin line

of red across the horizon. The moon would be coming up soon—full and bright.

In the hazy light of dusk, the old slave cemetery was a sepia-toned photograph of a time long gone but never forgotten.

"There aren't any crypts," I said.

"For slaves?" Diana opened the gate, which wasn't locked, so why have one? "You're kidding."

"But I thought people *had* to be buried aboveground."

"Only in the city, where burying them in the crypts prevents them from popping out of their graves and floating down the street when it floods."

Something that had happened in the past but thankfully did no longer.

"Out here the land is higher," Diana continued.

"By the swamp?"

"Sadly, yes. Besides, folks didn't much care if the slaves floated away. They weren't going to spend money on crypts for dead Africans."

"The inhumanity of man never ceases to amaze me," Edward murmured.

I guess he was an expert on that.

32

The three of us stood in a half circle around the only stone marker in the graveyard, as the sun dipped below the trees.

Edward shone a flashlight across the surface. The years of sun and wind and rain had worn off the name, if there'd ever been one there at all.

"You're sure this is it?" I asked.

"Only someone of extreme importance would warrant a stone," Diana said.

"That doesn't mean the voodoo queen was buried here."

"Look at this." She indicated the far side of the marker, and I bent down next to her.

Chalked Xs marked the white surface, just as they marked Marie Laveau's tomb at St. Louis Number One. People believed if they drew the Xs, scratched the ground three times with their feet, or rapped three times on the grave, their wish would be granted.

Obviously the person buried here had enough power to help devotees from beyond the grave. I only hoped she could help us.

"OK," I agreed. "You're certain this is *our* voodoo queen and not another?"

She straightened. "Why don't we ask her?"

"Do you know her name?"

"Not really."

In the process of unpacking my bag, I glanced up. "What do you mean, 'not really'?"

"She's referred to only as the woman of great magic. Is that a problem?"

"Could be. In everything I've read it says you must repeat the name of the dead three times to call them out of the grave."

"Is that what Mezareau did?"

My forehead creased as I recalled the symphony of names swirling through my head. "I think so."

"What do you mean, you think so?" Edward demanded. "Don't you know?"

I hadn't told Edward much about the night of the last full moon. I liked my head attached to my shoulders just the way it was.

"I know the ritual," I said, which wasn't an answer, but it was all that I had.

"What if we don't call her name?" Diana asked.

"Either she won't come," I threw out my arm, "or I might raise everyone here."

Edward cursed in German. "Out of my way." He elbowed me aside.

I frowned as he pulled a piece of paper from his pocket, then laid it atop the stone. He ran a pencil quickly back and forth across the page. Diana and I exchanged glances; she shrugged.

"What are you doing?" I asked.

"Grave etching. I used to do this as a teenager on a boring Saturday night."

Which, somehow, didn't surprise me.

"Her name was . . ." He frowned, straightened, and turned the paper in our direction.

The word *Mawu* had appeared in the midst of the pencil marks. Creepy.

"What's that mean?" Diana asked.

"Mawu was the creator goddess of Dahomey."

"Which was?"

"A great empire in West Africa where most of the slaves in Haiti came from. The Europeans referred to the area as the Slave Coast because the Dahomey had a great army and they conquered most of the tribes surrounding them."

"Then sold their enemies into slavery," Diana said.

"As well as their own people. The Dahomey were way ahead of the pack in getting rid of undesirables— namely sorcerers and priests. They didn't take orders very well."

"Which meant the religion was transported to Haiti."

"And from there it eventually came here."

"So the religion of Dahomey became voodoo?"

"Pretty much, with the addition of whatever other gods and goddesses the slaves wanted to add."

"All fascinating information," Edward murmured, "but what does it have to do with us?"

"Mawu wasn't just a creator goddess; she was also a goddess of the moon."

We tilted our heads upward and stared at the rising full white moon.

"I guess that explains why Henri was so freaked out by my name," Diana murmured. "He was cursed by a moon goddess; then I show up with basically the same name, different language."

"Funny he never mentioned the similarity."

"Henri didn't mention much beyond how he wanted to kill me, or screw me, maybe both at the same time, drink my blood, bathe in it, yada yada."

Henri had been a real laugh riot.

"He didn't seem the type to give a shit about the names of his slaves or what they meant," I said. "Knowing him, he changed her name to Susie and left it at that."

"Probably," Diana agreed. "Now that we know her name, let's get moving."

"How do you intend to put her back?" Edward asked quietly.

"Huh?"

"Once you raise the voodoo queen I cannot allow her to leave this graveyard."

"Someone might notice a dead woman walking," Diana said. "Even in New Orleans."

"There's, uh, something I didn't tell you about the *bokor*'s zombies."

Edward lifted a brow and remained silent, waiting.

"They aren't exactly zombie zombies."

"Cassandra," Diana said, "you aren't making any sense."

"They live again, as if they'd never died. They appear completely human."

The two of them stared at me as if I'd lost my mind; then they started to laugh.

"I'm serious!"

"OK." Diana managed to control her mirth; then she pointed to the grave. "Show me."

I glanced at the sky—completely dark, except for the perfectly round moon. I picked up the knife and slashed my arm.

"Damn it!" Diana exclaimed. "What are you doing?"

"The ritual." I let the blood drip into the bowl, then quickly wrapped my arm. "Back up."

I did as Mezareau had taught me, filling a second bowl with water from a bottle and sprinkling it in a circle around the grave—me on the inside, Diana and Edward on the outside. I shook my *ason* and recited the chant.

"Come back to us now. Come back. Death is not the end. Live again as you once lived. Forget you ever died. Follow me into the world. Come back to us now. Come back."

I slammed the rum, tossed the cup over my shoulder, and lifted the bowl full of blood. I waited for the dizziness that had occurred the last time, but it didn't come. Which was just as well. Since I had to complete the ritual on my own, I needed all my wits.

Tipping the bowl, I watched the blood tumble through the air and darken the ground that comprised the grave.

Nothing happened.

"The name," Edward murmured.

Oh, yeah.

"Mawu. Mawu. Mawu."

That worked like a charm.

The ground tumbled outward, the brown dirt marred with what appeared to be white sand. The earth trembled. I glanced at the others.

Diana was staring, horrified, fascinated—at me. Edward peered calmly at the ground. I followed his gaze and my mouth fell open.

What I'd first thought was sand had solidified into bones. That hadn't happened in Haiti, but then those people had been newly dead, not dust.

I couldn't tear my eyes from the sight. The bones moved on their own in a jerky march toward one another; when they met, they knit together. At any moment I expected to hear an old-time chorus of "Dry Bones."

The knee bone's connected to the thighbone.

I shook my head. Now I'd never stop hearing it.

A skeleton emerged atop the grave. Wet, sucking sounds erupted and flesh appeared from nowhere. Slowly, the figure took the shape of a woman and rose.

But she didn't look right.

Her hair had grown back in patches, leaving bald spots all over her head. The ebony flesh had returned, but not all of it, so there were holes here and there where white bone shone through. Her teeth were rotted, her eyelids closed. Would her eyes grow back?

"Oh, yeah, that's gonna pass for human," Diana muttered.

"Shut up," I said, and my voice shook. What had I done wrong?

The zombie's eyelids opened, and her eyes gazed into mine, dark, endless pools of sorrow. Make that: What had I *done*?

"Master," she said. "How may I serve you?"

"Master?" Edward murmured. "I don't believe I like the sound of that."

I didn't, either.

"You're Mawu, the voodoo queen?"

"Yes, master."

"Why are you calling me master?"

"You raised me from the dead to be your slave."

"No."

Her head tilted and part of her nose fell off. Diana made a gagging sound. I wanted to do the same.

"That is the only reason to raise a zombie. It is why we so fear becoming one."

"I don't understand."

"My people were slaves. Only death could release us. To become a slave after death is what we fear the most."

"Ask her," Diana interrupted. "We don't know how long we have."

"Mawu, you cursed a man. Henri Ruelle."

She wrapped her skeletal arms around herself and rocked. "I called on the moon to make him a beast."

"How do we unmake him?"

Her lips tightened and she spit out a tooth. Lovely.

"He was evil even before the curse. Why would you release him?"

Henri had been a people-owning, selfish prick of a rapist. But this wasn't about him.

"We know what he did to you," I said gently. "He deserved to be punished. But . . . Is it true that when Henri dies the next male in line becomes a loup-garou?"

"Of course. That is how these things are done."

"It's been a hundred and fifty years. There's a man and his son who don't deserve this."

"Is Henri still suffering?"

Elise had tried to cure him, but since Henri had been cursed and not bitten, the cure hadn't worked very well. Henri now spent a lot of time screaming mindlessly behind the bars of his cage.

"He suffers horribly," I said.

Mawu smiled, not a pretty sight. "Good."

"We were told only you could end the curse."

"No."

"Make her," Diana murmured, her face intense. "She's your slave."

I winced. "But—"

"Cassandra, think of Luc, if not Adam. Think of me. Order her to release Henri. That's why we did this."

I didn't want to force the poor woman to do anything; she'd been forced enough. But Diana was right. This entire fiasco of a zombie raising would be for nothing if we didn't get what we'd come for.

Edward encouraged me with a dip of his chin, so I did what I didn't want to do. "I command you to remove the curse of the crescent moon from the Ruelle family."

"I did not mean I would not, master; I meant I could not."

Diana made a soft sound of distress, and I lifted one hand to silence her. "I was told the voodoo queen who did the cursing could remove it."

"That is not true. Only by committing the ultimate sacrifice can a curse be lifted. Only then will Henri and his descendants be freed."

"What's the ultimate sacrifice?"

"Only Henri can decide that."

"Hell," Diana muttered.

"Exactly." Mawu turned her attention to me. "Is there anything else you require of me, master?"

I waited until Edward and Diana had moved off a few feet, then put their heads together and started to whisper, before I asked, "Do you know why you came back like this?"

"You called me out of my grave."

"The *bokor* who taught me the ritual raised the dead to live again—as warm, complete, breathing, thinking people."

She nodded and her earring came flying off. I moved closer, squinted. Make that her ear.

"I have heard of this. To change the shape of the dead—their very nature—a *bokor* who can change his or her very nature is needed. A *lougaro*."

My heart stuttered. The word was both familiar and slightly different.

"A what?" I managed.

"Shape-shifter."

"Werewolf?" I whispered.

"A *lougaro* can be anything."

Of course it could.

Edward was suddenly right next to me. "What did she say?"

Nothing I wanted him to hear.

"She said I was mistaken," I blurted. "The dead can't be raised to live as before."

"No shit," Diana muttered, but Edward contemplated me with an expression bordering on pity. I wondered, not for the first time, how much he knew.

"You must never raise the dead again," Mawu said.

"What about those who shouldn't be dead?" I asked.

"Who are you to say who should and should not die? Only the Gran Met can decide that."

In theory, I agreed with her. In truth, Sarah shouldn't be dead.

For a walking corpse Mawu was very perceptive. She grabbed my arm. I could feel every bone in her hand pressing against my skin. I fought not to pull away, afraid I'd take several of her appendages with me.

"Death is just the beginning," she whispered.

"Of what?"

"The next adventure in our path."

The far-off shriek of something large and furry made all of us turn our heads.

"Bobcat," I murmured, really hoping I was right.

Mawu's face became fearful. "Please put me back, master. Quickly."

"Do you know how to return her to the grave?" Edward asked.

I lifted my hand and blew salt into her face. A bright light nearly blinded me as she burst into a million silver sparkles. When I opened my eyes again, the voodoo queen was gone. I began to stuff my utensils into my bag.

"According to Renee," Edward said, "only a *bokor* can raise the dead."

"So?"

He stepped into the circle and pressed a silver crucifix to my forehead.

I jerked away. "Knock that off!"

"You just raised the dead, which makes you an evil sorcerer."

"You told me to!"

He sniffed. "That doesn't make you any less evil."

"I'm not evil. Or at least I'm not any more evil than the next person. And you can quit poking me with silver."

I wiggled my fingers, which I'd kept adorned in silver rings ever since I'd met Henri. Then I lifted my knife and pointed to the wound I'd made with it.

Edward shrugged. "Who is to say silver works on a sorcerer anyway."

33

Ten minutes later we drove toward the mansion.

"I really thought it would work," I murmured.

"You raised her," Diana said. "I've never seen anything like it."

"She wasn't much help."

"We know Henri has to commit the ultimate sacrifice to be cured."

"We just don't know what that is."

Together we sighed.

I left them at the mansion and returned to my shop. Letting myself in the front door, once again I missed the sound of Lazarus's slither. I was so alone here, and it was starting to prey on my mind.

Maybe it was all that had happened tonight, or all that hadn't. I was slightly hysterical at the loss of my dream.

Which might have been why I didn't notice there was a man in my room until he grabbed me. Hand to hand was not my thing; I was much better with a knife. Unfortunately, I'd left the weapon in my bag and my bag was still in the car.

Brains were clearly not my thing, either.

I stomped on his instep, heard a hiss of pain that sounded familiar, spun with the heel of my hand speeding toward his nose, and recognized the tangle of Murphy's hair in the silvery light from the full moon shining through my open bedroom window.

He caught my wrist. "Where've you been?"

"Dammit, Murphy." I tugged, but he wouldn't let me go, instead drawing me closer. "I could have stabbed you."

His free hand patted me down, lingering in places that would have gotten him a lawsuit if he'd actually been a cop. "With what? You don't seem to be carrying."

Suddenly I was so tired, so depressed, so damned sad and lonely, I wanted to cry. To my horror, I snuffled.

"Hey." He leaned down to look into my face. Tears spilled onto my cheeks. "What happened?"

"I—I—I raised the voodoo queen from the dead."

"Did you now? And I'd think that would be makin' you happy, not sad."

"Quit with the Irish," I snapped.

"Sorry."

"I raised her, but—"

Quickly I filled him in on the "but."

"You're saying the only reason Mezareau could raise such nonzombie zombies was because he was a werewolf?"

"Not a wolf. Leopard, I think."

"Right. Wereleopard. You bet."

"You don't believe me."

"Listen to yourself, Cassandra."

"You saw the zombies, the waterfall, the *baka*. Yet you balk at believing in a wereleopard?"

"I have to draw the line somewhere," he muttered.

"I killed him," I said. "And ruined any chance of ever seeing Sarah again."

"Maybe that's not so bad."

I shoved him away. "You've never loved anyone the way that I love her."

"Obsessively?"

"I'm not being obsessive; I'm being a mother."

"Same difference."

"I can't help it," I said quietly.

"I know."

"I thought you'd be lounging on a beach by now. Where have you been?"

"Around."

I lifted a brow. "How informative."

"I didn't think you'd want to see me." He brushed my cheek with his fingertips.

"Then why are you here?"

"Why do you think?"

I backed away, leaving his hand poised in the air, nowhere near my face. "For the diamond."

He lowered his arm. "I've already got the diamond."

"Where is it?"

"Safe."

"Diana thinks there's another member of the Egbo in town looking for the jewel. We need to give it back."

"Finders keepers."

"You *stole* it!"

"What's your point?"

I ignored the question because I'd had an idea. "If there's a member of the Egbo, the leopard society, turning furry and running around New Orleans killing people, that's a shape-shifter."

"Don't the *Jäger-Suchers* kill them?"

"Yes," I said absently. "But maybe I can get it to kill me."

"Cassandra," he said softly. "You're starting to worry me."

"Only starting?"

He didn't smile.

"I already know the ritual," I said eagerly, "and it works; I proved that. But if I need to be a shape-shifter to raise the *living* dead, then that's what I'll become."

"I won't let you."

"How are you going to stop me?"

He cursed in a language I didn't understand, shoved his fingers through his hair, then took a few steps toward the window as if he meant to leave. I couldn't blame him; I was irrational.

Instead of climbing out, he leaned on the sill, took a deep breath of the silvery night air, then laughed a little and turned.

He crossed the short distance between us before I realized he was coming, then yanked me into his arms and kissed me. I should have shoved him away, but I couldn't. I needed him to touch me, to make me forget for just a little while that my life sucked and probably always would.

His mouth devoured mine, rough, reckless, tongues and lips and teeth at war. He seemed as desperate as I was, and I wasn't sure why. But I wasn't going to ask, either, maybe have him decide that this was such a bad idea.

His hands were everywhere, clever fingers stroking, teasing, arousing. His mouth beat a moist path across my jaw, to my neck.

"Cass," he whispered.

I grabbed his head, lifted it, and muttered, "Don't talk," then crushed our lips together, tangling my fingers in his hair all the way to the scalp.

No one had ever called me Cass, probably because Cassandra wasn't even my name, but having Murphy call me that put an intimacy on this relationship that frightened me.

Murphy and I were lovers without the love, partners without the trust. Basically we were two ships that banged each other in the night. If I weren't careful, I'd sink to the bottom of depression ocean when he left. I couldn't let myself care.

Sure he'd come back, even after he had the diamond, but that was for sex. I wasn't so delusional that I thought a guy like Murphy and a voodoo priestess like me could ever find a life. Especially once I became a shape-shifter and raised a living zombie child.

I shoved that thought right out of my head. Talk about a mood killer.

In an attempt to feel something other than nothing, I focused on the sensations—his mouth, his hands against my skin, the drift of his hair along my cheek.

I stroked him through the loose khaki of his slacks, rolling my thumb over his tip, skated my fingernail down his length. He hissed in a breath and grabbed my wrist, but I twisted away.

Every time he tried to slow things down, I used all that I knew about sex, about him, to speed it up. Soon he was as crazy as I was and needed very little encouragement to toss off his clothes and tumble with me onto the bed.

Desperation clawed at my stomach, a desire to forget all in a mindless bout of sex, to feel alive when everything about me—my dreams, my child, my life—seemed dead.

My skin felt on fire, that familiar yet new sensation of being too small for my body. I put it down to the heat, the humidity, the arousal. I wanted to burst free, but I needed some help.

"Please," I whispered, and guided him to me.

At first he followed my lead. Hard and fast, he made me forget everything but him and me, together like this.

I was close to the edge when he stilled, deep inside. "Look at me."

I didn't want to, but he refused to move. Even when I arched my back, attempting to create the friction I craved, he just used his superior weight and strength to hold me beneath him in a suspended state of arousal.

My hair itched; my nose ached; my very fingernails tingled. The only way to make it stop was to come, and unless I looked at him, that wasn't going to happen.

I opened my eyes, ready to spit in anger, and he leaned forward, pressing his lips to my brow, my cheek, my chin. The gentleness of the gesture made my throat go thick with an emotion I refused to put a name to.

He sighed and tipped his forehead against mine. His hair shrouded our faces, creating a curtain that encased only us. Our breath mingled, his brushing my lips, making me shiver.

As the full moon spilled through the window, sprinkling silvery shadows everywhere, he flexed his hips just a little, just enough to touch me in ways I'd never been touched.

"Devon?" I whispered for the very first time, sensing something new, something frightening, just over the horizon.

The orgasm hit us both as the last thread of his name faded into the night. He shuddered in my arms; I shivered in his, and in the distance the shriek of a wild thing called to me.

Even while forgetting, I could not forget.

When the last tremors died, he rolled away, and I felt bereft. What was wrong with me? I'd never needed him to stay before.

I turned my head; he turned his.

"Thanks," I said, which sounded crass, but he smiled.

"Jolis yeux verts," he murmured, expression dopey with sleep.

"What does that mean?" I asked.

"Pretty green eyes," he said, and drifted away.

I slid from the bed and hurried to the mirror. Staring out of my face were the bright green eyes of a jungle cat.

34

My head erupted with a pain so great I fell to the floor
on my hands and knees, writhing as the agony continued. I tried to call for Murphy, but the only sound
I made was a feeble, animal-like whimper that was
drowned out by the distant bong of a clock striking
midnight.

I couldn't catch my breath; every inch of me was on
fire. I wanted to press my cheek against the cool tile of
the bathroom floor, but when I did it was as if something lay between my skin and the smooth surface, pre-
venting me from touching it.

Another wave of pain hit, and mercifully I passed out.

I awoke in an alley. Every voice on the street echoed
in my head; every scent made my nostrils flare. I stared
at the full moon framed by an ebony sky. The shiny silver disk seemed to ebb and flow, both sound and light;
I heard its song in the pulse of my blood.

And speaking of blood . . .

I breathed in deeply. Somewhere nearby, there was a lot of it.

Slowly I rose and saw the dead man only a few feet away. Something had torn out his throat. My stomach rolled, making a gurgling growl of hunger. Why did I suddenly smell meat?

I felt so strange, both dizzy and uncertain but at the same time stronger and ultra-aware. My limbs didn't want to obey my mind's commands. I could do nothing but crawl on all fours.

I tried to remember how I had gotten here, and the pain flared. I hung my head, shut out the bright moonlight until the agony receded and I could open my eyes.

Only to stare at the bloody paws on the ground in front of me.

I glanced up, expecting to come face-to-face with a leopard. But I was alone in the alley.

Once again I looked down. The paws were facing in the wrong direction to belong to anyone else but me.

I tried to laugh—I was dreaming again—but the sound that came out of my mouth was the furious call of a wild cat.

I backed away from the man—tempted to smell him, taste him, and that just wouldn't do. For all I knew, one little taste could make this dream real.

But wasn't that what I wanted?

I forced myself forward. The thought of what I was about to do excited and disgusted me. I was both leopard and woman. Priestess and *Jäger-Sucher*. Two natures, one mind.

As I lowered my head, my nose brushed the body, and the click of a gun split the silence.

I glanced up; a man stood at the entrance of the alley. The streetlight cast him in silhouette, but I knew who it was.

Edward didn't wait for me to explain—as if I could with my snout problem—he just shot me.

However, I'd started moving the instant I recognized him, and the bullet that had been meant for my head plowed into my shoulder. The sharp, slicing pain made me stumble, but since I didn't explode, I kept running.

I was down by the wharf, not too far from home. I kept to the shadows near the buildings, zigging right, zagging left, leaving Edward behind with ease.

People brain, cat body—if it weren't for the bloodlust, this wouldn't be so bad.

Moments later I reached my shop and jumped in through the open back window—a lot of things were much easier on cat legs.

Murphy was gone. Thank goodness for small favors. Because as soon as I was inside, I passed out again.

I awoke to the sun streaming across my face. The birds were chirping. I had feet, not paws. Life was good.

I rolled my shoulder—not a twinge—felt for a bullet hole, found nothing. Not only that, but the arm I'd slashed with a silver knife yesterday sported no bandage, no scab, not even a scar.

I rubbed at my forehead and something crackled. When I lowered my hand, dried blood marred my fingers.

As I ran into the bathroom, I kicked something small and hard beneath my bed. I didn't have time to wonder what it was; I barely reached the toilet before I threw up.

When I was through, I took a shower, brushed my teeth. Even before I looked into the mirror I knew what I'd see. My eyes had turned green, and they hadn't turned back.

The phone shrilled; my sharp, shocked intake of breath sounded like a shriek. I hurried into the bedroom and grabbed the receiver before it could ring again. The shrill sound made my head ache.

"I know what's wrong with your python."

I'd forgotten the problem with Lazarus when I started having problems with humanity.

The vet continued speaking. "Yesterday a technician forgot to put back one of the patients. Said patient wandered near Lazarus, and the snake flipped out."

"I'm not getting you. What patient?"

"Oh." He laughed. "A cat. Some snakes hate them. Lazarus seems to be one."

This news coming so soon after my nightmare that wasn't exactly a nightmare explained a lot of things.

"I don't have a cat," I said numbly.

"Maybe you held one? Then you'd smell like one. Snakes can be very perceptive."

Lazarus certainly was. He'd figured out what was happening before anyone else had.

My eyes had become greener even in Haiti, but I'd blown off the change as too much reflective, magical jungle.

My senses had sharpened. I'd healed a little faster. Of course nothing good genes and healthy living couldn't explain away.

Until last night.

I must have made the appropriate responses to the vet, because he said good-bye, and I hung up, then sat heavily on the side of the bed.

I'd hoped I'd had another dream, but what about the blood, the speed-of-light healing of my arm, if not my bullet wound? Had there been a bullet wound?

I slid from the bed and crawled underneath, fingers reaching for something small and hard, the something I'd kicked as I ran. It didn't take me long to recover the silver bullet. Obviously my body had expelled it when I shifted back into a woman.

"A handy talent to have," I murmured, tossing the thing onto my nightstand.

Looked like I didn't have to *become* a shape-shifter; I already was.

But how? I hadn't been bitten.

"Neither was Henri."

The sound of my own voice made me jump. Talking to myself probably wasn't the best idea, but I had no one else. If I told Diana what I suspected, she might tell Edward, and we already knew what he'd do about it.

"Shoot me with silver, although that doesn't seem to work."

There were still some holes in my logic. I'd thought I'd been unable to raise a living zombie because I wasn't a shape-shifter. Yet I was. So what had gone wrong at the cemetery?

The doorbell rang, and then it didn't stop. Either the thing was stuck or there was an emergency, either of which had to be dealt with, so I threw on some clothes and hurried through the store.

Since I figured the culprit was Diana, I threw open the door, flinching at the sight of Edward. I had expected him to shoot me again, but he was unarmed. How strange.

"Renee just called." He shoved past me without being invited. "People are still disappearing in Haiti. I thought you said the *bokor* was dead."

"He was. Is," I corrected.

"You checked?"

"Uh—"

"You didn't check?" he shouted.

"Not me personally." I'd been a little freaked over killing a man. "Murphy."

Edward scowled. "Did you at least shoot him with silver?"

"Shoot, stab, same difference, right?"

One of the first things Edward had taught me— silver works for man and beast. Although it didn't appear to be working on every beast.

"He did not explode?" Edward pressed.

"No."

"Men like the *bokor* never die easily. Especially when they are not men."

"You don't think he was a man?"

"Do you?"

"He wasn't a werewolf."

Edward stared at me for a minute, then murmured, "I shot a leopard last night, which didn't explode, either. The animal had just killed a man."

I made a soft sound of distress. The animal was me, and I had killed that man—though I didn't remember doing it. I didn't remember a lot of things lately.

Edward cast me a harsh glance. "You cannot be squeamish if you are to work for me."

I nodded and said nothing, but he didn't require any commentary. "We can't be sure that the victim won't rise. I shot him with silver, but that will probably not work. I am thinking wereleopards need to be shot with something other than that."

I was thinking the same thing.

"I will call Renee, set Diana to the research." He opened the door, and sunlight streamed over us both. With a scowl, he grasped my chin and lifted my face. "Your eyes. They were blue."

Son of a bitch! It wasn't easy being green. I'd forgotten my sudden change of shade, which was understandable. I didn't suddenly see everything through green-colored glasses instead of blue.

"My contacts," I blurted.

He squinted, peering at my irises. "You aren't wearing any."

"You rang the bell before I could put them in." I stepped out of his grasp, his clawlike fingers seeming to leave a dent in my flesh. "You know I'm in witness protection." He nodded; he'd known. "I started wearing blue lenses, figured it couldn't hurt."

Edward grunted and left, but he'd be back. Probably with twenty rounds of whatever it took to kill a wereleopard.

I had to sit down, so I stumbled to a chair, fell into it, then put my head between my knees and tried to breathe. Sure I'd wanted to be a shape-shifter, so I could shift the shape of my child from dead to alive. However, it hadn't occurred to me that in doing so I'd be changing the shape of countless others—from alive to dead.

I shuddered at the thought of killing someone, then drinking their blood, eating their flesh. If I was really a wereleopard, shouldn't I like it?

Werewolves turned evil when they turned. Why hadn't I?

The front door opened. Edward returning, no doubt, with second thoughts on my blue-contacts explanation. I was surprised he'd bought it in the first place.

I really should have gotten out of New Orleans while the getting was good, but now it was too late.

I lifted my head, prepared to explain everything, but the words froze on my lips at the sight of Jacques Mezareau.

35

"Priestess." Mezareau closed the door behind him, shutting out the light. "It's a whole new world for you today, isn't it?"

I could do nothing but stare at him. I'd suspected he wasn't dead, yet still it was so strange to see him.

He appeared just as he had in Haiti—linen shirt and trousers, dark hair combed just so, green eyes far too bright in his semidark face. The only differences I could detect in him were his shoes—sandals—and his turning up alive.

"Wh-why? How?"

"Your questions will soon be answered."

He smiled, and I was struck again by his precise and numerous teeth. I ran my tongue over my own. Were there more today than yesterday?

"First, Priestess, I have a question of my own: Where's the diamond?"

"I don't have it."

He backhanded me so hard I flew into a shelf of bottles and bones. Everything shattered but me.

"I know you have it."

I shook my head. Nothing rattled. Except for the glass in my ass, I was good.

"I don't." I wasn't going to tell him Murphy did, though I was sure he'd figure it out quickly enough. I needed to stall. "Go ahead and look."

Mezareau tore the place apart, and I let him. Though I wasn't sure how I could stop the man, and really what difference did it make? As he'd said, today my world was new, and in it I doubted I'd be able to continue as a voodoo priestess in the French Quarter, even if I managed to escape Edward's wrath.

The knowledge saddened me. I'd liked it here, when I could forget why I'd come.

"I tried to raise a zombie," I said.

"Let me guess." He smashed the glass on one of my display cases and tossed things hither and yon. "Your zombie wasn't quite right."

I remembered the voodoo queen's steadily disintegrating face. "I'll say."

"Only under a full moon at midnight, during a ceremony performed by a wereleopard, can the living dead be raised."

"No other type of shifter will do?"

"We are a select club."

No kidding.

"I *was* a shape-shifter," I said slowly. "I just didn't know it."

"No, you were not a wereleopard yet. The first transformation takes time. Didn't you notice the small alterations that came about bit by bit?" He waved a careless hand at my eyes.

I didn't bother to answer; I wasn't blind, although I had been a bit dumb.

"Until the midnight moon, when your first complete change occurred, you were not truly one of us and you did not have the power to raise a living zombie."

That made sense—or as much sense as anything else did lately.

"So, full midnight moon—" I held up one finger. "Ceremony performed by a wereleopard—" I flipped up another. "That's all there is to the spell?"

"That and the fucking diamond!"

A chill passed over me. "We need the diamond?"

"Why do you think I care so much?"

"It's expensive?"

He cast me a withering glare. "Considering I can raise the dead, do you think I lack for money?"

Good point.

He crossed the distance that separated us so fast I didn't see him coming until he was there. "Where is it?"

"I don't know."

This time I was ready, and I caught his hand before it smashed into my face.

"How did you do this to me?" I shoved him, and he stumbled back several feet.

He was strong, but now so was I. Being a wereleopard

had its uses. If it weren't for the need to commit bloody murder, I might like it.

"Why so angry?" He circled me like the beast he was. "You came to me. You asked me to share my secret."

I wasn't blameless. However, I did think it was common courtesy to tell someone before you turned them into a wereleopard.

"What, *exactly,* did you do?"

"Just a little curse." He tilted his head, the movement more canine than feline. "Nothing to be so upset about."

"I don't remember a curse."

Of course, after I'd drunk the *kleren,* I didn't remember much.

"More of a potion really."

Aha. That explained why I'd gotten loopy after drinking his rum and stayed sane after drinking my own.

"What was it?" I demanded.

"A secret passed down from my ancestors." I could tell by his smirk he wasn't going to give me the recipe.

"Are there more wereleopards running around somewhere?"

"Not yet." He leaned in close and took a deep breath. "You smell so good," he purred. "Perhaps we can create more of our kind in an intimate way."

"Yeah. That'll happen." I shoved him in the chest. This time when he fell back, he stayed there.

"You will change your mind." He licked his lips as his gaze wandered over me. I suddenly felt the need for a scalding hot shower and a bar of lye soap. "The longer you are a shifter, the more of a shifter you become. Soon you will be like me in all ways. The thrill of the chase, the excitement of the kill—it's better than sex."

His words made me shudder as I recalled dreams that hadn't been my own. "I remember things that haven't happened."

"I can walk through your dreams, Priestess. If you wish, you can walk through mine."

"I don't feel evil," I whispered.

He smiled. "You will."

"I killed a man."

"Last night? No. I did. But next month you may have the pleasure."

"What if I don't want to?"

"We must partake of human blood on the night of the full moon or go mad."

"But I didn't!"

"You did. You just don't remember."

I thought of how I'd woken up—blood on my hands, my face. I suspected he was right and I wanted to throw up again, but I didn't have the time.

"We may shift any night we wish," he continued. "On those nights, the hunt is just for fun."

"So we *are* like werewolves."

"I know nothing of werewolves, nor do I care."

"Silver doesn't kill us."

"Nothing can."

Somehow I doubted that, but I'd come back to it.

"Why a potion and not a bite?"

"We aren't diseased," he snapped.

"Just cursed."

"I prefer to believe I'm blessed."

"You would."

I considered what he'd told me. The shift wasn't the result of a virus, which meant Elise couldn't cure me, just as she hadn't been able to cure Henri.

When had I begun to consider a cure? Probably from the moment I'd seen the blood beneath my fingernails. Really, once I raised Sarah, I couldn't keep turning into a leopard under every full moon. What would the neighbors say?

"I didn't shift when the moon came up," I pointed out.

"Just as the sun is at its peak at noon, the moon is at its peak at midnight. The first shift requires such power. From that point onward, the power is in you." He brushed his hands together. "Now, the diamond."

"I thought we were all-powerful beings. Why do we need a stone?"

"The diamond focuses the moon and the magic. It was found in the motherland."

I frowned. "Germany?"

"You have been talking to Mandenauer too much. The diamond was birthed in the earth of Africa. The power of the ages is in every facet. When the Egbo was first formed, the diamond was the center of all. The members learned the secret to changing shape by staring into its sparkling center."

Sounded like BS to me, but then a lot of legends did.

"You're saying the Egbo was actually a leopard society, with real leopards."

"How do you think they kept the slaves in line?"

"Torture?"

"While that is great fun, seeing a man change into a leopard, tear out a few hearts, drink a little blood, always worked much better. There was also the very real threat they would be turned into a zombie."

"The Egbo turned people into zombies?"

"My dear, where do you think this all began?"

My front door rattled, then opened. Devon Murphy strolled in carrying two cups of coffee and a bag of *beignets*. Since when did he use the front door?

He didn't notice Mezareau and me in the shadows of the shop. He didn't notice the place had been trashed. He was too busy balancing the coffee and the doughnuts, trying to shut the door with his foot.

Mezareau's smile became predatory. His too-numerous teeth suddenly looked sharper. "Maybe you don't know where the diamond is, Priestess, but I bet he does."

Murphy spun at the sound of Mezareau's voice. He managed to hold on to breakfast, until the *bokor* swept everything out of his hands.

I sprang between them. "No," I said firmly. "He doesn't know anything."

"I had him detained," Mezareau said, in a voice that reminded me of Lazarus. "But he didn't have the diamond."

"He still doesn't," I said, desperate to make Mezareau

believe me. Murphy wasn't going to give the thing up, if he even had it anymore. He'd probably let the *bokor* kill him instead.

Mezareau just laughed. "He gave it to you, or most likely hid it in your luggage, then romanced it out from under you." He shook his head. "I thought you were smarter, Priestess, but you are still only a woman."

I gritted my teeth but let that pass. "I haven't seen the diamond since Haiti."

"Maybe this will refresh your memory."

I expected him to toss me aside, make a grab for Murphy, who'd been annoyingly silent through this whole exchange. Instead, Mezareau produced a knife made of dark stone, the handle wood. When he pressed it to my throat, my skin began to smoke, and I cried out.

"What the hell!" Murphy yanked me backward.

Slipping and sliding a bit until we got out of the puddle of spilled coffee, he then wrapped his arms around me from behind and tugged me close.

Mezareau lifted a brow. "I can easily stick this into her chest, and she will explode in a burning ball of fire."

I slapped my hand to my aching neck. "I thought you said nothing could kill us."

"I lie."

"What's going on?" Murphy demanded.

"He seems to have turned me into a wereleopard."

Murphy stiffened. "Cass—"

"I don't have time to argue. Even if you don't believe it, he does."

Murphy's chest rose and fell on a sigh. "You want your diamond."

"You always were sharp. Simply put, turn over my property, and I won't turn her into flambé."

I wondered if I could grab the knife before Mezareau buried it in my chest. I was quicker than I'd been yesterday, but Mezareau had been a furry feline longer. I doubted I was quicker than him.

I needed to move away so Murphy didn't get turned to ashes along with me. Or maybe I should continue to block his body with mine so Mezareau couldn't stick him with the knife? Sharp black stone would kill Murphy as easily as it would me, even without the fireworks.

Before I could decide, Murphy did. "I'll get you the diamond."

Mezareau appeared as shocked as I was at Murphy's easy capitulation. "I'll go with you."

"You think I left a jewel of that size in a hotel room or even a safe-deposit box? I left it somewhere secure, protected. Somewhere that someone I trust will move it the instant anyone else shows up but me, or even if anyone shows up *with* me."

"You've done this before." Mezareau kept his bright gaze on Murphy's face. "Fine. Bring me the diamond within the hour."

"It's not that close."

"When?"

"Tonight."

"We'll wait for you here."

"I need her to—"

"Spare me," Mezareau interrupted. "You think I'd let the priestess out of my sight? You think I give a shit what you need? I'm not stupid. Bring me the diamond or she dies."

I shook my head. The only hope we had of stopping Mezareau was keeping the diamond away from him. Even though I wasn't keen on the idea of helping him now, by next month I might be. Together we'd be unstoppable. We'd raise the dead until there weren't any left; then our army would march across the world.

"Don't do it," I said. "Better I die than he raises that army."

"I can't let him kill you," Murphy whispered, and then he was gone.

Hell. I should have told him to find Edward. The old man would know what to do. Now it was too late.

"More important than a diamond, Priestess." Mezareau's smirk made me want to smash something: How about him? "Aren't you pleased?"

I stared at the open front door through which Murphy had disappeared. "You won't kill me," I said.

"No?" He gave the word that annoying twist that only the French are able to manage.

"You had a reason for cursing me instead of someone else."

"Oui. You were chosen."

"By whom?"

"Me."

I rubbed my forehead. "*I* came looking for *you*."

"Because I wanted you to."

My hand fell away. "I don't understand."

"The voodoo community may be spread all over the world, but it's still very small. People talk; I listen. They began talking of you almost as soon as you started your training."

"Because I'm white?"

"Typical." He made a sound of derision. "As if that makes you special. It is what is in here." He tapped my forehead with one long fingernail. "And here." He did the same to my breastbone. "That matters. All that has happened was ordained long ago."

"All what?"

"You became who you are; you needed what I knew."

"But—"

"You possess the power necessary to make the dead rise."

"I thought that was in the shape-shifting and the diamond."

"And you. I couldn't turn just anyone into a wereleopard. You are favored by the *loas*."

"I've never done anything more powerful than anyone else," I protested.

"You sent your friend to Ife. Brought her out again with a piece of the moon goddess's garden."

Crap. How did he know about the time I'd sent Diana to voodoo heaven? That was supposed to be our little secret.

"Do you read minds?"

"No. But part of the magic in being a wereleopard is

being able to see and hear over a great distance—if someone happens to say my name."

"I knew it!"

"The power will come to you, too, eventually."

I frowned, uncertain I wanted to listen in on people's conversations—seemed a little evil.

No kidding.

"I haven't done anything great since," I hedged. "Ife was probably just an accident. A burp in the mystical universe."

"I sent the dead and you sent them away. Only a *mambo* of incredible power can do that."

He had me there.

"Then you conjured your daughter into my jungle."

The room was suddenly icy cold. "That was a dream."

Mezareau's too-green eyes narrowed. "Do your dreams often leave footprints?"

"Where is she?" I managed.

"She is still dead, Priestess, but for an instant she was with you. She can be again, forever, if you help me on the next midnight moon. Together we will raise my army."

"And then?"

His smile was a perfect imitation of the cat with canary feathers sticking out one side of its mouth. "Then I will give you the diamond."

36

I didn't believe for a minute that Mezareau would just give me the diamond and let me waltz out of Haiti. However, I wasn't going to tell him that.

The day passed slowly. Mezareau made me leave the Closed sign in the window. "Do you think I'm foolish enough to allow one of your *Jäger-Sucher* friends to just walk in and kill me?"

I *had* been hoping. There was only one problem.

"They think you're dead."

"Edward Mandenauer is no fool, either."

True. From the beginning Edward hadn't believed Mezareau was dead. But would Edward be able to figure out how to kill a wereleopard, then come back here in time to do so? As the day waned toward dusk, I had my doubts.

Looked like I was on my own. But that was nothing new.

I cleaned up the coffee, tossed the *beignets,* once my

favorite food. The scent of fried dough and sugar now turned my stomach. Pretty much everything did. Would I soon be able to eat nothing but raw meat? I'd never cared for it.

I got so bored, I began to sweep up glass and put my shop to rights. Mezareau spent his time paging through my library. I'd accumulated a lot of supernatural texts even before I'd begun to work for Edward. I'd always been interested in the bizarre. How else would I have come up with the idea of becoming a voodoo priestess?

Night fell; the moon rose. I was compelled to enter my courtyard and stare at the nearly perfect orb.

"Sometimes I swear it sings to me."

Mezareau had followed me out. He'd followed me everywhere today. I'd had to put my foot down at letting him follow me into the bathroom.

"Where's your friend?" Mezareau asked.

I'd started to believe that Murphy wasn't coming. What would Mezareau do once he figured it out? Tear apart the city, the county, the country, as he'd torn apart my shop?

"I'm right here."

I turned, and there he was in the doorway. Murphy had come back for me.

My stomach fluttered. He was risking his life and his future. No one had ever done anything like that for me before. What did it mean?

I glanced at Mezareau and my stomach stopped fluttering. What did it matter?

"Where's the diamond?" he demanded.

"Safe."

I thought I was far enough away to avoid getting a knife to my throat again, but I was still unfamiliar with the speed at which Mezareau could move. The blade burned my neck before I knew it was coming.

"I'm through fucking around," Mezareau snarled.

"OK, OK." Murphy removed the stone from his pocket. "Put the knife down, and I'll do the same with the diamond."

The sharp edge lifted just a little.

"As soon as he does, Cassandra, get over here," Murphy ordered.

The burn returned, and I hissed in pain.

"You want this or not?" Murphy snapped.

"You seem under the impression that you are in charge here. I could kill you with ease, Murphy."

"Not as easily as you think."

"Let's find out." Mezareau shoved me, and I stumbled on the uneven garden path, then fell.

When I glanced up, Mezareau had lifted his face and his hands to the moon. The silver glow streamed over him like a spotlight, and the edges of his silhouette shimmered, shifted, went indistinct.

The sheen from above seemed to shoot into his body, so bright I had to blink. When my eyes opened, a leopard stood where the *bokor* had been.

The beast appeared larger than the average leopard—not that I'd seen any except in the zoo. However, I didn't think they ran to six feet, plus a tail, or weighed near 170 pounds.

His coat was shiny, tawny, spotted—I could see why leopards had once been poached almost to extinction. I wouldn't mind wearing one of those on my back. Right now I'd kind of like to wear him—then he wouldn't be staring at Murphy out of hungry emerald green eyes.

Of all the things that might bother me about this leopard, the eyes bothered me the most, because just like werewolves' eyes, wereleopards' eyes were human.

The growl that rumbled from his throat sounded really pissed off. Murphy didn't appear scared. He was too busy staring at the beast with his mouth hanging open. I guess he believed in wereleopards now.

"Get inside!" I shouted, scrambling to my feet.

He didn't listen, didn't even glance my way, before he stepped into the courtyard and circled the leopard as the leopard circled him.

I looked for a weapon, spied the knife, thought better of it. Me with a knife, Mezareau with his teeth and claws, it wouldn't be pretty.

Instead I glanced at the moon and knew what I had to do. Quickly I lifted my face, my hands, hoping, praying, my magic would be enough.

Silver spilled down my body like a waterfall. I'd thought the moon would be cool; instead it was fiery hot, racing through my blood, bubbling beneath the surface, pushing me toward a change.

I waited for the pain—a crunching of bone, the shifting of skin, the sprouting from nowhere of fur, snout, and tail. Instead, fireflies of light sparkled all around me—a hundred thousand Tinkerbells. I swayed, closed my eyes, and when I opened them I was shorter.

Probably had something to do with the paws.

Mezareau crouched, ready to spring, and I launched myself at him. He ducked, and I flew over his back, skidding in the damp grass, slamming headfirst into a fountain. I wasn't used to this body yet, but Mezareau was.

I shook off the dizziness, no time for that, spinning just as the leopard launched himself into the air. They were too close to each other, too far away from me. I'd never reach them in time.

They say when you stare death in the face your entire life passes before your eyes. As I watched death sail toward Murphy, the times we'd shared tumbled through my mind.

Traveling through the mountains, sleeping under the stars, sharing our pasts, our pain, our bodies. I'd never shared with anyone else the things I'd shared with him. What would I do if I lost him?

I started to run, awkward in my new feet, but I couldn't just stand there and watch him die.

A second before the leopard hit the man, Murphy thrust his hand toward Mezareau's chest and the *bokor* exploded in a blazing ball of fire.

Murphy stumbled back from the flames, which were so bright and hot, Mezareau would be ashes in minutes. The knife clattered to the pavement as Murphy lifted his arm to shield his face.

How had he gotten the weapon? He must have taken

advantage of the momentary distraction I'd provided by launching myself at Mezareau to retrieve it. Murphy always had been both quick and smart.

I shied away from the heat, skittery, nervous, though the smell of roasting flesh interested me more than it should. I guess Mezareau's claim that I'd become more and more leopard, less and less woman, was true.

"That worked." Murphy glanced at me and flinched. "You wanna change back? You're freaking me out."

Change back? I hoped I could.

Lifting my snout to the sky, I imagined myself a woman. I remained a leopard.

I whined and pawed at the ground. The only person who knew the rules was barbecuing in my backyard.

"Maybe calling to the moon would work," Murphy suggested. "Seems like I've heard the call of the wild a lot lately. Mezareau must have been serenading us for a reason."

Probably just to scare everyone, but it couldn't hurt to try. I lifted my voice to the night, and somewhere in the distance a wolf howled.

Swell.

I didn't have time to worry about that, because suddenly I felt the heat, saw the sparkles, and an instant later I crouched in my garden, naked.

"Have to say I like this direction much better." Murphy handed me my clothes.

At least they weren't torn, as they would have been

if I'd been a werewolf. Bursting through seams and shoes must be a real pain. Literally. Magical shifting was so much neater.

While I dressed, Murphy collapsed on the rim of my fountain, leaning over to splash his face. "I didn't expect him to shift into a leopard."

"Have you been paying any attention over the past month? Wereleopard sorcerer. We've been over this."

"Gotta see to believe." He stood and brushed his fingers against the white streak in my hair. "What are we gonna do about you?"

"Me?"

"How do we make the leopard thing stop?"

I glanced at the ashes that had once been Mezareau. "You might have already stopped it."

I wasn't sure how I felt about that. If I wasn't a shape-shifter, Sarah was just dead.

"What do you mean?" Murphy asked.

"A lot of curses are broken when the curser dies."

"How about this one?"

I lifted my face, my arms, to the moon. Immediately the silver sheen crashed down; I felt the telltale heat, saw the shimmer at the edge of my vision.

"Then again . . ." I dropped my arms and thought about England. The heat fell away, and the sparkles died. "A lot of them aren't."

Like the curse of the crescent moon.

"You don't sound too upset about being a wereleopard," Murphy observed.

"I need to be. For Sarah."

"When are you going to give that up? You can't raise your child from the dead."

"Actually, I can, if you'll lend me your diamond."

"I didn't mean you aren't able to." His shoulders slumped. "I meant you can't. It isn't right." He took a deep breath and whispered, "I don't want you to."

"I can't just leave her there."

For several long moments there was silence between us. I didn't know what else to say.

"Why can't you start a new life?" he asked.

"As a wereleopard?"

"I'm sure someone with your power, with the re-sources of the *Jäger-Suchers* behind you, could find a way out of that."

"We probably shouldn't mention this to them. They tend to get all weirded out about shape-shifters."

"I can't imagine why," he muttered.

"I'll give the diamond back as soon as I'm done," I promised. "Or you could come with me to California."

I was shocked to discover how much I wanted him to. I'd been alone since I'd lost Sarah, alone until I'd found him. And while I couldn't bring myself to invite Murphy to share a life with me and my living zombie daughter, I couldn't let him go, either. Not yet.

"You think I'm worried about the damn diamond?" Despite his words, he seemed more defeated than mad. "Take it, Cassandra."

"No. I mean—I will for now. But you—"

"I thought I needed it, but I don't." He laughed, though the sound held no humor. "All I need is—"

Someone cleared his throat, and for an instant I imagined Mezareau had risen from the ashes. The bad guys just aren't as easy to kill as they used to be.

But the *bokor* wasn't standing in the center of my courtyard, holding the knife made of stone; it was Edward. I wasn't sure who was worse.

Edward lifted his gaze from the knife to me, then to Murphy. "Which one of you is a wereleopard?"

37

"Me," Murphy said, and Edward threw the knife.

The old man never waited around for explanations. Which was probably why he was still alive.

Without Murphy, I didn't want to be. I threw myself in front of him, shoving him in the chest, knocking him to the ground. The knife stuck in my shoulder with a thunk.

"Ouch!" I turned to Edward, but he was glaring at Murphy, who was glaring at me.

"Dammit, Cassandra." Murphy jumped to his feet. "You could have exploded."

But I hadn't. What the hell?

Without warning, Edward yanked the knife from my shoulder. I gasped at the pain but managed to grab his wrist as it descended toward Murphy.

"What are you doing?" I demanded.

"Diana discovered that only a knife made of black diamonds could end the life of a wereleopard."

Edward's voice came in fits and starts as we continued to struggle for possession of the knife. I was no longer strong enough to take it from him, and I wasn't sure why. I wouldn't be able to hold Edward's wrist away from Murphy much longer.

Murphy must have sensed this, because he plucked the knife, blade first, from Edward's hand. "Black diamonds. Those must be pretty rare."

"Extremely so in Africa, though more common in Brazil." The old man scowled at him. "You are not a wereleopard at all."

"No?" Murphy tossed the gory knife into the fountain.

"You touched the blade without burning." Edward turned his frown on me. "And you did *not* explode."

"No moss on you," Murphy muttered, but Edward ignored him to glance around the courtyard. His gaze stopped when it reached the pile of ashes. "Mezareau?"

"Yes."

He met my eyes. "You?"

I jerked my thumb in Murphy's direction.

"Hmph," Edward said.

Something soft touched my back. Murphy had taken off his shirt and pressed it to my wound. Sadly, the gash wasn't closing on its own. I was going to need stitches.

"Tell me what happened," Edward demanded.

"She needs a doctor."

Edward pulled out his gun and pointed it at us both. I told him everything.

"Only a wereleopard can raise the living dead." Edward set down the gun and picked up the diamond Murphy had placed on the low stone bench surrounding the fountain. "With a little help from the stone."

"Yes, sir."

"And the *bokor* cursed you to become like him on the next full moon, which was last night."

"That's the rumor."

Edward's lips twitched. I wasn't certain if I annoyed or amused him, but right now I didn't care.

"However, the black diamond knife, which killed Mezareau, did nothing to you."

"Is there a point to this?" Murphy demanded. "Wereleopard or not, she's only got so much blood to lose."

"I'm concerned," the old man murmured. "Cassandra has always had more power than she realizes. That, combined with Mezareau's knowledge and the near immortality of a shape-shifter . . ." He spread his hands. "I cannot allow her to walk freely in this world."

"You've got nothing to say about it!"

"There you are wrong." Edward snapped his fingers, and the courtyard filled with people. From the number of weapons I guessed they were *Jäger-Suchers*.

"Hold on," I said, fighting waves of nausea, pain, and dizziness. "The knife didn't make me go boom. I'm not healing in the blink of an eye. Let me see if I can shift."

The sound of several rounds being chambered made me freeze. I glanced at the sea of guns. "Little jumpy?"

"You think we'll let you shape-shift and tear out our throats?" Edward asked.

"I doubt you'll let me do anything of the kind," I muttered.

"But how will we stop you? Silver doesn't work on wereleopards; the black diamond doesn't work on you."

"So I'm supershifter. Lucky me."

A tall, willowy blonde shoved through the crowd. Her electric blue dress and snazzy black stilettos were both out of place and right in fashion. She carried no weapon, but then she didn't need one.

Elise was a werewolf.

You might think it odd that the most feared werewolf hunter had a granddaughter who turned furry; I know I had. However, the story of Elise and Edward was long, involved, and not exactly pleasant.

I'd met Elise once before, during the incident with Henri. We nodded a greeting, but I wasn't in the mood to be sociable. Blood loss from a four-inch gash in the shoulder can do that.

"She seems exactly the same as she did when I met her the first time," Elise murmured. "If she's evil, I can't see it."

"Because evil shows?" Murphy's voice was sarcastic.

"No." Elise flicked a glance at him, then away. "But I've gotten pretty good at smelling it."

His eyes narrowed. "Who is she?"

"Dr. Hanover, meet Devon Murphy."

"Excuse me if I don't shake hands," Murphy said. "I'm a little bloody."

Elise's blue eyes flared. "You probably want to lay off on the bloody," she said. "It excites me."

"Maybe I should have asked *what* is she?"

"Smart man," Elise murmured, but she didn't answer.

I would have, except Elise suddenly pressed her palm against my forehead, then closed her eyes. Since I'd seen her do this before, with Henri, I let her.

Seconds later, Elise lowered her hand and turned to Edward. "She's clean."

"Just like that?" he asked. "Usually there is a lot of 'Who am I? Where am I?' when you cure someone."

"I didn't have to cure her," Elise said. "She isn't a wereleopard. At least not anymore."

"You're certain?"

She glanced at me. "Go ahead and try to shift."

Edward made an elaborate "be my guest" gesture, so I lifted my face, my arms, to the moon.

No heat, no shimmers. The moon was just a moon, and I was just a woman. I let my hands fall back to my sides and glanced at Murphy. "I changed into a leopard, right?"

"And back again."

"OK. Just so we're clear." I suddenly had to sit down, so I did, on the ground at Murphy's feet.

"That's enough." He knelt at my side, worry creasing his brow. "We're going to the hospital."

"One moment," Edward murmured. "Elise, since when do your powers extend to anything other than werewolves?"

"I can only *cure* werewolves, and sometimes not

even them," she muttered. "But I still get the jolt with other shifters." She put her fingers to her forehead in memory. "Supreme ice-cream headache."

"And you know this how?" Edward demanded.

"I've been testing them."

"Them what?" Edward's voice had lowered, which somehow made him sound even angrier.

"You know as well as I do that there are a lot more things out there than werewolves."

"Sadly, yes," Edward agreed.

"I had a little time on my hands, so I thought I should check them out."

"Dr. Frankenstein," Murphy whispered, and Elise's lips tightened.

I should probably tell him that Elise could hear just about anything, but I didn't have the energy.

"What happened in between her shifting and her suddenly being unable to?" Elise asked.

"Besides the old man trying to kill me?" Murphy asked.

Elise gave a tired sigh and turned to her grandfather. "What have I said about killing first, asking questions later?"

"That it is a bad idea." Edward lifted his nose. "But I still find it to be a good one."

She stared at him for several seconds, and he stared right back. Eventually Elise gave up and glanced at Murphy. "If Edward tried to kill you, then why is Cassandra bleeding?"

"She stepped in front of the knife." Murphy's fingers tightened on my arms. I wasn't sure if he wanted to hug me or hurt me. Probably both.

"Ultimate sacrifice," Elise murmured, and I lifted my head.

"What?"

"I read the report from Diana. Only an ultimate sacrifice will end a voodoo curse."

"So?"

"You were cursed, too."

Damn. Why hadn't I thought of that. Except—

"My life means nothing to me."

Elise smiled gently. "But your daughter's does."

I froze as what she was saying became clear. Tears burned my eyes, and I turned my face into Murphy's bare chest.

"Cassandra, what is it?" His voice shook; he seemed really scared. I just shook my head, unable to speak.

"She can't raise her daughter now," Elise explained. "Mezareau is dead, and the formula for the curse died with him."

Murphy stiffened. "Hell."

"She saved you," Elise continued, "but the price was Sarah."

38

I passed out again, this time from blood loss, or maybe grief. For a woman who'd never fainted in her life, I was making quite a habit of it.

I awoke in the hospital with Diana at my side.

"Since when do stitches warrant a bed?" I asked.

"It wasn't the stitches that worried them but the fainting."

"Worried me, too," I admitted. "I'm going to lose my *Jäger-Sucher* ass-whupping card."

"I doubt that."

Silence settled between us. A silence full of questions, which I couldn't let continue.

"Sorry I didn't tell you everything," I blurted.

"What didn't you tell me?"

"About Sarah." I braced to fight the tears, but none came.

"If I'd lost a child," she said gently, "I wouldn't want to talk about it, either."

"You're very understanding." I considered her for a minute. "Am I dying?"

"No." She got up and went to the window.

"What aren't you telling *me*?"

"Murphy's gone. The diamond, too."

And that started the tears when Sarah hadn't.

"Damn it," Diana muttered, hurrying back to my side. "I should have kept my yap shut."

"No." I scrubbed my face. "I knew he wouldn't stay. I was surprised he came back in the first place."

"Elise really wanted to study that diamond."

"I bet."

"She took the black diamond knife instead."

"That might amuse her for a while." Though I doubted it. The black diamond knife was just pretty unless it was used on a wereleopard, and we appeared to be fresh out.

"Edward's in a serious snit," Diana continued. "He hates it when people disappear and he isn't behind it."

I had to smile at that.

The door opened. Edward stepped into the room. "Better?" he asked.

I sat up, wincing at the pain in my head and my shoulder. "Yes, sir."

"Excellent." That said, he got right back to business. "Renee went to the village—"

"She was able to find it?"

"According to her, the waterfall was just a waterfall, the cave just a cave, and beyond that there was more mountain with no jungle at all."

I guess that made sense. The waterfall had reappeared when we'd thought Mezareau dead, though he'd only been unconscious. His literal death must have made everything revert to its original state.

"What about the zombies?" I asked.

"The village was empty. Nothing but piles of dust, a few shards of bone."

"The magic died," I murmured, "when Mezareau did."

Which meant the zombies weren't really alive after all.

"Spells often fail when the spell caster dies," Edward agreed.

"But not curses," Diana muttered. "Noooo."

"If anyone tries to raise another zombie army," Edward said, "we need do nothing except kill the one who raises them."

"But that shouldn't ever happen again," Diana interjected. "Mezareau was the only one who knew how to create a wereleopard."

Edward sighed. "There is always another."

Diana cast a quick, concerned glance in my direction. She must be worried I'd leap out of bed and immediately try to find another way to become a wereleopard.

Maybe after I got rid of the headache.

"I have set my best trackers on finding Murphy," Edward said.

"Don't bother on my account."

If he didn't want me, I didn't want him.

"Your account?" Edward appeared puzzled; then his face cleared. "Oh, the sex."

Diana rolled her eyes. "Maybe the love?"

"You love him?" Edward asked.

"No."

Diana snorted and Edward's lips tightened. "I hate it when my agents fall in love. It's so messy."

"It's not messy," Diana snapped. "You get two agents where you previously had one. Don't be an ass."

Edward ignored her; maybe he was mellowing. Or maybe he just realized he *was* an ass much of the time.

"I was not looking for Murphy for you," he said, "but for the diamond."

"Good luck," I muttered. Edward wasn't going to find him.

"My second concern is you."

"I'm fine," I said.

"Not your health, but your magic."

"Sir?"

"You were made a wereleopard because you had power. Even though you are no longer a shape-shifter, you're still a voodoo priestess. You have raised the dead, which makes you a sorceress." He lifted his hand, even as I opened my mouth to argue. "I know I ordered you to do it; however, I do not want to be called back here to deal with you if you decide to run amok."

"Amok?"

His eyes narrowed. "Do you have any desire to rule the world?"

I snorted. "I can't even run my own life."

"Do *not* make me shoot you in the head, Cassandra."

"I'll do my best, sir."

Edward left without a good-bye.

"Are you going to stay in New Orleans?" Diana asked.

"Where else would I go?"

"Anywhere."

"Except you're here."

She smiled; I smiled. All was forgiven.

I got out of the hospital the same day, returned to my shop, and a week later was open for business.

I picked up Lazarus, who was going to be a daddy according to the vet, and the snake behaved as if he hadn't seen me in years, wrapping himself around my wrist and giving me all the love a snake could manage. He behaved as if I'd never smelled like a leopard at all—which worked for me.

We segued back into our routine—me working, him loving me and hissing at Diana whenever she stopped by. It was their thing.

I was busy; I was rarely alone, yet I was so lonely. Which was stupid. I'd been alone for years. It had never bothered me before. Of course I'd always had the promise of Sarah in my future. Now I wasn't sure what I had to look forward to.

And then one night, I found it.

I'd actually fallen asleep, a rare occurrence of late. I awoke to a breeze blowing through the open window next to my bed. But I hadn't left the window open.

"Why did you leave?" I asked.

Murphy materialized from the shadows. He was

thinner; his hair was longer. He'd found some new feathers. He looked almost like the man I'd met in the bar in Haiti, except that man had smiled and joked, traded accents. This one didn't.

"You hate me for taking her from you."

I sat up in bed and hugged my knees to my chest. "She was taken from me a long time ago, Devon, and it wasn't by you."

I sensed a sudden tension in him as he inched closer. I wanted to reach out, but I was afraid he'd run again. "How could you say your life meant nothing?"

"It didn't."

"You saved me, Cass. I was going nowhere fast until I met you."

"Ditto."

"I love you."

I smiled as I realized the truth. "Ditto."

He sat on the side of my bed. "Are you going to spend your life trying to find another way to get her back?"

I drew in a deep breath, then let it out. "No."

I hadn't admitted that until just this minute. Sarah was dead, and there was nothing I could do about it. Because raising my child from the grave was the act of a crazy person, and I kind of wanted to be sane. With him.

"You promise?" Murphy whispered.

"Yes."

His question, my answer, meant more than the words. They were vows we'd consecrate later. We spent the next several hours consummating them. It was what we were good at.

We were both drifting toward sleep when a final question woke me right back up. "Where's the diamond?"

"What diamond?"

I tilted my head and caught the shadow of a smile. "Oh, Edward's gonna love that."

Murphy's smile deepened as he fell asleep. Now I couldn't. The moon called.

I climbed out of bed and went into the courtyard, where I stared up at the perfectly round orb just as a faraway clock stuck midnight—the most powerful minute of the most powerful moon. I let the silver sheen wash over me as I said good-bye.

I'd never forget Sarah, but I didn't have to raise her from the dead for her to live in my heart, mind, and soul. She was my little girl, and no one could ever take that away.

Mommy?

She no longer wore her hated uniform but a frilly white nightgown.

Are you OK now?

"I think I am."

That's good. I couldn't go on to the best place until you let me go.

"I'm sorry."

Everything will be all right.

She'd told me that in the jungle, but I hadn't been listening.

The man with the pretty beads in his hair—I like him.

"Me, too."

He'll make a good daddy.

"What?"

Bye. Sarah began to fade and I let her. It was time.

I turned and Murphy was there. Something in his eyes made me ask, "Did you see her?"

"Yeah." He tilted his head, and his earring flashed silver beneath the moon. "What was that about me being a daddy?"

I considered what had just happened between us and what hadn't. Protection.

"I think we had a little accident."

He crossed the short space between us and pulled me into his arms. Leaning down, Murphy kissed my hair where it grew white, then whispered, "There are no accidents."

I smiled because I knew he was right.

Visit **www.panmacmillan.com** to read more about all our books and to buy them. You will also find features, author interviews and news of any author events, and you can sign up for e-newsletters so that you're always first to hear about our new releases.

www.panmacmillan.com

GIFT SELECTOR
YOUR ACCOUNT
WISH LIST
WAITING LIST

HOME | ABOUT US | IMPRINTS | TRADE/MEDIA | CONTACT US | ADVANCED SEARCH | SEARCH | GO

BOOK CATEGORIES | WHAT'S NEW | AUTHORS/ILLUSTRATORS | BESTSELLERS | READING GROUPS

Coming Soon...

Reading Groups

Competitions
Feeling Lucky?

Extracts
Sneak Previews

Interviews

Events
Meet Our Stars

Reviews
What The Critics Say

News & Awards

Editor's Choice
What We're Reading